CRIME ON THE FENS

Nikki Galena Book 1

JOY ELLIS

JOFFE

Published in paperback 2020
by Joffe Books, London
Revised edition 2016

www.joffebooks.com

First published by Crowood Press in 2010 as *Mask Wars*.

ISBN 978-1-78931-278-2

For my partner, Jacqueline.
Thank you for making Nikki real.

CHAPTER ONE

A night wind blew along the narrow alleyway, bringing with it the smell of ozone and red diesel. Nikki Galena leaned back against the rough brickwork of the derelict warehouse and wondered how many other women of thirty-six would feel quite so comfortable in such unpleasant surroundings. The backstreets that skirted the docks were no place for a lone female at any time of the day, but after midnight they were a definite no-go area. Nikki smiled in the darkness. Right now there was nowhere else she'd rather be.

She pushed the light button on her watch. He'd be here soon. She knew exactly what he'd look like, even though she'd never met him before. Worn denim jeans, a hooded jacket and trainers. It was like an unofficial uniform, except the jeans were sometimes swapped for sports pants, dark ones with stripes down the sides and a designer logo.

Nikki stared unblinkingly towards the entrance of the alley. The rain had stopped, but somewhere water was falling from a broken gutter, beating an uneven tattoo on the already wet flagstones. It was July, but summer meant nothing these days, and right now, Nikki didn't give a damn about the weather. She would have stood there and waited for Darren Barton if it had been a searing heat-wave, or below zero.

Nikki tensed. The sound of rubber soles slapping rhythmically on the slick pavement made the small smile spread further across her face.

She waited until he was a few feet from her, then stepped silently out, blocking his exit from the alleyway.

Darren jumped back and swore. 'Silly fucking cow! You scared the life out of me!'

'Sorry about that, Darren.'

The hooded figure froze at the mention of his name, then stepped a little closer, screwed up his face and stared at her suspiciously. 'I don't know you.'

Nikki stared back. 'No. You don't. But, I'll tell you something, you're never going to forget me.'

Her voice had become hard as winter ground, and Darren Barton suddenly seemed to decide that his earlier position, a few steps away from her, may have been the best one. 'Dunno what you're on about, so just bugger off. Get outta my way.' He tried to adopt a hard man pose. Hands deep in pockets and jaw pushed forward in a feeble attempt to look threatening.

'Can't do that.' In one swift move, she had Darren's arms behind his back and his cheek jammed against the brick wall. 'I'd hoped we could talk, but this way is fine by me.' She tightened her grip, and saw pinpoint specks of blood appear across the stubbly surface of the man's face. 'You see, I don't like you, Darren. Somehow I just can't cope with scumbags like you, scumbags who kill kids.'

The man groaned and tried to mutter something. Nikki held both his wrists in one hand, grabbed his hair and pulled his head away from the brickwork.

'I never killed no one!' His eyes rolled. 'Listen, lady! I dunno who you're after, but you got the wrong man!'

'Mm, don't think so.'

'What do you want?' The eyes still looked like a really bad case of hyperthyroidism.

'A name. That's all, I want you to give me a name. But first, let me tell you why I picked this exact spot for our little chat.'

The man's eyes narrowed.

'It's what's called a dead spot. No cameras. No CCTV. No passers-by. No interruptions. So, what else does that mean, Darren?'

'No witnesses.' The voice was just a gravely whisper.

'Exactly. Clever boy!'

'Maybe you should know that I got connections to some very nasty people. They won't be happy about this.'

Nikki laughed out loud. 'Believe me, the nastiest person you'll ever meet, is standing right beside you.' She spun him round and pushed him back against the wall. 'You carry a knife, Darren?'

He glowered at her, but said nothing.

'Of course you do. Your kind always does.' She stared at him, her loathing barely concealed. 'Now, are you going to take it out of your pocket and place it on the ground? Or am I going to have to get it off you?'

'I'll do it, alright? Just back off.' He may be a good foot taller than her, and weigh perhaps one and a half times her weight, but he had enough sense to know he would be seriously outclassed if it came to fighting dirty.

'Down here.' Nikki pointed to the wet pavement. 'Now, carefully kick it towards me, then back against that wall.'

She picked up the blade with a gloved hand, then pushed it into her own pocket. 'Right. Now, I need some information.'

'Oh no! I'm no fucking nark. And I'm clean right? I said before, you got the wrong man.'

Nikki ignored him. 'Do you know someone called Frankie Doyle?'

'Never heard of her.'

She raised an amused eyebrow. 'Is that so?'

'Yeah. Like I said, name means nothing.'

Before the man could take another breath, Nikki had leapt forward, one arm across his windpipe, and her knee jammed hard against his groin. 'So how do you know that Frankie is a woman?'

For the second time in five minutes, Darren's eyes practically exploded from their sockets. 'I, I guess I've heard of her.' He coughed painfully. 'But I don't know her. Really I don't.'

'So she's out of your league, is she?'

'Something like that.' He winced and tried to wriggle away from the unrelenting pressure that her knee was exerting. 'Lemme go. Please. I'll tell you what I know, though I'm warning you, it ain't much.'

Nikki leaned back a fraction, and the man gratefully exhaled stale breath. 'I've heard she hangs out with some new guys on the Carborough Estate. I hear they are a really tough bunch. Always got cash, and I mean a lot of cash. They've got mega funding from somewhere, but no one knows where.'

'Names?'

'No one knows *anything* about these guys. And there's only one real name on the Carborough, isn't there?'

'*Apart* from Archie Leonard.'

'Nah, they use tags.'

'Then give me a tag for whoever supplies Frankie, and I'll help you out of the mess you're in right now.'

'But I ain't in a mess, so I don't need your help, do I?'

'Oh, believe me, you do. Because you're in the brown and sticky stuff right up to your scraggy, and if I may say, very grubby neck.' She moved her knee a fraction and made to lean forward.

'No! There's this guy, calls himself Fluke. I think he's connected to the new gang. I don't say he supplies her, but he'll know who does. He's into everything.'

'Does this Fluke live on the Carborough?'

'I dunno, he kind of comes and goes. Like Frankie Doyle. They may even be an item.' Darren swallowed noisily. 'That's all I know, so you gonna let me go now?'

Nikki stared at him thoughtfully. 'Well, I suppose you have been helpful to me.'

Darren nodded furiously. 'Yeah. Gave you a name, didn't I?'

'Mmm.' She sighed. 'But sadly it doesn't work like that. Not with a stinking dealer.'

'I'm no dealer! Search me if you don't believe me!'

'Oh, I'm sure you've nothing on you,' she shrugged, 'because you sold your last batch to that skinny little tart who's been buying from you outside Harry's Club, didn't you?'

Darren's eyes narrowed.

'I see you remember her. White blonde hair, black spikes, too much make-up and no tits? She's one of ours, Darren. And the twenties that she gave you, the ones tucked up cosily in your wallet, are marked. Your prints will be all over the bag of crystal meth that you sold her, which incidentally, is already in an evidence bag and on its way to the police lab. So, along with that nasty knife you so kindly gave me . . . ?'

Darren's face screwed up into a mask of fear and anger. 'Stinking pig! You said you'd help me.' He almost spat the words at her.

'I lied.'

'You fucking set me up!'

'I did. And funny thing, but I'm not exactly eaten up by remorse.' She pushed harder against his groin. 'You see, in my book, if you deal drugs, you deal death. And me and my colleagues have to sit with the families, breathe in the heartbreak and the agonising pain that scum like you cause. And we don't like it, Darren. We don't like the fact that you make vulnerable kids turn to violence, to mugging old ladies to get money to feed their habit. A habit that you are *so* happy to fuel.'

'If they didn't get it from me, they'd get it from someone else!'

'Jesus! Don't give me that old crap! You're disgusting. You're like some flesh-eating virus infecting society, and making a wad of money out of your victims.' She jerked her knee forward and felt a small satisfaction from the ensuing scream.

'You can't do this! I'll have you! I know my rights!'

'Yeah, yeah, you shit-bags always know your rights. But proving this could be tricky, because we simply had a quiet chat, Darren, as my partner down there will testify.' She indicated to a shadowy figure sauntering slowly up the alley. 'And before he gets here, my scuzzy little friend, let me remind you of something. Tonight, I was just asking a few questions in an amicable manner. Don't *ever* let me get really angry with you, or you'll wish you'd been born in the Outer Hebrides and never left home, got it?' Her eyes bore into his. 'Oh, and before you start bleating about brutality, just be quite sure of what you're going to say, huh? Like who's going to believe a pusher who says he was terrorised in an alley by some woman half his size? Apart from which, I reckon it'd make your street cred rating slip down to somewhere around zero, don't you?' The knee gave one last jerk, and she turned away. 'Arrest him, Dave, then take him down to the station and sling him in the digger.'

The big man yawned, then slowly reached for his cuffs. 'What charge, guv?'

'You can start with this.' She pulled an evidence bag from her pocket, slipped Darren's vicious looking knife into it and passed it to her colleague. 'Then follow it up with unlawful supply of drugs. Tie up with WDC Cullen over that. He's all yours. I need to be somewhere where the air is a little sweeter.' With one last contemptuous look at the drug dealer, she turned her collar up against the rain, and walked back down the alley into the darkness.

* * *

It took only ten minutes to walk to the small basement flat that she hated to call home. She slipped the key into the lock, then paused, as a terrible lethargy overtook her. It happened every time. Out on the streets she was fine, she was great. At the nick, in the courts, in the cells, anywhere where she knew that she was doing something concrete to stop the drugs making their insidious way around her town, as a detective inspector, she was in control. But now, as the adrenaline slowed down, the camouflage fell away and she knew, behind that door, she was just Nikki Galena, a lonely woman who dreaded the working day coming to an end.

She gripped the key and began to turn it. It was as if every ounce of energy had left her. The key weighed a ton, and she had all the strength of a week old baby. With a supreme effort, she pushed open the door, went inside and flipped the light switch.

Nothing that she loved greeted her. An estate agent would have called it minimalist, in fact, it was mind-numbingly Spartan. The front door opened directly into the living room, off that was a bedroom with what the landlord laughingly called an en-suite, and a kitchen/diner with French windows that opened into a tiny, private courtyard garden. And that was the only part of the miserable place that Nikki had some mild affection for.

She pulled off her damp jacket and threw it over the back of the room's only chair, then went through to the kitchen. Exhausted as she was, sleep never came easy. Her body was shutting down, but her mind was in overdrive. She needed help to switch off, and for years it had been in the form of single malt. Now she couldn't even do that. If she got a call, a lead, anything that may bring another result, she'd have to be ready to go at a second's notice, and you sure couldn't do that if you'd had enough units to detonate a breathalyzer.

Nikki opened the fridge and peered inside. The top two shelves were lined from back to front with dozens of small bottles of wine. Red, white and rosé. French, Italian, Australian. Sweet, dry, sparkling. Neat little bottles that held one wine glass full to brimming. Just enough to relax the mind, but not enough to dull the senses.

She selected a Grenache and tipped every last drop into the only glass in the cupboard. Normally she would have sat in the garden and planned her next day's hunting, but tonight the rain thwarted her.

The lounge housed a lonely chair, a large metal frame futon with a huge soft blanket thrown over it, and something that probably started life as a corner unit for a television. At present, it held a phone charger, a telephone book, a lap top computer and a lamp with multicoloured glass shade that screamed out faux-Tiffany.

Nikki slumped onto the futon and tucked her legs beneath her. As always she had felt the initial rush of relief at having prepared the way for another pusher to face the legal system, but it was never enough. Not anymore. There were too many dealers, too many drugs out there.

She sipped her drink and thought how radically things had changed over the last few years. Greenborough had always been a pleasant rural market town. To some it still was. One mile from the outskirts in any direction, and you were in the fenlands. One more mile to the east, and you were on the coastal marshes. It was fairly big, as market towns go, and the tidal river running right through the centre made it busier than some. But then there was the port. Small maybe, one end for the cockle fishing boats, and the other recently expanded to take in real ships again. Freighters and cargo vessels made their way in from the North Sea, through the Wash and into the estuary of the Wayland River. And with the extra jobs, the new opportunities and the illegal immigrants had come a frightening increase in the drug trade.

The wine buzzed reassuringly on her tongue, and she took another sip.

Drugs, the bane of her life.

Nikki placed the glass on the floor, pulled one of the big cushions round, nestled her head onto it and wondered how she had become this extraordinary avenging angel, waging a one-woman crusade on the drug dealers. At times like this, the low moments, she wished with all her heart that she could give up her battle, but she couldn't. She didn't have much else left. Her mother had died, her father was in a nursing home and hardly recognised her, her husband Robert, had left her, and her daughter blamed her for *everything* that was wrong in the world.

Nikki smiled when she thought about Hannah. Yes, no matter how bad things got, she still had her daughter to consider. Okay, the girl wasn't at home anymore, but that didn't mean she didn't love her or care deeply what happened to her. She closed her eyes. It was far too late now, but whatever happened tomorrow, she would make time to ring and see how she was. Behind her closed eyelids she saw pictures of the dark, almost black hair, the deep brown, often angry eyes, and the clear, smooth olive skin that all her friends would have hocked their iPods for.

The picture faded. Maybe she should give up this rented dump. For the sake of her daughter, maybe she should go back to their family home on Cloud Fen. Clear out the old cottage. Gut it. Make it nice. Make it somewhere to call home again.

Nikki yawned. She'd been here before. Juggling thoughts, what ifs and maybes. And it always came back to the fact that it would mean less hours on the streets. Less hours delousing the town of two-legged vermin. Living here she was a only few moments' walk from their lair, or the rat runs that led to it. Cloud Fen was a twenty minute drive from the nick, slow moving tractors and agricultural equipment allowing. And that just wasn't acceptable.

She yawned again. It should be funny, but it wasn't. You would have thought that her single-minded dedication to jailing the bad guys would have made her something of a hero in the eyes of her colleagues, but it had had the reverse effect. No one wanted to work with her anymore. They resented her passion, refused to accept her rather unorthodox methods and called her unreasonable. Well, they called a lot of things actually, and none of them pleasant. But then they had lives, didn't they? Families, friends and activities outside the force. She just had the force, and her crusade.

Nikki pulled the blanket around her and vaguely wondered when she had changed her bed linen last. Not that it mattered, because she never slept in the bed. She only went into the bedroom at all because the shower was off it, and her clothes needed to hang somewhere. She hated the pokey dark room with the low ceiling and the mud coloured carpet. She hated it most of all because it was the only room with a photograph in it, one she could never bring herself to hide in a drawer. One she loved with all her heart, but could hardly bear to look at.

CHAPTER TWO

At the same time as Nikki's drug pusher was being processed by the custody sergeant, a young woman was picking her way hesitantly along the dark seabank. The track was muddy and uneven, full of waterlogged trenches and gullies, and although she knew it well and carried a pretty useful torch, it really wasn't a good place to be at night.

She shivered, pulled her short denim jacket tighter across the thin skinny T-shirt, and thought that maybe she had made a mistake in rushing out here to meet him.

In daylight, it was different. She hated the town, and whenever she could she would escape to this strange water-world. Out here, you could look across the vast stretch of marshland, see flocks of migrant seabirds and hares and rabbits, and no people. In the distance you could sometimes see the silver-grey waters of the Wash, and you could always see the clouds. Wonderful sky-scapes, full of magical, billowy, fluffy, windblown clouds. She believed it to be almost mystical, with its ever-changing light and the elusive mists that would creep across the Fens like wraiths.

Tonight however it did not seem mystical. The girl shivered and wondered how somewhere that she loved so much, could suddenly feel so threatening.

She paused and looked along the long straight track that was the seabank. The black outline of the old pumping station looked stark and menacing against the paler, indigo night sky. She should be able to see him by now. He always used a powerful lantern with a red shield to set up the Newtonian Reflector telescope on its mount, and get it aligned on the heavens.

But she could see nothing, and something about that darkness bothered her. So did the fact that he had sent her a text. It was *so* out of character. He liked to talk, not send electronic messages. In fact, he was the only person she knew that owned a fountain pen and used ink from a bottle.

From the moment that she received his message, she had felt puzzled. Earlier, as she pulled on her rambling boots, she had wondered about the uncharacteristic secrecy. It just wasn't his way. He would visit her, or ring if pushed. He'd blurt out something about the tilt of Saturn's rings, or he'd got some brilliant new lens and some deep-sky viewing would be showing some glorious double stars that she just *couldn't* miss. She knew that most people considered him a freak, but where they saw an anorak, she saw someone driven by passion, and that was something she could relate to.

She stopped and tried to ring him, but his phone was switched off. Her anxiety increased. If she took the message at face value, he had seemed desperate that she meet him. But where was he? And where was his dog? It almost always followed him out to the marsh. Something was wrong. She shivered, and then a scary thought crossed her mind. There were no stars tonight.

Fear flooded through her. Oh God! She had been a fool, and now she needed to get off the marsh. If he wanted to see her, he could damn well . . .

Something far darker than the night was roughly pulled over her head, and an arm snaked around her throat, forcing her neck backwards and her throat to close. She jerked her arms and legs frantically kicking and beating uselessly at her unseen assailant, then a rushing noise filled her ears and bright lights exploded behind her eyelids. Abruptly, the roaring sound became everything, and she felt her legs stop their dancing and her arms fell uselessly to her sides. Her fight for air became almost impossible, and she slipped from the iron grasp, to fall silently into darkness.

CHAPTER THREE

Nikki knew the superintendent was looking for her, but suspecting yet another bollocking, managed to evade him for most of the day. Now she had run out of excuses, and found herself grudgingly making her way to his office.

Superintendent Rick Bainbridge peered at her over thin wire-rimmed glasses. 'Come in. Sit down.'

His icy tone spoke volumes. She walked across the room to the waiting chair, drawing in a long slow breath and preparing herself for the onslaught.

'Know what these are?' In one hand the super held a thick pile of reports, each of which he carefully placed, one after the other, like giant playing cards, on his desk.

'Fan mail?'

'You know it bloody isn't! And this is no joke anymore.' He threw the remaining papers down. 'Complaints, Nikki! Damned complaints!' He sat back in his chair and shook his head. 'And this time, I'm not sure whether I've got the energy or the inclination to try to bail you out.'

Nikki opened her mouth to reply, but decided against it. Better to let him rant for a bit. He'd cool down eventually, he always did.

'I'll be frank with you, Nikki, I'm running out of detectives who will work with you. And, considering the fact that you get more arrests than the rest of the bloody teams put together, that is one ridiculous situation to be in.'

'Dave and I get along, sir.'

'Dave Harris is uniform, he's not a detective, and he's only tagging along with you, because he's too damned lazy to get his finger out and do some proper police work.'

'Well, it wasn't my fault that DS Salter decided to move to the West Country.'

The super glared at her. 'It was, and you know it! And she's still not sure if Truro is actually far enough away.'

'Unfortunate clash of personalities, sir.'

The super's eyes rolled up towards the ceiling. 'Oh please! This is not a game! Now, will you just cut the snide comments and wake up to the fact that this time,' he slammed his fist down on the desk, 'this time, it's serious.'

Nikki blinked, and felt a jolt of concern. This wasn't following the usual pattern. She looked up, and saw an uncharacteristic mixture of concern, anger and frustration on that familiar craggy face.

'There's no easy way to say this, but top brass are talking about disciplinary action.'

'What!' Nikki's jaw dropped. 'Oh, sir! I know my methods are a bit extreme sometimes, but, Jesus, we *have* to get the dealers off the streets! You know this area is over run with drugs, you can't just pussyfoot around with these villains. I just play them at their own game, hit them where it hurts, and I get results! Good results! *You* know that, sir.'

'Of course I know it! I've been protecting you and damn near perjuring myself for years! And why? Because I happen to think you're a damned good copper. And you, Inspector, know full well that I need you. But you just can't go on acting like a bloody loose cannon, I know you've got your reasons, and that's all very well for crime thrillers and cop films, but not here in the Fenland Constabulary. To get an arrest, you rampage through the rule book and disregard everything. You *have* to back down. Can't you get it into your head that there are such things as human rights, political correctness, bullying, racial abuse. God, the list is endless, and it's me who has to scurry around behind you clearing up the mess.'

The superintendent exhaled loudly, then sighed and opened a drawer in his desk. He pulled out two small shot glasses and a half bottle of Scotch. With another sigh, he filled both glasses then passed one to her. 'It's the end of the day, and if ever I needed this, it's now.'

Nikki stared at the amber liquid and bit her lip. So, either Rick Bainbridge was going for a well-earned Oscar nomination, or the shit had really hit the fan. He'd read the riot act on many occasions, but *never* like this.

In her mind's eye she saw the orderly rows of tiny wine bottles in her fridge, then she looked back at the super's scarlet face, and downed her drink in one.

'So what was the final straw?' The old familiar taste of whisky hit her like a painful memory, one you couldn't ignore. 'Which one of my many misdemeanours actually broke the camel's back?'

'Nothing specific, Nikki, it's just the sheer volume.' He pointed back to the heap of reports.

Nikki closed her eyes and hoped that when she opened them the super would have re-filled her glass. She squinted hopefully, but the glass remained empty.

Perhaps it was time to test the waters and maybe call his bluff.

'Sorry to say this, sir, but if there had been anything that would actually stick in that pile of paperwork, the Complaints and Discipline Investigator would have dragged me into an interview room by now, and my warrant card would be in your drawer, along with that very nice bottle of Scotch.' She pushed her glass hopefully across the desk.

'It's no trick, Nikki. You are in real trouble, the powers that be are sincerely pissed off.' He splashed more whisky into their glasses. 'Now they've firmly wedged me between a rock and a hard place, so I'll tell you this straight. The message I've been given is that you fall in line, or move on. So, you really have to help me out here, or it goes out of my hands.'

'Maybe I should move on.' She hardly recognised her own voice. It was not a 'poor me' statement, and it was not for effect. There was a deep desolation in her words; an emotion that surprised even her.

'Oh, sod that for a game of soldiers.' The super sipped his Scotch and ignored her comment. 'I have no intention of losing you, Nikki Galena, but I do have one last ditch suggestion.' He placed the shot glass back on the desk and stared at her intently. 'I've had a volunteer.'

Nikki's eyes narrowed. *No one* ever volunteered to work with her.

'Detective Sergeant Joseph Easter from Fenchester has asked for a temporary transfer, so . . .'

'Holy Joe! Oh, no way! I could *not* work with him.'

'He's a bloody good detective!'

'Right! With a huge emphasis on the word, *good*, no doubt.' Nikki grabbed at her glass and threw a mouthful of the fiery whisky down her throat. 'Volunteer! Oh yes, I can see what his game is!'

'And ?'

'He knows my reputation and he clearly wants to take Good Cop/Bad Cop to a brave new dimension! Or maybe he's after the conversion of the century, and believe me, that would rival that of St Paul on the road to Damascus!'

'So you know something of the Bible, do you? I thought maybe you only read Butterworth's Police Law, or Zander on PACE?'

'Very funny! I'm not a bloody heathen, I would just prefer a detective for a sergeant, not a lay-preacher.'

For the first time since she walked into the room, Nikki noticed the hint of a smile on the superintendent's face.

'Give it one month, okay? And I guarantee that you'll find there's more to Joe Easter than what the mess room gossips would have you believe.'

Nikki gritted her teeth. This was a disaster, but she was very aware that the super had been loyal enough to throw her a lifeline, even though a great deal of pressure had been exerted on him. She took a deep breath. It would appear that he wasn't the only one between that rock and a hard place right now. 'One month? Is that a calendar month or four weeks? Because if there's a choice, I'd prefer the four weeks.'

'Don't push it, Inspector.' The superintendent tilted the remaining spirit in the flat bottle backwards and forwards and raised his eyebrows. 'Are you walking home tonight?'

Nikki pushed her glass forward. Sod the tiny bottles in her fridge. 'I am now.'

* * *

Rick Bainbridge watched Nikki leave, and let out an audible sigh. He knew so much more about her than anyone else. He'd known her since she was an eager young probationer, full of all the right things that would make her a great officer. But then she had volunteered to take a distress call, and had finished up cradling a dying teenage girl in her arms in a rat infested basement. It was something that changed her life for ever. It screwed up both her marriage and her head, and it sent her off on a personal vendetta that had waged constantly from the moment the youngster died, to the present day. If she had never raised her hand and volunteered for that particular job, Rick was sure that Nikki Galena would have been weighed down with brass, gold braid and respect by now. She certainly wouldn't be the hard-nosed loner, the scary enigma, that she'd become over the last years.

Rick stood up, picked up his jacket and briefcase, and walked slowly to the door. He would hate to lose her. She practically kept their arrest target going single handed, but now the ice had become too thin for him to support her for much longer. And at this late stage in his career, he couldn't afford to sink below the water line with her. He turned off the light and closed the door. The partnership with Joseph Easter was their last chance. Because if they both went down now, there was no one left to throw them a line.

CHAPTER FOUR

As 5 a.m. approached, Greenborough police station still buzzed with activity. WPC Yvonne Collins flopped down gratefully into a mess room chair and watched as her partner, PC Niall Farrow unclipped his heavy equipment belt and lowered it gently to the floor.

'Maybe if you put on a few pounds around your gut, you'd be able to cram a load more gadgets on that thing.' She stared at her crewmate in exasperation. 'Something useful like an AK47, or the kitchen sink, maybe?'

'I like to be prepared,' said Niall smugly.

'You're a copper, not a boy scout! And if you jam anything else around your waist, there won't be room for us both in the patrol car.'

'Lighten up, Vonnie. One day I'm sure you'll be grateful for my excellent selection of equipment.' He grinned at her.

'In your dreams, Sunshine.' Yvonne smiled as she pulled off her hat and placed it on the chair next to her. Her crewmate's constant exuberance amused her. Niall was only two years into the job, and still viewed every moment as a great adventure.

Yvonne was nearing fifteen years' service and had a more pragmatic approach to her job, usually praying for peace and goodwill to all men, something she rarely got to see.

'So, how many mask-related incidents do you think have occurred tonight?' asked Niall, leaning back and stretching.

'Well, we've had three, haven't we? One mugging, a couple of joy-riders and that group of masked kids trying to break into the chippie. I'm not sure what the other crews have had.' Yvonne thought about the spate of petty crimes all committed by youths wearing horrible rubber masks, and gave a little shiver. 'Those things are obscene. I just wish we knew where they were coming from.'

'Yeah, it's weird, isn't it?' Niall went to the coffee machine and sorted through his pocket for some change. 'Started with a few school kids wearing them to scare the shit out of each other, now they are all over town. Someone must know what the devil's going on.'

Yvonne accepted the coffee that Niall handed to her. 'Thanks. I need this. Let's hope we've seen the last of them for this shift. Those masks give me the creeps.'

'Collins! Farrow! You've got a shout! Now!' The sergeant's voice echoed down the corridor and into the mess room.

Yvonne grabbed her hat and jumped up. 'Bugger! Grab that bloody ton of hardware off the floor, Niall. Here we go again!'

* * *

As Yvonne and Niall chased more masked hooligans around the town, Nikki walked slowly down the corridor to CID. She was very early, but sleep had evaded her and seeing the dawn rise over the nick was distinctly preferable to spending one more waking moment in her miserable flat.

She could hear the murmured comments of the officers on duty, but she did what she normally did, and ignored them. She didn't need a crystal ball to know what they were saying. News travelled fast through the station and she had a fair idea that a book had already been opened on how long Old Nick and Holy Joe would last as a team.

Nikki pushed open the door to her office and decided that she would not be placing a bet. She took off her jacket, flung it over the back of her chair, and went straight back out to get a coffee. She wanted some time to herself before her new sergeant arrived. She just wished they'd let her go solo. When she worked alone, she was at her best. Now they were pairing her with . . . ? Nikki stared at the steaming brown liquid dribbling into the beaker and wondered. With who, exactly? She knew very little about Joseph Easter. As the super had said, everything she knew had come straight from the mess room, and that was not the most reliable source. As she picked up the beaker and placed it in a holder, a wry smile crossed her face. And if Sergeant Easter believed everything he heard about *her* via the grape vine, he would probably be expecting to meet the Medusa herself.

Maybe she should use the next hour to do a little sleuthing about him. Then again, that would be something of a pointless exercise. The super had made her position perfectly clear, she was going to *have* to try to work with him, so she may as well draw her own conclusions as they went along. She just hoped that the subject of religion would not creep into their conversations. She wasn't sure how she'd react to being told just how great God was, when as far back as she could remember, the Almighty had taken a backseat when it came to helping her out. Perhaps some nice, clear ground rules should be the first item on her agenda.

She pushed through her office door, trying not to spill her coffee, and saw an untidy pile of rubber masks lying on her desk.

'Oh shit!' She muttered, picking up a memo from the night shift crews. Fifteen of the hideous things confiscated in just one night!

She glanced at her watch and wondered if the super would be in yet. He'd asked to be kept informed about them, and clearly they were becoming more than just a nuisance.

She flopped down at her desk. It would be a little while before he arrived, certainly long enough to do a search. Not on Joseph Easter, but on someone from a different investigation, a rather private one that she had been discreetly running for a very long time. Nikki switched her computer on, drummed her fingers impatiently on the desk while she waited for it to boot up, then punched in her password. A few screens later and she was where she wanted to be. She carefully typed in FLUKE, and waited.

Damn! No one known to them used that particular tag. She tried FLOOK, in case she had misunderstood the spelling, then widened the search, but still nothing. Nikki closed the programme and went onto the Internet, but after half an hour's hunting, gave up. Only a rock band of that name, one that Hannah had been a fan of, jarred off any sort of recognition. Nikki signed off the computer, and sat thinking about her daughter. Hannah loved the kind of music that destroyed both eardrums and brain cells in one hit, and for a moment Nikki could hear herself screaming "Will you *please* turn that rubbish down!"

She sipped her coffee, and wished that her daughter was still at home. She missed her. She missed the mess, the noise, the arguments, the tantrums and the tears. Funny really, she missed all the things that she had spent years complaining about. Nikki swallowed another gulp of her drink and glanced back at her watch. No time to start wading through the mud and mire of the past, the superintendent should be in by now, and she needed to get her brain back into work mode.

One more hour, and the good Reverend Easter would arrive. Nikki felt a despondency creep into her. Hell, she didn't even know what he looked like! Probably short and paunchy, with receding hair and a permanent holier-than-thou expression. Not that that mattered much to her. She glanced down at the masks, and thought maybe everyone wore a mask when it suited them. She certainly did, come to think of it. And why should she be worrying about the arrival of the newest addition to her shabby little team? If the jungle drums were correct, he'd just be another lamb to the slaughter, and if he had the balls and stamina of his pre-decessors, he'd be breaking the speed limit all the way back to Fenchester before nightfall. With a sigh, she picked up her coffee and one of the masks, and went to find the super.

* * *

Superintendent Bainbridge lifted it up with a finger and thumb, and stared at the mask with distaste. 'What the hell is it supposed to be?'

'Part rat, part rotting corpse. And its origin is hazy, to say the least.'

'Lovely. So why can't we trace the source?'

Nikki drew in a long breath. 'Beats me, sir. They don't show up legitimately anywhere. Not in fancy dress hire places, or in novelty shops, or suppliers catalogues, nowhere.'

'What about the Internet? That's where practically everything comes from these days, isn't it?'

'First place we looked, sir, but we got a big fat zero.'

'So how do these kids get hold of them?'

'Sounds ridiculous, I know . . .' Nikki ran her fingers through her hair and exhaled, '. . . but they just seem to turn up. Everyone we've interviewed has denied buying or purposefully acquiring them. They just seem to have come by them somehow, and being the opportunists that they are, have used them for whatever mischief or devious little crime they were planning on committing.'

The super frowned. 'And is there any connection between the youngsters who have been using the masks?'

'Not really. The kids come from different schools, dif-ferent areas of the town, even different ethnic groups.' She shrugged. 'The first users were a bunch of school kids nick-ing their classmates dinner money. Then they appeared on the Carborough Estate where some little scrotes were play-ing some sort of scary knock-down-ginger and putting the frighteners on whoever opened the door. Then we had a couple of handbag snatches with kids wearing them, and a mugging over near the railway station. Now, they are all over the place.'

'And last night?'

'PC's Collins and Farrow left me a memo, sir. One little toe-rag that they brought in, called the mask by a name. Called it a *Griffyx* apparently, then clammed up tighter than a duck's backside. WPC Collins Googled it, but found nothing. I'll have a word with them before they go off shift, sir, maybe . . .'

'Sorry to interrupt, sir.' The big frame of Jack Conway, the duty sergeant appeared in the doorway. 'I've had the dean of the Fenland University on the blower. One of his third-year students is missing. She's twenty-one apparently, and I told him the score regarding mispers, but he wondered if you'd give him a ring. Said you know him.'

The superintendent frowned. 'Mm, I do. Did he leave a number, Jack?'

'Yes, sir, got it right here.' The sergeant handed him a note and left.

As Nikki made to follow him, the super called her back. 'Hang fire, Nik. Let's just check this out. I've known Kenneth Villiers for years, he's been a staunch supporter of everything we've been trying to do with the youth of Greenborough, both financially and with practical help. One thing I do know about him, is that he's not the type to panic over one wayward student.'

For several minutes Nikki listened to a one-sided telephone conversation, but from the super's tone, and the grave expression on his face, she knew he was taking everything that he was being told very seriously. After a while he slowly replaced the receiver in its cradle, and said, 'I don't like the sound of this. I'm aware this young woman is not considered at risk, or indeed even vulnerable, but Dr Villiers is quite certain that something has happened to the girl.'

'What's the situation?'

'Her name is Kerry Anderson, she's twenty-one years old, in her last year, taking a BA in photography. Star pupil, preparing to go on to post-graduate level. Apparently she went out late on Monday night, which is not unusual, but she failed to show up for a field trip yesterday, which was *very* unusual.'

Nikki thought carefully, then said, 'Well, I know we'd normally refer him to the Missing Person's Bureau, but if this Villiers is such an important benefactor, would you like me to make a few low-key enquiries?'

The superintendent flashed her a concerned glance. 'I'm not sure that's a good idea.'

She leaned forward, knowing full well that the super was remembering the old case that nearly sent her off the rails. 'I'm okay with it, honestly.' Her eyes pierced him with their intensity, then she lowered her voice to almost a whisper. '*Please* don't keep protecting me from every case that involves young women. I have my new sergeant as from today, and all I'm doing, apart from my constant battle with the drug dealers, is playing with bloody Halloween masks! Let's face it, sir, ten to one, your student has buggered off with the boyfriend and discovered that nookie is far more fun than seminars, tutorials and lectures.' She mustered a pathetic smile and pleaded. '*Please*, super, let me do this.'

The man's eyes narrowed. He looked as if he was precariously juggling his head and his heart. Finally he seemed to make some kind of a decision, and he nodded. 'Okay. Maybe you're right. Just be sure to take your new sergeant with you, it'll be a way of getting to know him.'

Like hell, she thought, but managed to freeze frame her smile for a little longer. 'Thanks super. As soon as he's here, we'll get onto it.'

CHAPTER FIVE

Detective Sergeant Joseph Easter stood by his parked car and looked across at the police station. It was about as different to his old patch as a Morris Minor to a Ferrari Enzo.

Fenchester nick was a 1920s piece of history, while this sparkling edifice of steel and smoky glass was strictly ultra-modernism, and bloody ugly with it. He grinned to himself. And that was just fine. He needed everything to be completely different. And this was about as different as it got.

He was early, but then he always was. And probably not a bad thing. First impressions and all that. But should he really be suffering from nerves, at the age of thirty-eight? He considered his own question, then decided that, under the present circumstances, *anyone* would be suffering from nerves. Joseph bit his lip. One month here. That was the agreement. He just hoped he was doing the right thing. He took a deep breath and straightened his tie. One more thing to do before he went in. He removed his mobile from his pocket, flipped it open and pressed a speed dial number.

'Hi there, sweetheart, it's Dad. I've no idea of the time where you are, but I wanted you to know that I'm going to be working out of Greenborough for few weeks. With a new boss and she's got something of a reputation, but hopefully we'll get on. Uh, that's all I guess. Hope you're okay, and I'm on the same number if you need me. And I love you. Always have and always will.'

He shut the phone and closed his eyes for a moment. A face swam behind his eyelids. Long, light brown hair and huge hazel eyes. Uneven dimples and very white teeth. *Yes, I love you. But sadly, it looks as though I have just run out of excuses for not going in to that arty-farty tin can of a building and introducing myself.* Before he opened his eyes, he muttered a few quiet words to himself, then strode across the paved courtyard to the front entrance.

Joseph stepped inside, looked around, and was forced to smile. It may be a high-tech modern building, but the clients who frequented it were exactly the same as those in Fenchester. They just stood out as being even more grubby and smelly against the shining safety glass and clean, acrylic painted walls. In his old nick, they kind of blended into the worn and faded flooring, the chipped woodwork and the high, dark stained ceilings.

Joseph walked briskly up to the reception desk. 'Detective Sergeant Easter to see Superintendent Bainbridge, please.'

The briefest hint of amusement that crossed the woman's face was not lost on him.

'If you'll just wait a moment, sir, I'll take you up.' She turned away and called loudly for someone to cover the desk for her. Instantly he saw a sea of curious faces look his way.

As they walked across the foyer towards the lifts, she said, 'The super will be very pleased to see you, sir.'

'Why? Is something going down?'

The woman raised an eyebrow. 'No, no. It's just that CID are not up to full strength at present. DI Galena's *last* sergeant re-located to the West Country, you know.'

She gave him a sidelong glance as they moved into the lift, and Joseph stifled a grin.

'Yes, I heard. Lovely part of the world.'

'Mm, lovely.' The woman gave him an overly innocent look, and said, 'You *are* going to be working with DI Galena, aren't you?'

The lift sighed and stopped with hardly a shudder, which made a very pleasant change from flights of stone stairs with rickety brass rails. He flashed her one of his brightest smiles, and thought, you know full well I am, my friend, but if you want to play, that's fine by me. 'Oh yes. And I'm *really* looking forward to it.'

The eyebrows lifted again. 'Second door along, sir. And good luck.'

The lift doors closed silently, but he could have sworn that he heard a soft giggle coming from inside. Joseph paused and considered that perhaps his name should have been Daniel, because this felt very much like the entrance to a lion's den.

He gritted his teeth, took a long deep breath, and knocked on the door.

* * *

As Joseph waited tentatively outside the superintendent's office, a commuter train pulled out of Greenborough station. None of its occupants took notice of the two sullen-faced youths who sat on a graffiti-covered bench. As the train moved slowly away, they glanced at each other, then left the seat and silently slipped down the steep bank at the end of the platform, and disappeared into a scrubby area full of weeds and broken concrete.

'Can you see them?' One boy whispered urgently.

'Give us a chance!'

Crouching low, although there was little chance of being spotted in this godforsaken spot, they searched between the stunted, windblown shrubs, and untidy piles of builder's waste.

'Got it!' The taller of the two cursed and scrabbled his way through a thicket of nettles and brambles to where he could see the sack. It was an orange nylon bag, the sort that held onions or other root vegetables. Something often seen discarded beside the acres of arable fields, or in the rubbish that collected beside railway tracks.

The boy dragged it out and pulled the drawstring tie open. 'Wicked!'

'How many?' The smaller boy squatted down beside him and peered into the bag.

'Twenty or more.'

'Yee-ha!' Whooped the younger one. 'Hey, Marcus? What if we try to make something out of this lot? Even just a fiver on each? What do you think?'

'I think you have shit for brains, arsehole! You know the score. These things come and go. No money *ever* changes hands, right? The only ones who get anything, are you and me, and that's for making sure things are done right, so don't forget it!'

'Well, it's still risky, ain't it?' The younger one looked peeved. 'If we got caught . . .'

'Don't be a total turd, Mickey! No one's going to catch us, and if they did, what exactly have we done?' He shrugged. 'We've picked up a sack and looked in it. Last time I drew breath, there was no law against that. So,' he glowered at the other boy, 'we take these to the arranged places, and forget all about them, until we get another call, okay?' He drew a plain sealed envelope from the sack, opened it and handed his friend a couple of notes. 'Just don't get greedy, Mickey, this is money for old rope, and you know it.'

The boy took the money and counted it. 'I suppose. It's just that my granddad told me never to pass up a chance to make a fast buck, that's all.'

'It'd be a very deadly buck, man. The last one you'd ever make. I've been told what would happen if we cock up, and it ain't nice, believe me.'

Mickey's already pasty face, blanched a shade paler. 'So, what's it all about? Why all this big secret shit?'

The older boy grabbed Mickey's shoulder, fingers biting deep into his flesh. 'Look, do you want that cash? Or do I find someone else to help me? Someone who can keep his fucking trap shut for longer than twenty seconds at a time, and not keep asking fucking stupid questions!'

'Okay! Okay! Back off! I'm sorry, alright? Just get off me, and let's go make the drops.'

Without another word, the two boys gathered up their precious bag and made their way to a crumbling wall at the back of the yard, where they scrambled over, and disappeared into the copse beyond.

* * *

Nikki strode down to the front desk. The new recruit would be here shortly, and as she obviously could do nothing to alter that fact, she'd get in first and leave him a message to report directly to her office.

'*When* Detective Sergeant Easter arrives, please tell him . . .'

'Oh, he's already here, ma'am.' The officer feigned surprise that she should not know this fact. 'He arrived over half an hour ago. He's with the superintendent.'

Nikki bit back a retort, settled for a muttered "thank you", and turned on her heel. She really should have known that Mister Efficiency would be early.

For a moment she felt very tired. Very tired of what she had become. She had never set out to be the Fenland Constabulary's number one harridan, over the years it had just kind of turned out that way. When the people you worked with are not as driven as you are, it's inevitable that you end up resenting each other. And now the super would, no doubt, be sitting in his office, sipping tea, and prepping the new boy for what he should expect from working with Old Nick.

She pushed open the door to CID, then halted abruptly, as she saw Superintendent Bainbridge talking to a tall, fair, floppy-haired man.

'Ah Nikki! Excellent! Excellent!'

The bogus bonhomie that the big man was exuding was almost sick-making, and Nikki was forced to recall that this was her last chance in the eyes of top brass.

'I'd like you to meet your new colleague.' He turned to the man and said, 'Detective Sergeant Joseph Easter, this is Detective Inspector Nikki Galena.'

The hand was already outstretched and waiting. As she shook it, she fought to conceal her surprise. Her initial impression of Joseph Easter was a very long way from anything she had expected. The face was almost familiar, not because she had ever met him before, but from a grainy black and white photograph that had hung on her daughter's bedroom wall when she was going through her "deeply misunderstood and unfairly burdened with the worries of the world" phase. The man bore an uncanny resemblance to Rupert Brooke. Older, sure, but the ghost of the dead poet called out from behind the eyes of the policeman. Even more astounding than the unexpected good looks, was the fact that rather than looking paunchy and pious, he was downright sexy.

'It's an honour to work with you, ma'am.' Joseph looked her directly in the eyes, and Nikki found it hard to hold their gaze. 'Even if it is only for a month.'

For one weird moment, she actually believed him. Why didn't she feel that he was taking the piss? Surely he had to be? Jesus, she hated it when she felt confused about people. She needed to take back control; then she'd feel more comfortable. 'Four weeks, actually, Sergeant. And although I hate to break up the party, I think the pleasantries can wait. We have some enquiries to make about a missing young woman.'

'And I think a quick guided tour of the station should come first, Nikki. After all, Joseph is a stranger here.' The super threw her a warning glance.

'No, no. That's okay, sir.' Joseph shook his head. 'DI Galena is quite right. I can find my way around as we go along. No problem at all.'

The superintendent stepped back and raised his hands in surrender. 'Then over to you two. And keep me informed on everything. Good Luck.'

Nikki wondered which one of them would need it.

'Take that empty desk by the window, Sergeant. My office is over there.' She pointed to the corridor. 'The coffee machine is on the landing by the lifts. The karzy is at the end of the hall and the canteen is in the basement. Guided tour over. Now, I like my coffee black, strong and no sugar, sort that out and then meet me in my office in two minutes.'

As she closed her door behind her, she leant on it for one moment, and blew out a long whistling breath. Joseph Easter was *nothing* like she had imagined!

In two minutes, he was tapping on her door, then placing a beaker of coffee on the coaster on her desk.

'Sit down. There are one or two things we need to get perfectly clear before we start.' She fixed him with one of her best, unblinking stares. 'I never asked for this. I like to work alone. I am not easy to work with, in fact, according to most of this bloody station, I'm damn near impossible, *and* I deeply suspect your motives for coming here.'

Joseph returned her stare. 'Fair enough. But you know that my old Inspector, Val Hughes, was forced to retire?'

'Yes. She was injured working the Castor Fen murders.' Nikki wondered where this was going.

'We had a very good working relationship, ma'am. But I'm afraid I did not gel too well with the officer who took her place.' He shrugged. 'I wanted a change, ma'am. A clean break. Something completely different.'

Nikki looked at him steadily. 'Do you see me as a challenge, Sergeant?'

The detective seemed completely unfazed by her question. 'No, ma'am. I don't. But I know a little of your record, like your Queen's Commendation for Bravery? You are driven and passionate, and your methods may not be the same as mine, but we want exactly the same outcome. We want the bad guys off the streets, and put away for as long as possible.' He paused. 'I know you take a lot of flak because of the way you work. Well, I take it because of the way I am.'

Nikki leant forward, her elbows on the desk and her chin resting in her hands. She saw no deception in those curiously dark eyes.

'So, are you prepared to work with someone, who in order to catch a villain, risks her job almost every time she steps outside the station?'

'In this job, we all have to take risks.'

'And would you be prepared to back her up? Even if she lied, cheated and threatened in order to get an arrest?'

'Although I would never compromise my own ethical beliefs, I'm sure everything depends on ones interpretation of the particular situation, doesn't it, ma'am?' There was a hint of mischief in the voice. 'As long as I saw some kind of justice there, I would want to support my senior officer to the hilt.'

'But would you respect her?'

Joseph dropped his gaze for a moment. 'Respect can only be earned.'

'Mm.'

'May I ask one favour?'

Had she been any other woman at the station, or maybe even one or two of the blokes, she would have found herself melting. 'You can ask.'

'If I endeavour not to moralise over your actions, or draw your attention to the rule book too often, would you be kind enough never to bring religion up in conversation?'

Nikki kept the feeling of enormous relief out of her tone, and said, 'The conversations that we will be having, Sergeant, will be entirely professional. I'm not here to make friends or indulge in chit-chat, so rest assured, it'll be my pleasure. Now, can we start work?'

Joseph nodded. 'That's what I'm here for, ma'am.'

* * *

Fifteen minutes later, Joseph and his new boss, entered the CID room.

'Okay, this is the team. Such as it is.' DI Galena indicated to the two other occupants of the room. 'Sadly, you will discover that you have come to work with the most dysfunctional bunch in the whole of the Fenland Constabulary. This is PC Dave Harris,' she pointed to a large, middle-aged man with thinning hair and a shirt that looked as if it had never met up with an iron in all its life. Dave raised a hand to Joseph and nodded vigorously, as if he was completely agreeing with the 'dysfunctional' comment.

'He's on loan from uniform,' continued the DI. 'The super thinks he only wants to work with me because he's a lazy bastard and knows that he can spend most of his time hanging around doing sod all, while I do all the hard graft.' She looked at Dave, who was still nodding, although with considerably less conviction. 'Maybe that's right, or maybe I know different.' She turned to the other officer. 'And this is DC Cat Cullen. Frankly, she's a bit of a Billy No-Mates, too. She's only here because no one else would have her. Her inability to get in on time doesn't go down too well with most team leaders.'

The woman said nothing, but threw Joseph a "Poor sod, what have you let yourself in for?" look.

'But,' conceded the DI, 'if you want a genius to go undercover, she's your woman. Send her out on a bit of recon and even our own surveillance boys don't recognise her. Frankly, her own mother wouldn't know her.'

'Talented, ain't I?' said Cat with a grin.

'Whatever, and it pains me to say this, but nice work helping me to nail Darren Barton.'

'That slime-ball! Believe me, it was a sheer delight, guv.'

Galena suddenly turned and looked directly at him. 'And this is Detective Sergeant Joseph Easter, here for one month, *maybe*, on loan from Fenchester. And with your reputation, Joseph, you should fit in a treat.'

Joseph smiled. After all, he *had* been warned. And so far, DI Nikki Galena was delivering everything that he had expected.

'Right. Sit. And listen. Two things. One, we are still trying to find the origins of those damned masks. Dave, you fill the sergeant here in on them later. And two, the super has given us a low-key investigation to carry out.' She perched on the edge of a desk and picked up a thin file. 'It's less official, more a favour under the old pals act, unless we discover otherwise.' As she looked at her small team, Joseph noticed an odd look in her eyes. He wasn't sure what it was, but it looked very much like pain.

'We have a missing student. Now, I know all the reasons why a twenty-one-year-old would skip a few classes, but the dean of the uni believes that in this case, it's too uncharacteristic to ignore. He is certain that she's either met with an accident, or been taken by someone.' The DI skimmed down a brief report with her index finger. 'As the dean coughs up regularly for our fund raising projects, the super thinks we should check her out. So, this is how I suggest we proceed. First, I'll go speak to the dean. Sergeant, you come with me. We'll check out the girl's living accommodation. I understand she lives on campus. If we are concerned, we'll speak to her friends, then we'll decide where to go from there. Meantime,' she glared at Cat and Dave, 'if you two can manage to stay awake long enough, keep plugging away at those bloody masks!'

CHAPTER SIX

Dr Villiers was in the foyer waiting for them. He moved quickly forward, hand out stretched. 'Thank you for your time, officers. I know it's not the normal procedure, but I really appreciate it. Please, come to my office, and I'll explain why I'm so worried.'

Villiers was stick thin, but exuded energy. He gave the impression of being able to take on the London Marathon with no notice or training. Nikki and Joseph sat down, but he paced as he talked.

'Brilliant student. Incredibly sensitive to light and shade. Kerry's picture composition is almost a natural thing: the sort of young person who, without doubt, has chosen the right career path to follow.'

Nikki's usual impatience welled up, she wanted to get down to the nitty gritty, but recognised that the man felt he should explain himself fully.

'And that is one of the reasons that she just would not have missed the field trip to Derbyshire yesterday. The whole trip was organised around a particular place that she herself had designated as a superb spot for landscape photography. The pictures that she hoped to take were going to be used in her final presentation, in her portfolio. *No way* would she have missed it.'

'Does she have any particular problems, sir?'

'None that I know of, Inspector. She seems very well balanced.'

'Friends? A particular friend here?'

'She's generally popular, but strangely, has no one that I would call a best friend.' He frowned. 'But I think that may simply be because she is so passionate about her course. She's something of a rare breed, truly dedicated. Her supervisor has high hopes that Kerry will go a very long way.'

'Boyfriend?'

'No one from the university, but she does spend time with a young man from one of the marsh villages, I understand. I wouldn't know if they were actually a couple, but frankly I'd doubt it.'

'Do you know his name, Dr Villiers?' asked Nikki, deciding that he would be her first port of call.

'No, I don't, but I'm sure one of the students will be able to help you.' He handed her a typed sheet. 'I thought this might help. It's a list of students who are probably closest to her.'

'What about her family? Do her parents know that she has missed classes?'

The dean looked worried. 'Not exactly. The secretary rang them earlier, on some pretext, just to ascertain if she was there, but they said that they were not expecting to see her until next Friday for some family birthday.'

'Didn't they get concerned, if you didn't seem to know her whereabouts?' asked Joseph.

'Third-year students have a fair amount of free time for their studies, Sergeant. There's a greater emphasis on independent learning. We don't keep them locked up.'

'What is her background, sir? Family well off?'

'Absolutely not. They live on the Carborough Estate. Kerry came here by way of a scholarship and a grant. Her school work and examination results were exemplary.'

Nikki's eyes widened. 'A kid from the Borough making it to uni, now that's refreshing!'

'Not every child from a poor background finishes up as a mug shot, Inspector. A few have enough drive and inclination to move upward.'

'Not many. Sadly, we spend most of our life seeing the other end of the spectrum.' Nikki stood up. 'May we see her room, Dr Villiers?'

'Of course, but they don't have rooms anymore, the modern version is called a pod or a cube. And if it's alright with you, I won't come with you. My visits to the student's quarters are kept to the minimum, and my presence would definitely cause speculation that something is amiss.'

'And ours won't?' asked Nikki.

'You aren't wearing uniforms. Lots of people come and go through the living centre.' The dean opened the door. 'Excuse me, I'll go and get you a pass card.'

'There goes a seriously worried man,' muttered Joseph, as the door closed.

'Wouldn't you be, if this kid is the A-class swot that he reckons she is?' Nikki walked to the window and looked across the acres of grounds, and whispered, almost to herself. 'I've got a very bad feeling about Kerry Anderson.'

* * *

Joseph looked across the campus and his eyes widened. 'This has all changed beyond recognition! An uncle of mine used to live in one of the old houses in Blenheim Road.' He indicated to an area beyond the perimeter wall. 'You could see the art college, as it was then, from his bedroom window. It looked like some rambling old mansion house in lovely parkland. Nothing like this!'

'Ever heard of progress?' Nikki was in no mood for giving talks on Greenborough's regeneration over the last decade, and thankfully, Joseph took the hint.

The student living quarters bore no resemblance to any student digs that Nikki had ever seen, and she'd seen a few grubby rooms in her time. Ultra-modern, the main entrance opened onto a large communal space with a central hub that housed chairs and tables, and a bank of ovens, refrigerators and store cupboards. Several students were making snacks, getting hot drinks or generally hanging out there. A series of corridors radiated from the central core, and off these, were the student pods.

Using the swipe card, they let themselves into Kerry's private domain.

For a student, it was unnervingly tidy. The bed was made, and there was very little clutter of any kind around. It seemed that Kerry's only concession to traditional student living was to cover the walls with pictures. But hers were very professional pictures.

'Bloody hell! Villiers was right.' Nikki studied an atmospheric black and white study of a derelict windmill. 'She's damned good. I suppose it's her work?'

'I'd say so.' Joseph looked from picture to picture. 'With the probable exception of these.' He pointed to a collection of postcard sized photographs.

Nikki squinted. 'What are they? Stars and stuff?'

'They are astro-photos, taken through a telescope, and to get quality like this, someone was using some pretty expensive equipment, I'd say.'

'Not her?'

'Wouldn't think so. Unless she keeps her telescope and accessories somewhere else. There's no room for that kind of stuff here.' He looked around, then added, 'And frankly, science, astronomy and cosmology enthusiasts who would be capable of taking shots like this, tend to be male.'

'Sexist!'

'Far from it. I'm actually admitting that geeks, nerds and anoraks are generally blokes. She clearly has an interest in the subject, or she wouldn't have the photos, but I just feel, looking at these other pictures, that she's more artistic, more into moods and atmospheres.'

Nicely side stepped, Sergeant Easter! 'Right, well, let's see what we can find. You take the living area and I'll take the bedroom section.'

Nikki had never been inside a pod before, and was impressed. Within the small area was a living space with desk and workstation, a bedroom with roomy storage boxes, hanging space and cupboards built around the bed, and a full en-suite. The windows in both rooms were floor to ceiling, giving the small apartment a bright and airy feel. There were no cooking facilities except for a narrow breakfast bar with a microwave and an electric kettle, but she guessed the communal hub provided everything they needed for eating and socialising.

She thought about her own early years, and decided it was best not to try to make comparisons, because there seemed to be none.

She began to sift through Kerry's belongings, and felt a pang of nostalgia at seeing the young woman's bright, trendy clothes. Every drawer was neatly packed with carefully folded T-shirts, blouses, camisoles, shorts and underwear.

Why hadn't Hannah been as tidy as this when she was at home? It would have meant a lot less heated arguments, that was for sure. She picked up a make-up bag, took out a lipstick and undid it. She twisted the base. Same colour as Hannah's favourite. She glanced at the label and knew that she would see the words, "Seriously Sexy Pink". She put it back and tried to push thoughts of Hannah away. Instead she stole a surreptitious glance at Joseph. Sadly she found nothing to complain about regarding his search techniques. He was annoyingly thorough, methodical and careful.

'I've found a birthday card for her father.' Joseph called out.

'The dean mentioned a family birthday. Has she written in it?'

'Yes. She says, "Have a great day, old man! See you for a birthday drink on Friday. Love and kisses. K." Oh,' his tone altered, 'ma'am, I've just found her credit cards, student card and some cash.'

Nikki felt a cold shiver snake across her shoulder blades. 'I said that I had a bad feeling about this.'

Joseph gave a short sigh and held out a piece of paper with a scrawl of handwriting across it. 'Look. She's even left herself a note to ring someone about a workshop next week. Hardly the thing to do, if you are planning on doing a bunk.'

'Right, I think it's time we spoke to some of her colleagues, and in a very informal manner, Sergeant, I don't want any of these kids panicked.'

'Don't worry, ma'am. I can do softly-softly rather well.'

'Why doesn't that surprise me? Come on, let's start with the *neighbours*.'

* * *

An hour later, they made their way back to the car.

'You drive,' she threw Joseph the keys, 'while I bring the super up to speed. I assume that if your uncle lived around here, you can find your way back to the nick without needing satnav?'

'I'll try my best, ma'am.' He adjusted the seat, clipped on his safety belt and listened as his boss spoke to the superintendent.

'Yes, sir. It looks as though your academic friend may be right. Her room shows no signs at all of anything being out of the ordinary. Kerry has taken nothing with her to indicate that she was planning on going away, and she was seen leaving the student's block at around midnight on Monday. She was wearing casual clothes, carrying only a shoulder bag and wearing hiking boots.'

After a short break in her side of the conversation, she said, 'No, not unusual. Midnight is far from late for a student, sir, and her friends say she would often go out with her camera taking night studies, although the boots do indicate that where ever she was going, it certainly wasn't clubbing.'

There was another silence, then the DI said, 'I agree, sir. So if she hasn't met with some kind of an accident, on

41

whatever clandestine excursion she went on, I'm forced to think the worst.' She flipped the phone closed, 'The super has already checked round the local hospitals, and zilch.' She sat for a while, chewing on her lip. 'As soon as we get back, I'll ring Villiers to make sure that no one goes into that pod. I would normally get uniform to close it up, but until we know a bit more, we still have to keep this unofficial. Our bloody budget doesn't extend to our chasing round after every kid who goes on a three day bender.' She gave a short sigh. 'Not for one minute do I believe that's the case here. However, our next task looks as if it will be speaking to the parents.'

Joseph glanced across and saw her face harden. No one liked this part of the job. He loathed it, but looking at her, he had the feeling that DI Galena hated it as much as he did.

Without thinking, his foot eased further down on the accelerator. He was starting to feel as uneasy as his new boss.

CHAPTER SEVEN

'What do you think of this, Davey-boy?' Cat threw a catalogue onto Dave's desk.

'Whoa! I'm not sure the old ticker is up to looking at that kind of thing! Where on earth did you get it, and what's it got to do with the investigation?' Dave tried hard not to look at the abnormally large-breasted woman in the shiny red rubber catsuit.

'Shot in the dark, but I called into that adult shop down Carvery Lane.' She threw him an accusatory look. 'Nothing kinky, just checking for masks.'

'And?'

'Well, if they ever send me undercover to an S & M club, I know exactly where to buy my outfit, that's for sure! But, I digress. The bloke who runs it, Jimmy, he imports all his masks, via a wholesaler, from China. Hardly surprising, I know, but listen to this. Apparently there's a big market in really scary hand-made ones. Made here in the UK.'

'I've just been looking at them on the web. They are horrific! Look at this one.'

He double-clicked the mouse and a hideous, rubber horror mask appeared full screen.

'That is kid's stuff, mate, believe me. Take a look at this, if you've got the stomach.' Cat flicked through the brochure to find the right page. 'What about that?'

Dave visibly recoiled.

Cat hid a sly smile at his reaction. 'Effective, isn't it? Apparently made of quality latex, and all individually designed and hand-painted. They are full head covering and are moulded from a human head to get a life-like effect.'

'Who the hell would buy something like that?'

'Any freak who has sixty quid to spare, and fancies looking like a flesh-eating nightmare from hell, I suppose.'

'Sixty quid!'

'Get one of your own design made up, and it will be more like a hundred.'

Dave closed the catalogue. 'Well whoever is spreading ours around the town didn't spend that kind of money, surely?'

'Of course not. These tacky things,' she pointed to the dead-rat-man mask on the desk, 'are rubber, and nowhere near the quality of this.' She jabbed a finger at the brochure. 'What I'm saying is that it *is* possible to get these things made to order. And Jimmy told me you can even get a DVD from the Internet that tells you how to mould and cast your own. Not an easy process, but it can be done. Maybe I'll download it and find out what equipment you need. Checking out the suppliers could be my next avenue to follow.' She picked up the magazine and flicked through it. 'Wow! Gorgeous outfit! I wonder how you would get that on, or more to the point, how you'd get it off.'

'Please!' Dave closed his eyes. 'Remember my heart!'

Cat grinned and shut the book. 'Okay, in the interests of your cardiac health, I'll change the subject slightly. Has anyone got any further with the name Griffyx?'

Dave shook his head. 'No, nothing. I've Googled it myself but can't find anything on any variation of spelling.'

'Means nothing to me, but I can ask around on the streets.'

'I wouldn't, well not until you run it past the guv'nor. Don't want to give anything away. So far it's the only info we've had on the damned things.'

'Yeah, you're probably right. Maybe I'll try a few searches of my own. It sounds like something from a computer game to me.' She logged into her computer and while she waited for the search engine, said, 'So, what do you think of the new boy?'

'Sergeant Easter? Well, not what I was expecting, that's for sure. Seems okay. And *so far*, pretty resistant to the boss's acid tongue.'

'Well, I think he's hot! If he's what religion is about, Hallelujah! I'm converted.'

'You are a lost cause, Cat Cullen. And I'd keep that observation to yourself, if I were you. If anyone hears you talking like that, they'll have you up for discrimination of one sort or another.'

'Okay, okay, you boring old fart! But I still think he's hot. Now, let *me* try. Come on, Mister Griffyx, show yourself.' She punched in another search and sat back to watch the monitor screen. 'You know, it's weird when you think about it.'

Dave looked up.

'I mean, it's just *kids* who seem to have these masks, and it's not hard to get a kid to fess up if you lean on him a bit.'

'I catch your drift. You mean that so far, not one has as much as squeaked about where they come from. So . . . ?'

'So they really *don't* know, do they? Which begs the question, what the hell is some adult doing scattering nasty masks around for kids to pick up?'

'Niall Farrow reckons it's a publicity stunt. Maybe the forerunner to some kind of new gimmick thing. You know, the "must have" gizmo of the month.'

'So why *give* them away?'

'A sprat to catch a mackerel. Get 'em hooked, then start charging the earth for them.'

'Sorry, but I think that's total crap.' Cat snorted. 'What sane parent is going to fork out good money to make their kid's face look like road kill?'

Dave grimaced. 'For some of the little shites we get in here, it'd be an improvement.'

'Maybe, but—' Cat didn't have the chance to finish as the desk phone shrilled out.

A moment or two later, she replaced the receiver and bit her lip. 'That was the guv'nor. She's on her way back. She wants us in her office in ten minutes.'

Dave pulled a face. 'That doesn't sound too good. Is it about the missing girl?'

'I think so, my chubby little friend. So, if you need a coffee or a bun, I'd go get it now. My gut feeling says we are going to be very busy.'

* * *

Nikki jumped out of the car, leaving Joseph to lock it and chase after her to the back door of the station. She knew that the sooner they acted the better the chance of finding the girl and she was not going to waste one damned second. For once, the drug dealers slipped from her thoughts, and Kerry Anderson moved in.

She punched in the security number and pushed the door impatiently. 'What was the name of that boy she spends her time with?'

'Her 'pod' neighbour said he's called Kris, spelt with a 'K.'' Joseph breathed hard as he caught the door before it closed on him. 'Lives in Barnby Eaudyke.'

'Surname?'

'Brown.'

'Does her friend think they are lovers?'

'Definitely not. She said they are just mates.'

'Yeah, right, well I wonder if Mr Kris with a 'K' sees it like that?'

As they ran up the stairs to the CID room, Nikki's mind was already in overdrive. Kris Brown was obviously their starting point. And the parents needed to be told. And then . . .

'Inspector Galena!' A WPC ran up behind them. 'Superintendent Bainbridge wants to see you right away, ma'am. He's in your office.'

Without replying, Nikki turned and hurried down the corridor.

* * *

Rick Bainbridge stood up as they entered. 'Shut the door.' His craggy face looked even more war-torn than usual.

Nikki's jaw jutted forward. 'What's happened, sir?'

'Some ramblers walking the seabank found a mobile phone. They also found this.' The super placed an evidence bag on the desk.

'What is it?' Asked Nikki, peering through the clear plastic.

'A light meter,' Joseph said sombrely. 'Used by serious photographers.'

'A photographer, like Kerry?'

The super ran a meaty hand through his hair. 'I don't think there's too much doubt about that. Most happy snappers are all digital these days.' He paused. 'But we have one piece of good luck here, although the phone was damaged, the lab reckon they will be able to retrieve information from it.'

'Right, so we now know she's been abducted.' Nikki drew in a deep breath, 'It's time to get the official wheels turning.'

The super held up his hand. 'Yes, but before we open the floodgates, Inspector, I want to know, one hundred per cent, that the phone belonged to her.'

'It has to be hers!' exploded Nikki. 'Her friends say she often goes up the seabank, either taking photos or sky watching with her little 'mate,' Kris. And she was last seen wearing hiking boots, what more do you want?'

'Confirmation,' said the super patiently.

'Sir! You know the time scale for finding abductees. The first twenty-four hours are crucial! And we've already lost valuable hours . . .'

The superintendent reached for the ringing phone. 'It's the lab,' he muttered holding his hand over the mouthpiece. After a few short words, he hung up and looked from her to Joseph. 'It's Kerry Anderson's alright. The last message she received, *and* the last call she made, were both to and from the same person.'

'Don't tell me,' Nikki was already making for the door, 'Kris Brown.'

CHAPTER EIGHT

The word 'village' conjures up a certain rural quaintness, but as Nikki and Joseph drove into Barnby Eaudyke, they found nothing of the sort. The cottages and houses were scattered in meagre clusters, and every one of them edged the vast arable fields that ran all the way down to the marsh. The narrow lane that served as the main road was clogged with mud spewed up from the tractor tyres, and chickens roamed at will across the pocked-marked asphalt.

The Browns' cottage sat a little way back from the road. The front garden had mainly been given over to a shingle car-parking area and turning space, and the cottage itself, although not exactly ramshackle, could have used a hearty dose of TLC.

'Hardly chocolate box, is it?' said Joseph, looking at the weather-bleached paintwork.

'What do you expect!' Nikki snorted. 'These are farm worker's places. And this is the Fens, not the cosy Cotswolds. They work god-awful hours to just about scrape an existence. So, along with the east wind and the North Sea—'

'Okay, okay, I get the picture.'

Nikki swung the car into a lay-by, intended for church business, and they walked back.

In the absence of a bell, Joseph rapped hard on the wooden front door.

A dog barked sharply, and then they heard a voice call out. 'It's open. And Swampy doesn't bite.'

Joseph pushed the door, and was greeted by a small brown and white spaniel that barked excitedly, then fled back into the cottage.

'We're looking for Kris Brown,' called out Joseph.

'Then you've found him.' The young man was tall, skinny in the extreme, and had a floppy mop of almost black hair and thin wire-framed glasses. 'What can I do for you?' he asked, mildly suspiciously.

Both Nikki and Joseph produced their warrant cards. 'We'd like a word please, Mr Brown.'

Nikki watched the eyes. After looking closely at their cards, he looked up and she saw the suspicion had been replaced by confusion. He shrugged, then stood back from the door.

'I suppose you'd better come in.'

The door led directly into the sitting room. He pointed vaguely towards two armchairs that flanked the fireplace. 'Sit down, if you want to.' He perched on the arm of an over-stuffed sofa and stared at them. 'So what's this about?'

'You are a friend of Kerry Anderson, Mr Brown?'

'Yes.' The eyes narrowed slightly.

'When did you see her last?'

The vagueness fell away. 'Kerry?' He said sharply. Now there was concern, in both his expression and his voice. 'Has something happened to her?'

'Well, we thought perhaps you may know the answer to that, Mr Brown.' Nikki didn't take her eyes off him. If he was acting, he was bloody good. But then Nikki had seen some award winning performances in her time.

'Well! Has she had an accident, or what?'

'Can you tell us when you saw her last?' repeated Nikki.

The young man's Adam's apple jerked convulsively in his throat as he swallowed.

'I, well, I . . .' He rubbed his forehead. 'Oh yeah, it was the day before yesterday.'

'And where was that, Mr Brown?' added Joseph calmly.

'At the Hub.'

'At the university?'

'Yeah. She wanted to talk to me, and as she had some spare time before one of her lectures, we grabbed a coffee.' He pushed his glasses further up onto the bridge of his nose and stared straight at Joseph. 'Look, man, if something's happened to Kerry, you have to tell me.'

'We don't have to tell you anything,' said Nikki flatly. 'So what did she want to talk about?'

'Uh, nothing really, well nothing important.'

'Let us be the judge of that.' Nikki's tone was edgy. 'What did she want?'

Brown tugged nervously at the hem of his baggy sweatshirt. 'I . . . I can't remember.'

'Oh come on! Kerry asks to see you, to talk, and you can't remember why?'

'We just chatted. She talked about her dad, and what she'd bought him for his birthday, and she said she was looking forward to the field trip to the Peak District. I filled her in on some new gamma-ray bursts that have been discovered by ESA's Integral satellite, and that's all, really.'

'Thrilling! And you didn't think to ask her why she specifically needed to see you?' Nikki didn't bother to keep the derisory tone from her voice.

'But we often have a coffee. It was nothing new.' He frowned. 'Kerry sometimes likes to just off-load, you know? And she knows that she can to me.' He stared directly at Nikki. 'People think it's all so easy for her, but it isn't.'

'Okay. So what sort of mood was she in?'

Brown thought for moment. 'Upbeat about the field trip, but . . .'

'But?' asked Joseph.

Brown didn't answer immediately.

'My sergeant asked you a question,' growled Nikki.

'Well, I didn't think too much about it at the time, but now,' he rubbed hard at his temple, 'now, I get the feeling that something could have been bothering her. The fact that she was all fired up for the trip kind of masked it, but on reflection, maybe she was *too* hyped up.'

It was Nikki's turn to frown. She'd played this all wrong. She'd given Kris Brown too much time to work out a retrospect scenario where Kerry was already worried about something. Time to move on.

'So, when did you speak to her last?'

'But I just told you!'

'No, Mr Brown, you told me when you last *saw* her, not when you spoke last.'

'That was it! I haven't spoken to her since.'

'No phone calls? No text messages?' Nikki kept her voice expressionless.

'No, none.'

Nikki frowned. 'Do you have a mobile phone, Mr Brown?'

Kris Brown looked at her as if she were in need of mental care. 'Yeah.'

'Can I see yours, please?'

'Sure.' He moved across to a row of coat hooks by the front door and pulled a light jacket down. He plunged his hand deep into the pocket, then pulled it out and tried the other pocket. 'That's odd,' he murmured, almost to himself. 'I thought . . .'

'Having trouble finding it, sir?' asked Joseph. 'I thought you young people were super-glued to your phones?'

Brown frowned. 'Not me.'

'Why? Bit of a loner, are you? Not many friends? Except Kerry of course.' As Nikki stared at him she saw him begin to gnaw on his bottom lip. And she wasn't sure if he were nervous, frightened, or just acting at one of the aforementioned emotions.

'I think I have a right to know what has happened to Kerry.' There was a tremor in his voice.

'Where were you last night, Mr Brown?'

He tensed. 'I was here.'

'Was anyone with you?'

'I was alone. My mother was away last night.'

'And, is there a father?' Joseph's tone was gentler than Nikki's, and it irritated her.

'No. No father.

'And your mother was conveniently 'away'?' barked Nikki.

'It wasn't convenient, whatever that means. She's a rep, for a sports equipment company. She's often away. Now will you please tell me what the hell is going on?'

Nikki noted the shaking hands and the reddening cheeks. 'We need to find your phone, Mr Brown. Perhaps my sergeant should help you look for it?'

'If it's not in my pocket, then I've lost it.' Kris Brown sat back on the sofa and stared belligerently at them. 'I hate the things. I'm always losing it. Sure you need one living in a place like this, but I don't often use it, and I never text!'

'We have reason to believe that you texted Kerry Anderson last night.' Nikki paused to see what effect her next words would have. 'That would be just before she disappeared.'

The man gave a sharp intake of breath. 'Oh shit! But I never sent her a text! It wasn't me!'

'I'm sorry, Mr Brown, but in the absence of someone to confirm your whereabouts last night, and the fact that you cannot produce your mobile, I'm afraid we are going to have to ask you to come with us to the station.'

Nikki glanced at Joseph. 'Get him to sort his dog out, then take him to the car, Sergeant. I need to ring for uniform to get out here. I want a thorough search for that missing phone, and any other evidence of Kerry Anderson being here.' She turned to Brown. 'Can we have your permission for that? Or do I need to get a warrant?'

The man offered no resistance. 'Do what you have to, no doubt you will anyway. But I promise you, I haven't seen

Kerry since we met for coffee. And I would never hurt her, never.'

'Because you love her?'

'Love her?' He blinked in surprise. 'I don't love her. She's my friend.'

'Well, perhaps that's how she wants it to be, but maybe you'd like a bit more, Kris? Did you make a move on her and she didn't like it? Is that how it was?'

At first he didn't answer, then Kris Brown threw her a look of utter disgust. 'I said she's my friend. And I meant it.'

As Joseph walked him to the car, Nikki pondered on the intonation Kris Brown had placed on the words, *my friend*. There was a peculiar 'singular' sound to it, and she was left with the distinct feeling that Kris's other friends were few and far between. If indeed, apart from Kerry, there were any.

As she locked the door, she decided that she was going to need a lot more time with that young man. There had been something in his voice when he talked about Kerry Anderson, something clingy and unhealthy. Like he knew her better than anyone else. Like he worshiped her. Nikki shuddered slightly. She knew from past cases, one in particular, that that kind of relationship could go horribly wrong.

* * *

Mickey lay on his side on the unmade bed, and stared at the mask held tightly in his hand. He should never have taken it. The orders were very clear, and if Marcus found out, the older boy would knock seven bales out of him. And that would be the end of all that lovely cash.

He felt the spongy rubber with his fingers, then smiled possessively at it. He'd just have to make sure that Marcus *didn't* find out. He'd hide it, and wear it when he was alone. Like now.

The boy gave a little shiver of excitement. So far he had not had the opportunity to put it on. Now that his dad was down the social, and his mum had gone off with some friend, he had the place to himself.

Mickey sat up, and taking the mask with him, walked across to the wardrobe. Inside the door was a long narrow mirror. Mickey looked at himself with interest. He sure didn't look like the kind of kid who had nearly £200 stuffed in a shoebox beneath his bed. He grinned, then pulled the mask over his thick thatch of corn-coloured hair. He positioned the eye slits, then looked once again in the mirror.

The second he saw himself, he gave an involuntary yelp, and breathed in a great gulp of stale, rubber smelling air that made him cough.

It was horrible. And exciting, at the same time. Sort of powerful! He felt a cramp-like thrill grip his stomach and churn his lunch into mush. Yeah, this was so cool! He stared at himself again and knew it had been worth the risk.

* * *

Superintendent Bainbridge was waiting in the CID room when Nikki got back. He seemed to have aged ten years since her trip to Barnby Eaudyke. 'WPC Collins and I have seen the parents. I don't have to tell you what kind of state they are in.'

He didn't. Nikki had dealt with enough frightened and bereaved parents to fill a small theatre. Plus she had had more than her own fair share of heartache with Hannah.

'Have they thrown any light on what may have happened, sir?' she asked.

'Right now, they are too shocked to string a sensible sentence together. WPC Collins and PC Farrow have volunteered to wait with them until the designated Victim Support Liaison Officer gets there.'

'What about the seabank? Where they found the mobile? Has that shown up anything?'

'Plenty, and none of it good.' The super frowned. 'The whole area has been trashed. Probably to cover up footprints or signs of a struggle.'

'Yet they left the phone and that gadget thing behind?' Nikki questioned.

'The ramblers found those some way down a steep bank that drops away from the path to the marsh. You'd never see them in the dark.'

'What about tyre tracks, sir?' asked Joseph. 'They had to get out to the seabank somehow, and I doubt they walked.'

'Yes, there are tracks. Too damn many,' growled the super. 'Some kids on off-road bikes were out there doing wheelies, or whatever it is they do on those wretched machines.'

'Convenient.'

'I don't think it's connected. The kids go out there regularly, scaring the shit out of the wild-life.' The super leaned back against the wall. 'As soon as Collins and Farrow are back in the station, I'm calling a meeting. This is your case Nikki, but I'm pulling in all the help I can get, and,' he paused, looking directly at her, 'I think, under the circumstances, our best hope is to go public immediately, do you agree?'

Nikki thought for a moment, then nodded. 'It could be costly if she turns up tomorrow with a hangover and a tattoo that she doesn't remember getting, but I guess we can't afford not to.'

The super straightened up. 'Then I'll inform top brass. And I'd appreciate it if you and Sergeant Easter went back to the campus and spoke to Dr Villiers in person. We're going to need a pretty big team down there to talk to the students. Arrange things with him and I'll see you all back in the meeting room in an hour.'

Nikki pulled a face. 'Could someone else go? I really need to speak to the occupant of Interview Room 2.'

'Kris Brown?' The super halted mid-way through the door. 'Is his mother here yet?'

'On her way, sir,' said Joseph. 'Probably be here in about an hour. She was in Grantham when I managed to contact her.'

Nikki glared at Joseph. 'But there's no reason on earth to wait until she arrives before we interview Brown. He's not a bloody kid!'

Joseph raised his hands in mock surrender. 'That's not what I was implying. I just answered a question, ma'am. And for what it's worth, I'm with you.' He looked back to the superintendent and raised his eyebrows. 'If Brown knows where Kerry is, I don't think we should waste a single moment.'

Nikki opened her mouth, then shut it again. She wasn't sure if it was the man's gentle voice and unshakable calm that was rattling her, or simply that she wasn't used to people agreeing with her.

The superintendent gave them both a stony look. 'And *I* say Brown waits until you've been to the university. He's not going anywhere, and some time alone, not knowing exactly what we know or are planning, may just scare him into talking to us.'

Nikki gritted her teeth. And that wasted hour could mean life or death to Kerry Anderson. If she were right, time alone was normal practice for Kris. It wouldn't worry a loner like him one iota, let alone scare him. But she was going to get nowhere by arguing, so they'd better get back to the university, and fast.

With a muttered word that could have been anything, she picked up her bag and made for the door.

CHAPTER NINE

'Those poor parents. What it must feel like to know your child is missing.' Niall shook his head, then suddenly started forward. 'Hey! Vonnie! Look over there!'

Yvonne Collins looked, then swerved the police car across the oncoming traffic and into a side road that led to the Carborough Estate. 'Little sods! Radio in for some help for that woman. She's clearly not injured, so I'm going after the kids who mugged her!'

'You'll have to put your foot down, Von. Another few hundred metres and the rabbit warren opens up and we'll never catch them!' Niall gripped the dashboard as Yvonne accelerated forward.

'What the dickens do you think I'm doing?' she muttered, as she deftly missed an overturned rubbish bin. 'Jesus! These street kids get worse! In broad daylight with a police vehicle in full view, they snatch a handbag and take off on bloody bikes.'

Niall swiftly reported their position and what had occurred, then flipped off his radio. 'Someone's on their way to the victim.' He puffed out his cheeks. 'Not that she'll be able to give a description. They are wearing those damned masks, aren't they?'

'Oh yes, just look!'

Ahead of them, spinning his bike around as he entered a narrow alley way, a masked youth was staring defiantly straight at the police car, and sticking up his middle finger in customary salute.

'Too late,' cursed Niall. 'We'll never find him now.'

'Don't bank on it.' Yvonne floored the accelerator and cannoned straight past the alley. 'There's a chance they are heading for the flats, and those connecting alleys all meet on Fisher Street. I may be wrong, but it's worth a shot.'

'Stick on the two tones before we kill someone!'

'What, and let half the estate know we're coming? Like hell.' Yvonne flung the car expertly around a corner. 'And I have no intention of killing anyone. Unless I get my hands on those little shits, that is.' She straightened up and the car leapt forward.

'If I can just get across to the recreation ground before them, we may . . .' Yvonne broke off, and braked hard. 'Oh hell! Take a look at that!'

Ahead of them was an open expanse of concrete, unofficially used for parking, but right now there were no cars, just youths. Two gangs, squaring up to each other like warring tribes, all ugly faces and aggressive posturing. There was little difference between them when it came to age and attitude, the only thing that separated them was that one gang were wearing masks.

Niall was already on the radio when the taunting stopped and the fists came out.

'Tell them we need back up!' shouted Yvonne, as she prepared to jump out of the car. 'Meanwhile, I'll do what I can.'

'No!' Niall's voice blasted in her ear. 'Not this time, Vonnie. I'm all for getting stuck in, but look at them! Someone's going to get badly hurt out there, and I'd prefer it not to be us.'

'We've got to try.' Yvonne opened the car door. 'For exactly the reason that you just said, someone's going to get hurt, and we have to try to prevent that happening.'

'Oh shit! Next time I volunteer us for overtime, remind me of this, will you?' Niall swung open his door to follow her. 'At least you've got a voice that could be heard the other side of the Humber Bridge.'

Together they waded in and began pulling some of the less committed thugs from the pack, and by the time two more police cars arrived, they were left with a heated core of some ten kids. Vicious kids who had the red mist in front of their eyes, and were giving up for no one.

'Leave 'em to the Cavalry!' called out Niall, as he yanked a stick-thin youth from the back of another. 'We've done our bit, and it looks like half the station has turned out to mop up.'

'Yeah,' gasped Yvonne, as she propelled another young-ster towards the car. 'You could be right!' Cars and vans were pouring into the estate, and the teenage rioters were now running in every direction to get away. 'Blimey! Even Old Nick and Holy Joe have made an appearance. What the devil did you say was going down here?'

Niall grinned. 'Mm, it seems I may have over-reacted somewhat.' He pulled the skinny youth towards him. 'What's this all about? Don't tell me you're actually fighting over those damn masks?'

'Sod off! It ain't nothing to do with me. Got caught up in it accidental-like.' The boy wiped a dirty sleeve across his blood stained lip.

'Really?' said Niall. 'And I thought it was *you* that jumped on that other ugly little kid over there!' He looked across at Yvonne. 'Well, how wrong could I be? I could have sworn that I saw this poor innocent lad smack the other one with a knuckle duster!'

'What the knuckle duster he just slipped into his jeans?'

'That'd be the one.' Niall gripped the boy tightly, pulled the offending implement from his pocket, and pushed him towards the car. 'You're coming with us, chum.'

As the teenager stepped forward, something slid from beneath his jacket and fell onto the pavement.

Yvonne picked the mask up with distaste. 'Yours?'

The boy struggled to get free of Niall's iron hold, and when he failed, he threw her a baleful look. 'Give it back, pig!'

'Sorry, poppet. But even though it suits you far better than me, I think I'll keep it. Now, get in the car! There's a comfy little cell back at the nick, with your name on the door!'

* * *

'Is everything against me right now?' Nikki fumed. 'Why the hell you had to come this way to get to the bloody university beats me!'

'I'm not local,' said Joseph reasonably. 'It's the only way I remember. And we couldn't ignore an assistance call, now could we?' With little or no effort, he frog marched two youngsters towards a waiting police van.

'I know that!' Nikki dodged a flying missile, then wrestled a youth twice her size to the ground and knelt on him until a uniformed constable dragged him up and cuffed him. 'But the timing stinks!'

Joseph had just relinquished his hold on his two charges and was making his way back to her, when she heard him call out.

'Ma'am!' Over there!'

She spun round and saw one boy rip a mask from the face of another, then turn tail and run from the brawling group. The boy who remained, screamed and fell to the ground, blood oozing through his T-shirt. 'Jesus! He's been stabbed! Someone call a paramedic!'

Before she could get to the boy, two other officers were with him. 'Help's on the way!' called someone, and Nikki turned to see Joseph hurtling after two youths, one who was still carrying the stolen mask.

'Oh shit! That silly bastard's going to get himself killed!' She cursed under her breath, then raced after him.

The two boys fled down a narrow alley, one of their usual get-away routes, but found it blocked by a stationary delivery truck. With nowhere to go, Joseph and Nikki were on them in seconds.

'Come here, you little turd!' Nikki threw herself against the shorter of the two, the one who had stolen the mask, and slammed him roughly against a garage door. Air escaped from his lungs in a loud gasp, and she snapped her cuffs neatly around his wrists. Carefully she slipped her hand into his pocket and withdrew a sticky-bladed flick knife. 'Oh, you are *so* nicked.'

Holding him firmly, she turned to see Joseph lifting the taller boy from the gutter by his jacket collar.

'You too, sunshine,' said the sergeant brightly.

She exhaled loudly. 'Let's get these two scrotes back to the van, then . . .'

Before she could finish, she heard a grunt, and as she turned, she saw Joseph flip the boy into some weird straight-armed lock position that immobilised the youth totally. Before she could even speak, she heard the sergeant whisper, 'One more move towards your pocket, and you'll wake up with both shoulders dislocated, and your arms ready for plaster casts, understand?'

The boy's eyes widened to an impossible size, but all he could do was groan.

To her total surprise, Joseph moved with lightning speed and swapped his grip from one hand to the other, never for one micro-second losing his hold on the boy, or slackening the vice-like grip. The detective then slipped his free hand into the jacket pocket and withdrew it, holding a wicked looking blade.

Nikki's jaw dropped. 'I bet you didn't learn that move in Bible Class!'

Joseph's eyes snapped up, and for a moment she really didn't like the expression that flashed across his face. Then, just as swiftly, it turned to one of reproach. 'I thought we had an agreement?'

'Sorry, sorry. Just an observation! That was nothing I've ever seen taught at Police Training School, and it's not the kind of thing you learn when sorting out the lager louts on a Friday night either.'

Joseph remained silent, then pushing the terrified boy ahead of him, made his way back down the alley.

Nikki followed, still wondering at what she had just witnessed. She was tough. She pulled no punches, and had been close to overstepping the mark on far too many occasions, but that was in a different league altogether. It wasn't just the unorthodox move, it was the sheer speed, not only of his actions, but of his assessment of the situation.

What you saw was most definitely *not* what you got with Detective Sergeant Joseph Easter. Nikki remembered that strange, ice-cold look he'd given her, and shivered.

CHAPTER TEN

Nikki sped through the arrangements with the dean, and hurried back to the police station. Inside, she stopped and stared at Joseph. She had given him two chances to talk to her, to and from the campus, but he had chosen to say nothing.

'A word in private, Sergeant.' She said, then marched up the stairs to her office.

'Close the door.' She flopped into her chair and pointed to one on the other side of her desk. 'Do you have anything you'd like to share with me, Detective?'

Joseph sat down slowly, but stared at his hands, rather than at her. 'Don't we have a suspect to interview?'

'Yes we do, and you're wasting time by avoiding talking to me. As soon as you've told me what the hell all that was about, we go interview Mr Brown, okay?' She narrowed her eyes. 'And until that happens, we sit here for as long as it takes.'

The silence that followed was almost tangible, then Nikki's patience ran out. 'OK, so you were in the military?'

Joseph lifted his head, and she saw no anger in his face, only sadness.

'That was another life. I'm not that man anymore.'

'From what I saw earlier, I think maybe you are.'

'No, I'm not!' exclaimed Joseph. A look of intense pain suffused his face. 'Really. I'm not. It's just that sometimes you chance on a situation, and the old ways, the indoctrination, the reflex, whatever you like to call it, just takes over.'

'Lucky it did, Joseph. I had no idea that little shit had a knife. He could have killed either, or maybe even both, of us. And for that I thank you.'

Joseph shook his head almost violently. 'Forget it. It never happened.' He looked her full in the face. 'And if you want to thank me, just let this go. I really don't want to talk about the past, and I'd appreciate it if the team and the other officers here *never* know about my background. You know that regular career police officers don't like squaddies who turn copper. In fact, some of them hate us. So . . . ? Please?'

Nikki tilted her head to one side. Maybe she was getting even more bitter and twisted, but recently she had found herself quite enjoying seeing someone squirm. But this was different. Joseph Easter was different. And strangely, she felt no pleasure, just a sad sort of discomfort for him. Certainly there were a dozen questions running through her head, but now was not the time to ask them. Not with a girl missing.

She nodded, and to her surprise, found herself giving him the first smile that she could remember handing out for a very long while. 'I think we have a suspect to interview, don't we?'

* * *

The rest of the day passed in a blur, and by nightfall every available man and woman was out hunting for Kerry Anderson. Local media had been contacted and the superintendent had made an impassioned plea on national television.

Kris Brown had told them no more than they already knew, and his distraught mother had painted them a picture of a sensitive, highly intelligent, but slightly introverted, home-loving boy. Something more on a par with St Francis of Assisi, than a cold-blooded abductor of pretty girls.

Then at eleven thirty, Nikki received a call from one of the villagers from Barnby Eaudyke. A call that meant she would have to let him go.

'There was a fox around, Inspector. That's why I kept going out into the garden. I have chickens, you see.'

'So what time did you actually see Mr Brown, Mrs Roper?' asked Nikki with something like exasperation.

'Well, off and on from around seven thirty, right up until two o'clock, I suppose. I saw him when I checked my hens. He has an 'observatory,' Inspector. Big posh shed with an opening window, if you ask me, but our Kris is something of a celebrity in the village. He's an astronomer, you know. Nothing he don't know about stars and stuff. Sometimes he's out there all night.'

'Yes, and . . . ?' Nikki tried to keep her cool.

'Well, I saw him going in and out, didn't I? Moving his telescope around. Oh yes, and once, close to midnight, his dog started barking. Must have smelt the fox, I reckon. So he had to be there all evening, Inspector.'

'And, to your knowledge, he was alone, Mrs Roper?'

'Well, I can't swear to it, but I never saw anyone else.'

Nikki thanked the woman for her help, then slammed down the receiver and swore out loud. 'Fuck it! We're going to have to let him go.' She puffed out her cheeks in exasperation.

Joseph shrugged. 'For what it's worth, and I know he's unlike any other twenty year old kid I've ever met, but I really don't think he knows where Kerry is.'

'Since when did you become the county profiler?' enquired Nikki.

'I know I'm no psychologist, but his body language didn't exactly scream out 'I'm a liar,' did it?' countered Joseph.

Nikki leaned back in her chair and rubbed her temples. 'Oh God! I need some sleep. But how can I walk out of this station with a girl missing?'

'We have to. Wherever Kerry is, she needs us to be one hundred per cent on the ball. And as most of the Fenland Constabulary are out there looking for her, there's little left for us to do right now.' Joseph yawned and examined a darkening bruise on his wrist. 'Plus, as we've just spent a happy hour brawling with Carborough thugs, I think we can grab a few hours shut-eye without too many recriminations.'

'Oh shit! The boy who got stabbed! I'd better get down to the hospital and check on him.' Nikki could feel the shadow of a headache forming behind her eyes.

'I rang while you on the phone, ma'am. He's conscious and stable. He's got two uniforms with him until he's well enough to interview, so you can relax over him.'

'Nevertheless, that kid got stabbed because of one of those bloody masks. I need to get those evil things off the streets before something even worse happens.' She gave him a look full of frustration. 'There are not enough hours in the sodding day!'

'My digs are near the hospital, I can call in, if it helps? A couple of hours rest will charge me up again.' He stood up. 'If that's all right with you, ma'am?'

Nikki nodded. 'Would you? That injured kid may just be scared enough to tell you something about the masks. It's worth a try, and I have no doubt you'll be a damn sight more compassionate with him that I would be.'

'No problem. See you later, guv.' Joseph walked to the door.

'And Sergeant?' she called after him. 'About earlier. I won't be mentioning it again, but thank you. I still believe your actions may have saved our lives.'

Joseph Easter didn't answer immediately, but he paused in the doorway, then threw her a small smile. 'Anytime, ma'am.'

Nikki sat for a while. Her first day with her new detective sergeant had been quite something. And he was certainly a far cry from what she had been led to believe. She frowned. Maybe, for her own safety, she should make it her business to find out more about him. One thing was certain, he was a man who had deep dark secrets.

Nikki gave a short bark of laughter that echoed around the empty office. If anyone should know about keeping secrets, it was her.

Yeah, when it came to talking about the past, let's hear it for Nikki Galena, the Queen of the Sealed Lips!

She yawned. Just one more thing to do, then it was a hot shower and a few hours' sleep. She flipped open her phone. Maybe it was the horror of having a young woman missing on her patch, maybe it was tiredness, or maybe it was the flashback she kept getting of her new sergeant immobilising a thug in the time it took her to blink, but she needed to see Hannah. She flicked down to 'H' and pressed 'call.'

Sure it was late, but she really needed to talk to her precious daughter, and a quick visit might do them both good.

After a just few words, Nikki grabbed her coat, and went out into the night.

* * *

The corridors were almost empty and dimly lit. Energy saving, Joseph supposed. Whatever, it gave the rambling old hospital an eerie feeling. His footsteps sounded oddly loud as he tried to locate the lifts, and several times he found himself glancing over his shoulder.

The injured boy, Callum Lodge, had had a close shave but was out of danger. Sadly he had little inclination to talk to the police, even if they had saved his life. The youth had been both scared and aggressive, but Joseph had managed to extract a few more snippets of information about the masks. And then Callum had mentioned a name. Well, a street tag. It wasn't much, but it may help. He'd check it out first thing in the morning.

Joseph cursed softly, and decided that he must have taken a wrong turn. If it had been Fenchester Hospital, he could have done it blindfold, but this place was a maze of unfamiliar clinics and corridors. After a while, he was forced to admit to himself that his usually reliable 'bump of direction' had failed him. He was on a long straight passageway that he certainly did not recognise from his trip in.

He walked along it for a while, hopeful that he would find a Way Out sign, then to his relief he spotted two nurses hurrying out of a door at the end of the corridor ahead of him. He accelerated towards them, but by the time he got there, they had disappeared.

He scanned the walls for a hospital plan, a fire drill map, anything that would get him back to the foyer and the car park, but he found nothing. He'd clearly wandered into a completely different wing, and now he felt both tired and pissed off.

'Can I help you?'

The voice was like an answered prayer.

'I just want out.'

'Don't we all, man!' laughed the male nurse. He flashed the whitest of teeth, then pointed to a set of double doors. 'Go through there, past the High Dependency Unit and you'll see the lifts. Down one floor, turn right, go 100 yards on, and freedom is yours!'

Thankfully Joseph made his way through the doors, then froze in his tracks.

Going towards one of the rooms some way ahead of him, was his new detective inspector.

For a moment, he queried his observational skills, but as he watched the back of the woman, he knew he had not been mistaken. It was definitely DI Galena.

For some reason, he pulled back and waited for her to go inside.

His mind raced. Why was she here? Had she decided to talk to Callum anyway, and then got as lost as he had? He doubted that very much. This was her patch. She wouldn't get lost on her own turf. And her stride had been confident. She knew exactly where she was going. He moved slowly forward. And where exactly was that, he wondered?

Almost tiptoeing along the deserted corridor, Joseph approached the room that he had seen her enter.

The door was shut, but there was a small glass window set in it.

Keeping to one side, so as not to be noticed, Joseph glanced inside.

Nikki Galena sat holding a young woman's hand in hers. The girl, just a teenager, lay unmoving in the bed. He could see Nikki's mouth working as she talked animatedly, but there was no similar response from the girl. In fact, as far as Joseph could see, there was no response at all.

Joseph swallowed hard, and moved back. He had just witnessed something that was intensely private, and he truly wished he hadn't.

Sucking in air, he put his head down, moved swiftly past the door and headed for the lifts, but not before he caught sight of the small handwritten name plate to one side of the closed door.

It simply read, Hannah Galena.

CHAPTER ELEVEN

Nikki had only managed to snatch a few minutes sleep in between tossing and turning uncomfortably on her sofa. Earlier, when she had finally arrived home, she had felt better. It always helped to talk to her daughter. And she was sure that she'd seen signs of improvement in Hannah. The nurses had not agreed, but then they wouldn't. It wasn't up to them to give what may be false hope. But a mother knew best, didn't she?

She had curled up under her blanket believing, as she always did, that one day she would get her beautiful daughter back.

But then the dark thoughts had descended. Thoughts about Kerry Anderson. Would her parents ever get *their* beautiful daughter back? The clock was ticking, and they still had nothing to go on.

And then there were the other disturbing thoughts about Joseph Easter. Since the fight on the Carborough Estate, she had been seeing flashes of how her new sergeant had conducted himself. Those lightning fast moves were not right. And those later comments about being a squaddie? No squaddie she'd ever met had that kind of reflexes. And they were always proud of their regiment, far more so than their place in the police force. That was why they were often disliked, because their allegiance was always, first and foremost, the army. And Joseph wasn't like that at all.

As Nikki locked her front door and stepped out into the early morning air, she wondered if she should talk to Rick Bainbridge about him. After all, the super had made some comment about there being more to Joseph Easter than met the eye. Perhaps he knew something she didn't. She shook her head and carefully stepped around a torn rubbish bag that had deposited its stinking contents across her path. She really couldn't afford all this, she needed to keep her whole focus on Kerry Anderson, not pondering about her sergeant's dubious origins. With a grunt of irritation, she quickened her step and headed towards the police station.

* * *

As Nikki headed for work, Marcus and Mickey slipped quietly away from the Carborough.

'Usual drop?' asked Mickey as he struggled to keep up with Marcus' long-legged stride.

'Not this time. Things are heating up, so they've changed the location.' The older boy looked almost haggard in the early morning light. 'And you're dead certain that your mum and dad don't suspect anything?'

Mickey frowned. 'They don't give a shit what I do.'

'You know what I mean, muppet! You are being careful, aren't you?'

Mickey pulled his hood further over his face. 'Don't worry! Dad's back on the bottle. He was drinking until three, and me mum's buggered off until he sobers up, so everything's cool.'

'It better be. We can't afford the slightest slip.' Marcus lowered his voice. 'Especially now the war has started.'

'Mask Wars! Yeah!' Mickey did a little skip and punched the air with his fist.

'Shut up, you stupid little shit!' He lifted his hand to his forehead and glowered at the younger boy. 'I've had it up

72

to here with you! You're a fucking liability, you know that? Why the hell did I pick you, of all the kids on the 'Borough?'

'Cos no one gives a flying fuck about me. And I've got the face of an angel, which always helps.'

Marcus gave a hopeless sigh. 'Yeah, I guess. But will you please keep your voice down. In fact, just shut it until we get there.'

'Where are we going?'

'I told you to shut up! You'll know soon enough. And hurry up, we only have fifteen minutes to get there.'

They walked the next half mile in silence, then Marcus slowed his pace, and looked around. Ahead of them was a narrow walk down to the river bank. Not the popular bit, where joggers fought for breath and early-bird commuters took a short cut to the station, but a dingy, shadowy track that ran beneath a railway bridge and stopped at the back of a disused bedding factory.

'Neat,' whispered Mickey. 'No one goes down here, except for a piss.'

Marcus ignored him and strode off towards the dark tunnel. He had almost disappeared before Mickey chased after him.

'Can you see anything?'

'Yeah, they're here. Shift your arse and come and help me.' Marcus had pulled an Adidas Sports bag from his shoulder and was ripping open a large cardboard box. He removed a fat plain envelope, then grabbed a handful of the familiar rubber masks. 'Here, get these into your rucksack! We don't have long.'

Mickey jammed the masks into his bag, then hoisted it over his back while Marcus zipped up his own, then returned to dispose of the box. He tore the cardboard into pieces and dunked it into the sluggish river water. When it was well soaked, he screwed it up some more, then stuffed it under some straggly brambly bushes on the edge of the river. 'Let's go.'

Pushing the smaller boy ahead of him, Marcus headed back up to the road. 'Now, we have another change of plan, Muppet-face. Come with me, and don't ask any questions.'

He pulled Mickey roughly around by the shoulders, and glared at him. 'Or this really will be your last job, understand?'

Mickey saw the cool stare and understood perfectly.

* * *

When Nikki arrived at the station, the car park was heaving with vehicles, police officers and volunteers, all heading out to the marshes and the places that were impossible to search at night.

'Nothing yet?' she asked a weary looking Dave Harris.

'No, ma'am. The second wave is just moving out now, they are still concentrating on the campus and the marshlands around the seabank, where her phone was found.' Dave yawned. 'Now you're back, guv, I'll take a bit of a break, if that's okay?'

Nikki pushed her way between a group of searchers in high-vis jackets, and into the foyer. 'Have you been here all night?'

'Yes, ma'am.'

'But what about . . . ?' Nikki frowned and lowered her voice. 'Sorry, but shouldn't you have gone home long before this?'

'She's okay ma'am, but thanks for thinking of us.' He gave her a tired smile. 'I've arranged a carer, just to cover me, short-term like.'

'Surely there's enough bodies here to comb the Fens, without you.'

'Can't dodge the issue when there's a kid missing, can I, guv? And I wouldn't want to either.'

Nikki lightly touched the big man's arm. 'I know, but you have your own problems, and they don't go away because something big is going down here. You go get some sleep, and look after yourself, you hear?'

Nikki watched him go, his shoulders sloping down and his step more a shuffle than a stride. She was the only one who knew about his home life, and she really felt for him.

'Ma'am?' Joseph was striding up the corridor. 'Got you a coffee.'

'What the hell time did you get in?' she asked with something like annoyance.

'Ten minutes ago.' He balanced the mugs in one hand and held the office door open for her with the other. 'Did you sleep?'

'No,' she said sharply, wishing she could tell him that he was partly to blame for her insomnia. 'I've sent Dave home. Is Cat still here?'

'Yup. She's onto something regarding the components required to make rubber masks. She's found a wholesaler of the raw materials.'

'Good, and what did you find out from the victim of yesterday's knife attack?'

Joseph stared at her thoughtfully for a moment, then flopped into a chair. 'Well, the masks really do just turn up. Dumped around the estate or in schools or recreation grounds. Callum swears that no one knows where they come from.'

'And you believe him?'

'No reason not to.' Joseph sipped his coffee. 'He started off all tough, then when he realised I was prepared to take residence beside his bed, he started talking, probably just to get rid of me.'

Nikki gave a long sigh. 'So he's told you nothing that we didn't already know.'

'Not quite. He gave me a name.'

'What?' She leant forward eagerly.

'Well, a street tag. I haven't had a chance to run a check yet.'

'And? What the hell is it?'

'Fluke.'

Nikki choked back a gasp.

'You know him?' It was Joseph's turn to look surprised.

'I know enough to say don't bother running that check. You won't find anything.'

The sergeant jutted his jaw forward. 'So you've already had a lead on him?'

Nikki leaned back in her chair. 'With regard to this case, no. And sadly I don't know a damn thing about him.'

'Then maybe I should get down to the Carborough and make a few enquiries?'

'And you think they'll talk to you?' She gave a short laugh. 'I don't think so!'

'Someone may. One of the mothers perhaps.' He shrugged. 'They will have been pretty shaken up by a young kid getting stabbed.'

'Oh get real, Sergeant. On the Carborough, it's a common occurrence. And right now, we have to concentrate on Kerry Anderson.'

'*She* came from that estate,' said Joseph pensively. 'Do you think there may be a connection?'

'I can't make one, personally.' The thought had already crossed Nikki's mind. 'Kerry comes from the northern side, not an area known for trouble, well, not anywhere near on the scale of that around the flats or the south side.' She pulled a face. 'And how would a hard-working young student possibly be connected to a spate of petty crimes committed by a load of masked yobs? It doesn't make sense.'

'Oh, that's another thing that Callum said. He overheard this Fluke mention something called 'Mask Wars.' He doesn't know what it means, and it's only the intensity of that fight yesterday that made him think about it.'

'Mask Wars?' repeated Nikki softly. 'They'd risk their lives for a crappy piece of rubber? Hell, I know some of these kids have had half their brain cells devoured by alcohol and crack, but this is plain insanity.'

'I agree,' sighed Joseph, 'But as you said, we have Kerry to worry about, so what now?'

Nikki finished her coffee and stood up. 'Back to the university, I want to get up close and personal with her friends. Someone knows more about her relationship with 'Kris with a K' than they've let on.'

'You really don't trust him, do you?' Joseph grinned at her.

'He's a weirdo. And I don't trust weirdos.'

* * *

As they arrived at the University of the Fens, the sun was just coming up. A green-gold glow suffused the glorious old trees that were a legacy of days gone by, with an almost magical luminescence.

'This is really beautiful,' mused Joseph. 'My university was an inner city, concrete monstrosity.'

Nikki swung the car into a tight parking space and killed the engine. 'My heart bleeds for you.' She slammed the door. 'Didn't quite get that sort of education myself. Had to work for a living.' She marched on ahead of him, but couldn't help but wonder how many squaddies had ever gone to uni. 'We'll split up. You take the students to the right of her pod, I'll take the left, and anything you think may be useful, call me. With luck, they'll still be half asleep and easier to interview.' The door to the Hub swung soundlessly open. 'See you back here in half an hour, Sergeant, and we'll re-assess.'

* * *

'Nothing much, ma'am.' Joseph perched on a high stool and looked across the Hub. 'They all know Kris Brown by sight, and one or two have seen his astro-photographs, which I'm told are 'Awesome!' But no one believes that Kerry and Kris are an item. In fact most of them laughed at the notion.'

'Same damn thing with the ones I spoke to,' grumbled Nikki.

'One point, though,' said Joseph. 'A guy called Lewis, who was organising this field trip with Kerry, mentioned that Kris had been mugged recently.' He rubbed his chin with his forefinger. 'Probably not connected, but worth asking Mr Brown about it, don't you think?'

'As good a reason as any for taking another trip out to Mr Weirdo's place.' Nikki stared around at the small clusters of students gathered in the meeting place. 'He's still my number one, even if his mother believes he's a modern day saint.' She looked back at Joseph. 'Anything else?'

Joseph pulled a face. 'Nothing specific. I just get the feeling that no one here really *knows* Kerry,' he paused, then said, 'and how many girls do you know who have no close girly mates to gossip with?'

Nikki nodded. She understood exactly what her sergeant meant. The kids were shocked by Kerry's disappearance, but their reaction had been more detached than she would have expected. If Hannah had disappeared, Nikki was pretty sure that her girlfriends would have been distraught, throwing every kind of teenage histrionic known to man. 'If she's a Top Swot, perhaps her contemporaries don't like her? Maybe they're jealous of her good grades or the attention she gets from the tutors?'

'Could be, but it didn't seem that way. There was no animosity there, I just didn't get the reaction I was expecting.' Joseph shrugged. 'Maybe I'm just out of touch with youngsters these days.'

There was a strange wistfulness to his voice that was not lost on Nikki, but now was not the time to wonder on the enigma that was Joseph Easter.

'Right, then it's back to the station.'

As they reached the car, Nikki's phone rang. After a few curt words she hung up.

'Problem, ma'am?' Joseph's face was apprehensive.

'More trouble on the Carborough. A group of masked yobs have torched a car.'

'Are we required, ma'am?'

'Not this time. Uniform has got it covered.' Nikki looked thoughtfully at her sergeant. Was there a hint of disappointment there? Or maybe it was relief? It was hard to tell. 'So, I think it's time we paid a visit to Kerry Anderson's mother and father.'

Joseph took a deep breath, then nodded resignedly. He clearly had no more liking for facing grief-stricken parents than she did.

As they got into the car, she tried to conceal the small private smile that played on her lips. So, maybe she and her strange sergeant had one thing in common after all.

CHAPTER TWELVE

The Anderson's pride for their daughter screamed all around the small terraced house. In most rooms, photographs, diplomas, certificates and press cuttings practically replaced wallpaper. And that made the absence of the girl herself even more poignant.

Sergeant Lucy Wells, the Family Liaison Officer, had a brief word with them in the kitchen before they spoke to the parents.

'Mr Anderson is very quiet, but I think he's more switched on to the gravity of what's happened than his wife. She's a bit flaky, convinced it's a great big mistake, and her daughter will come marching through the front door at any moment.'

'Well, we can't blame her for that, can we?' said Nikki flatly.

'Of course not, but I'm worried about her. Apparently she's not strong at the best of times, and this has been one hell of a shock for her.'

'I assume her doctor has seen her?'

'Oh yes,' said Lucy. 'She's got a bucket load of pills for her nerves, but I'm still keeping a close eye on her.'

'And you have no suspicions about the father?' asked Nikki, knowing the sad statistics about the abductor being a close family member.

'If it's him,' Lucy raised an eyebrow, 'I'll give up my career and go cut cauliflowers for a living.'

'Okay, well, we won't over do the questions, but maybe they know something that could help us, even if they don't think it's relevant.'

In the living room, the Andersons sat close together on a floral patterned sofa. Lucy introduced them, then went to make some tea.

'Can you tell me why Kerry is in halls of residence, when you live so close to campus, Mr Anderson?' asked Nikki.

The man rubbed at the stubble on his chin, and sighed. 'We argued about that, the wife and me. But it came down to the simple fact that we live on the Carborough. It's hardly the kind of place where a youngster can get some peace and quiet to study.'

As if on call, a police siren echoed across the estate, and that was soon joined by several more.

'That's the norm around here, and this is the quiet part.' He added miserably.

'We know, Mr Anderson. Our uniforms spend as much time here as they do in their own homes, and I take your point, but I thought universities usually kept those rooms for students from out of the area?'

'The principal, Dr Villiers was very kind. He made an exception considering her unusually high pass marks and her dedication.'

'This can't be happening! Not to my Kerry!' The mouse-like woman on the sofa suddenly flared up like a re-born phoenix. 'Who would want to hurt her? She's a good girl!'

'Mary, Mary.' Hugh Anderson's voice sounded horribly tired. He patted the woman's shoulder gently. 'We have to try to help these good people. They are as worried about our lass as we are. So no more outbursts, my darling, because they really don't help.'

Mary Anderson slumped back, almost disappearing into the cushions. 'I'm sorry.'

'There is no need to apologise, Mrs Anderson, no need at all.' Joseph's voice was full of real compassion. 'It's us that should be sorry. We cannot begin to know what you're going through, but if we are to find Kerry, we have to ask you to help us.'

The woman shook her head slowly from side to side. 'I just don't know what we can possibly tell you.'

Nikki saw that she was close to tears. 'Well, just tell us about Kerry. Her likes, dislikes, friends, hobbies, pets, anything you can think of, just talk about her to us.'

They talked for over half an hour, and Nikki began to build up a picture of the missing girl. Kerry, it seemed, was not a social student, and although likable, she was so unusually single-minded, so totally committed to her photographic studies that they overpowered even the need for close friends, and something about that image disturbed Nikki.

Back in the car, she turned to Joseph and abruptly said, 'Didn't have a lot to say, did you, Sergeant?'

She felt the temperature drop a few degrees before he answered.

'Not something I enjoy.' His words were clipped. 'Frankly, I'd rather face a few tooled-up thugs in a dark alley.'

I bet you would! she thought, but said, 'Well, at least what you did say seemed to come from the heart.'

Joseph did not answer this time, so she continued. 'So, regarding Kerry. Did you get the feeling that she would have sold her soul to get away from the Carborough?'

Joseph turned the key in the ignition. 'I did. And all things considered, it's a marvel she stayed on the straight and narrow. She had to have some special kind of strength to remain focused on getting to uni. I dread to think where she would have ended up if she'd relinquished her dream.'

Nikki nodded thoughtfully. 'Some of the names that her parents gave us; contemporaries from junior school years, they would not mean too much to you, but I can assure you, that as young adults, they are regulars in the Custody Suite.' She sucked in air. 'And the name Frankie Doyle was something I never thought I'd hear from anyone in connection with Kerry Anderson.'

'Why? Is she known to us in some way?'

'She's known to *me*,' said Nikki through gritted teeth.

'And not in a nice way, I guess?' Joseph stared at her enquiringly.

'She's poison. She hurts people. Innocent people.' Nikki stared out of the windshield. 'And I've never managed to pin a bloody thing on her.'

She felt an involuntary shiver chase down her spine. Her own enquiry, the very private one that she'd successfully kept under wraps for so long, was suddenly becoming entangled with the hunt for Kerry Anderson, *and* with this bloody mask war, whatever it was.

She bit down hard on her lip and glanced across to the man sitting next to her. No matter what his reputation said about him, he was the most astute officer she'd worked with for years. He was no fool, and she'd be a fool herself to try to deceive him. The problem was just how much was she prepared to tell him. And because of his secrets, she couldn't totally trust him. Her mind went into overdrive. She clearly needed some time to work that one out, so all she could do at present was stick to basics.

'One thing though, one of my sources reckons Frankie Doyle's started mixing with some very nasty people, so hopefully, she'll get out of her depth and slip up. And I'll be waiting.'

Joseph raised an eyebrow. 'Then it sounds like Kerry was *very* lucky to get away from them.'

Nikki bit her lip again. '*If* she did.'

* * *

'You won't believe this, ma'am, but Archie Leonard is here to see you!' The civilian from the front desk pounced on them as they entered the station. 'He's been here for ages.'

'What the hell . . . ?' breathed Nikki.

'Even I've heard of him,' muttered Joseph from behind. 'The godfather of the Carborough!'

'Well, this is a first. You'd better sit in, Sergeant. It could be interesting.'

'Try to stop me.'

'But first,' Nikki pulled Joseph to one side and dropped her voice to little more than a whisper, 'just so that you know, Archie Leonard is no mindless thug, okay? He's been the King of the Carborough for as long as I can remember. His family have lived there since it was built, but he's an 'old school' crook, if you know what I mean?'

'What, one of the Heroes and Villains Brigade?'

'Yeah, even when I was a rookie, he was 'the man.' But you knew where you stood with him. Life was like a massive game called 'Them and Us,' and when they won, we worked harder, and when we won, they threw up their hands and coughed to it.'

'Surely it was never really like that? No one said, "Fair cop, officer, I'll go quietly." did they?' Joseph's eyes widened.

'Not quite, but Archie Leonard and his two brothers earned quite a bit of respect back then.' Nikki ran a hand through her hair. 'Yes, they were villains, and people did get hurt, no denying that, but they never went in for violence for violence sake. They were damn clever criminals, and anyone who managed to stick a conviction on one of them was pretty well thought of.'

'And I've no doubt you've had your moments with the Leonard family?'

'Off and on over the years we've had the odd run in, but I thought you should know what kind of man Archie is before you draw any conclusions about him.'

'Okay, I'll bear that in mind. So, any idea why he's here?'

'None whatsoever, but I *do* know he won't be behind the violence on the Carborough. That's not his way, and he has family and friends living there.'

'Right.' Joseph flashed her an intrigued smile. 'Let's go see what the man wants, shall we?'

CHAPTER THIRTEEN

If Joseph had had any preconceptions as to what the godfather was like, they would have been blown away the moment he entered the interview room.

Archie Leonard sat at the desk, sipping black coffee. Three other empty beakers were lined up on the table in front of him. Joseph smiled inwardly at the understated indication to the inspector as to exactly how long the man had been waiting.

Joseph did a quick appraisal, and noted a man who would have looked totally at home in a courtroom, but not in the dock. Archie Leonard would have been the one dressed in a red robe and wearing a curled wig. He was straight-backed, good-looking in a greying, distinguished way, and had piercing, intelligent bright blue eyes.

Nikki strode into the room and straight up to Leonard.
'Archie! How are you?'

Joseph remained close to the door and silently observed the greeting. He hadn't been in Greenborough long, but DI Galena was giving this high ranking criminal, the warmest smile he'd seen her stony face produce since he'd met her. And just as surprising, the feeling was clearly reciprocated. Leonard had clasped her outstretched hand in a two-handed grip and was pumping her hand up and down with obvious warmth. There was history here and Joseph wondered what the hell it was.

When Leonard finally let her go, he sat back down, and drew in a deep breath. His gaze then whipped round to Joseph.

'And you are?'

The voice was deep, and although Joseph wasn't sure, he thought it held the slightest hint of an accent. He waited for moment, then realised that his boss wasn't going to introduce him. 'My name is Detective Sergeant Joseph Easter. I'm temporarily assigned to work with DI Galena, sir.'

'Ah, Joseph A good name. My eldest boy is called Joseph, isn't he, Nikki?' There was an almost conspiratorial lift of a thick grey eyebrow.

The DI chose to ignore whatever that implied and simply nodded. 'But you haven't come here to discuss the family, have you, Archie?'

'Actually I have.'

There was a long silence, then she said, 'Look, I know that you'd rather eat broken glass than walk in here voluntarily, so it has to be serious. What has happened?'

The man seemed to shrink, as he said, 'Lisa Jane's missing.'

'Your brother Frank's daughter? The pretty one with the long, dark hair?'

'*All* our girls are pretty.' He looked at the DI reproachfully, 'but yes, the long dark hair. My lovely Lisa Jane.'

'How long has she been gone?' She was clearly shocked.

'Two days. She was going to a new club with her friends, but she never arrived.'

'For God's sake, Archie! Why didn't you come to me sooner?'

The man looked excruciatingly tired. '*You* know how we do things, Nikki. The family wanted to sort it.'

'I know you *never* involve the Old Bill, but Hell-fire, man, this is Lisa Jane we're talking about.' She swung round and looked Joseph straight in the eyes. 'Lisa Jane Leonard. Nineteen years old. Beautiful. Dark brunette, brown eyes.'

'Small scar below her left ear, and a tattoo of a butterfly on her right shoulder blade,' added Archie painfully.

'Right. So sit, Joseph, and get down what Archie has to say.' The DI jabbed a finger at the chair next to her.

Joseph frowned. 'Shouldn't I put a tape in, ma'am?'

'No, you shouldn't.' She looked hard at him. 'No tapes. Just you and a pencil, okay?'

Now was not the time to argue. Joseph nodded, took out his notebook and obediently began to write.

It took very little time to note the relevant details about Lisa Jane. She had left home, all excited and dressed to party, then disappeared.

'And you have no idea who might have taken her, if, of course that's what has happened?' asked the DI.

'Of course I have enemies, but not the kind who would do this.'

Honour amongst thieves, thought Joseph, *I wonder?*

Archie Leonard continued. 'We wondered if it had something to do with some new outfit that are haunting the Carborough. But,' Archie raised his eyebrows and shrugged, 'to be honest, we don't even know if they actually exist.'

'How so?'

'It's all just vague hints and rumours that *someone* is muscling in on us, but that's not the way it works.' He looked at the DI. 'You know the score. The new boss declares his intention. He steals your deals, messes up your jobs and leans on your personnel. It's the standard preliminary before the full turf war begins.'

'And you've had none of this?' asked Joseph.

'No, Sergeant.' Archie looked at him carefully. 'And as you will appreciate, I have a lot of seriously heavy connections, but *no one* can give me either a name or a face.' He shook his head. 'It is our way to settle our own problems, but this is something I just can't fix, and I will *not* risk my niece's life by sticking to age old gangland rules.'

'You know I'll do whatever it takes to help you, Archie,' said the DI solemnly.

'I know. That's why I came to you. But Nikki,' he stared at her intently, 'no press yet. Whatever you do, you'll keep it low-key, won't you?'

Joseph watched as his boss took a long intake of breath. 'As I said, I'll do what I have to, in the best way that I can. The bottom line is that we get Lisa Jane back.' She stared at Archie for a time then said, 'Can you tell us anything about something called Mask Wars?'

'Ah, those damn kids! But that can't have any bearing on my girl going missing, can it?'

'Probably not, but it's costing us time and manpower, and that takes us away from much more important issues, if you see what I mean?' Her eyes never left those of the older man.

He nodded shrewdly. 'I'll do what I can, but those idiots in the masks listen to no one, not even me. They are just brainless waste of space kids.' His brow drew together into deep wrinkles. 'The base line is that one gang has them, the other doesn't. They are a prize that they fight over. Simple and stupid as that.'

'So where do the masks come from, Archie?'

He threw up his hands. 'No idea, and I've had more pressing things on my mind to care.'

The DI smiled. 'I know. Same here. But I need to put an end to it, before someone else gets stabbed, or dies.'

'I suppose you do.' Archie Leonard stood up. 'Now I have to go, no one knows I came to see you, but I'll see what I can find out about your masks.' He gave her a weak smile. 'Nikki? Find my girl? Please.'

The DI gave him her card. 'Private mobile number. Any time, day or night. Trust me, and take care, Archie.'

* * *

After Archie Leonard had been escorted out, Joseph and his boss returned to the interview room. The DI closed the door, leaned back on it and let out a long sigh. She then stared at the floor until Joseph began to wonder if she were all right. To break the silence he said, 'That can't have been easy, to walk in here and ask for help.'

'You've no idea!' She walked over to one of the chairs and sank down. 'He's broken every underworld law there is by turning to us.'

'So do you know anything about this mysterious new outfit?' Joseph flopped into the chair opposite her and wished he wasn't so out of his depth. In his own area he knew all the names, knew what was going down, but in a different manor, it was difficult and frustrating.

The DI thought for a moment, then shook her head, 'Not much. An informant told me he'd heard rumours about a new gang. Vicious, violent and wanting a patch of their own. Maybe they are looking at the Carborough?'

'Then surely we know exactly where to look for the girl's abductors?' asked Joseph in surprise.

'There's just one tiny problem. Just like Archie, we don't know who they are.' She frowned. '*And* as there have been no prior direct threats to him or any of his family, these shadowy newcomers really may just be myth.' The DI bit her lip. 'Our biggest problem right now is how we deal with it, when Archie doesn't want Lisa Jane's disappearance broadcast.'

Joseph shifted uncomfortably, knowing they were wasting time. 'Well, whatever he wants or doesn't want is irrelevant as we now have *two* girls missing. We have no choice but to work fast, do we? So what next?'

The DI leaned back in her chair and stared at him. 'Carefully, that's how. We don't just rush out there like headless chickens. This is delicate stuff, Joseph. Lisa Jane is a lovely girl, but she's still a member of a close knit gangland family.'

Joseph calmed his mind and thought about it, then realised what the media might make of it, and the hype they could splash across the tabloid press. Something that could severely hamper their enquiries into both disappearances. He looked back at the DI and saw deep concern etched on her face. 'You like Archie Leonard, don't you?'

For a moment he thought she was going to tell him to mind his own damned business, then she nodded.

'Maybe *like* isn't quite the word I'd use, but as you said before, our paths have crossed in the past. A while ago he helped me out with something,' she shrugged, 'and although I was able to reciprocate on another occasion, I still feel I owe him.' She took a deep breath. 'Whatever, he loves Lisa Jane and he's distraught about her, and we have to do all we can to find her.'

'Naturally. A missing girl is a missing girl, no matter what her background,' said Joseph.

'Of course but the politics of this could be a minefield, and I don't want anyone telling me how to run the enquiry.' She abruptly stood up and her face was set with a grim determination. 'I'm going to see the super, and beg him to keep this from the press. And the longer he can sit on it, the better.' She walked to the door, then turned back to him. 'This may have nothing whatsoever to do with the disappearance of Kerry Anderson. Apart from this possible new gang, Archie has made a lot of enemies in his lifetime, one of them may be less honourable than he thinks and may have decided it's payback time,' she paused, 'but no matter how simple that sounds, my gut says different. How say you?'

Joseph didn't even need to think about his answer. 'Two missing girls. Same time frame, same area location, too much of a coincidence. I believe they are connected, ma'am. My gut says the same as yours.'

CHAPTER FOURTEEN

After seeing the superintendent, Nikki decided that she needed to pay another visit to Barnby Eaudyke, and Kris Brown.

As she drove, Joseph stared out across the miles of flat, open fields that edged the marsh.

'Do you really like this place?' he asked.

'It's my home. I love it,' replied Nikki simply.

Joseph nodded. 'I guess seeing 360 degrees of sky has its good points, but don't you find it a tad . . .' he looked for the right word, 'overpowering?'

Nikki shrugged and gently reduced her speed as they approached a hump back bridge over a dyke. 'You can breathe out here. When I was a probationer and I'd had a bad shift, I'd go up to the seabank, be on my own and get my head back together. I know exactly why young Kerry likes to go there.'

'Or, she did. It looks like her last trip could have been a bad, if not fatal, mistake.'

Nikki drew in a long breath. 'Let's just stick to the premise that as we don't have a body, she's still alive, shall we?'

'I want to believe that, it's just that time is slipping away, and . . .'

'No need to go on. I'm fully aware of the ticking clock, *and* the statistics regarding missing youngsters.' She gritted her teeth, then said, 'I wonder if Kris Brown knows Lisa Jane Leonard?'

'Doubtful. I can't see that a beautiful, young model would see much in a skinny anorak who spends his nights with a telescope, can you?'

'I've been thinking that there could be a tenuous connection.'

Joseph's eyes narrowed. 'Tell me.'

'Frankie Doyle.' Nikki found even saying the name difficult. 'Lisa Jane knew her, they were the same age, and Archie told us that they lived quite close when they were kids. Kerry knew her. Her parents said they went to the same school. Ergo, Kris may know her too.'

'But that doesn't mean that Kris would also know Lisa Jane?'

Nikki pulled a face. 'I said it was tenuous.' Before Joseph could answer her, the radio crackled into life and they heard her call sign. 'DI Galena. Over.'

'Ma'am. It's Sergeant Jack Conway. What's your position, please?'

'Siltmarsh Lane, on route to Barnby Eaudyke.'

'We've had a call from the farmer who owns Amber Drove Farmhouse. He's reported finding the body of an IC1 female in one of his barns. Can you attend?'

Nikki stiffened. 'On our way, Sergeant. ETA two minutes.' She floored the accelerator.

* * *

Amber Drove Farmhouse was an imposing stone building with a collection of massive barns and numerous outbuildings and glass houses. The whole place was meticulously neat and reeked of old money.

As Nikki parked close to a stable block, the farmer hurried out to meet them. As she got out of the car, she noticed the pale face of a woman, probably the man's wife, staring at them from a downstairs window of the house. From the look on her face, finding bodies was clearly not in the country diary for a Tuesday afternoon.

Nikki flashed her warrant card and made the briefest of introductions.

The farmer was a big, broad-shouldered, florid-faced man, 'I'm Nigel Grieves. God, you got here quickly! I only rang 999 a few minutes ago!'

'Has this area been checked by the search parties yet?' asked Nikki.

'No, although I had a call yesterday to ask me to look in all my outbuildings. Which I did, but somehow I forgot the lower barn. It's just a shell, and it's so inaccessible that I left it until last, then I got side-tracked.' The man looked apologetic. 'I'm sorry, but running all this can be pretty demanding.'

'So where is she, Mr Grieves? Can you take us to her?'

'Of course. This way, Inspector.' The man moved off towards the stable. 'Know how to ride one of these?' He pointed to two quad bikes that sat on the edge of the field.

'No problem,' said Joseph.

'Then you take that one, and follow us.' He jumped on the first bike and switched it on. 'Hope you don't mind riding pillion, Inspector.' He patted the seat. 'But it's the fastest way to get out there.'

'Out where?' shouted Nikki over the noise of the engine.

'Bottom field. By the Amber Fen drain. As I said, it's just a wreck of an old barn, and I'm preparing to demolish it.'

Nikki wanted to ask him to describe the girl, but the two revving engines meant she would have to wait and see for herself.

Nigel Grieves checked that she was ready, then accelerated out onto the narrow path across the fields.

Joseph spun his bike around, and with considerable skill, caught them up.

It may have only taken about three minutes, but the track was rough and uneven, and as Nikki hung on grimly, she wondered if they would ever get there. Finally the dark, dilapidated hulk of a barn drew closer, and she began to worry.

Would it be Kerry Anderson, or Lisa Jane, or maybe another girl, one they didn't even know about? Whoever it turned out to be, Nikki was not looking forward to walking into the gloom and seeing a dead youngster. She swallowed hard. After everything that had happened in the past, she was going to need every ounce of her strength just to walk in there, and as the bike pulled up, her feelings of deep concern turned into dread.

A silence fell over the vast landscape. In the distance she could see the Wash, glistening and sparkling. A light breeze whispered across her skin, and she stared at the decrepit old barn. This disgusting, decaying building was not fit to be the last resting place of a lovely young woman, no matter who she was.

'She's at the back. She's lying on some old hay bales.' Nigel Grieves' voice held a hollow tone. 'I'd rather not go in again, if you don't mind. I'm no coward, mind you, but I've got kids of my own, and . . .'

Joseph leaned forward and gripped the man's shoulder. 'We'll take it from here, sir. No need to see more than you have already.' He gave the man a serious kind of smile then added. 'Would you go back to the farmhouse and wait for our colleagues? This is a pretty remote spot, I would think it'll take them about fifteen to twenty minutes from town.' He looked around. 'I assume there is no other way to get out here?'

The man shook his head. 'No. The seabank veers around towards the coast about a mile back. The way we came is the only route, I'm afraid. And you won't get any normal vehicle out here either, you'll need something that'll go off-road.'

'You get back, sir. We'll radio in and get a 4x4.'

'You're welcome to use some of the farm vehicles.' Nigel Grieves climbed back onto the quad bike. 'Eh, there's one thing I haven't mentioned.' He paused and looked at them, suddenly uncertain of himself.

'And what's that, sir?' Nikki was getting very bad vibes from the man.

'When I phoned in, I couldn't describe her, because she's wearing some kind of horrible mask. Shocked me rigid, I can tell you. I only knew she was a young woman from her clothes and her body shape.'

'Okay,' said Joseph gravely. 'You go now, sir.'

Grieves didn't need a second telling, and he rode way, earth flying up from the thick tyres, and with not as much as a glance back. The man was more than glad to be leaving his wreck of a barn and all that it concealed.

Nikki wished she could do the same. Then she took hold of herself. There was no way around it. She pulled on a pair of gloves.

'Come on, Sergeant. Let's get this over with.' She moved forwards, knowing that she looked far more in control than she really was.

It took a moment or two for their eyes to grow accustomed to the gloom inside the old building. The floor was littered with detritus, and they had to pick their way between shattered packing boxes, heaps of decaying root vegetables and small piles of bird shit.

'Watch where you walk.' Joseph had moved ahead of her, and his voice had taken on an air of command. 'There are bits of old farm machinery here. An unprotected blade or spike could shear clean through your ankle.'

He's back on patrol, thought Nikki, and suddenly she was glad to have him with her.

Slim shafts of light criss-crossed the barn, where the sun had found its way through the gaps in the broken and rotted walls. Dust motes swam in them, giving the whole place a strange, surreal effect.

As they carefully moved forward, the smell of decaying vegetation and musty wood turned into something else, something far nastier.

Nikki almost gagged. It was a smell she never got used to. She glanced across to Joseph, but like an automaton he was still moving forward, his face set like stone. Nikki sighed. Gentle and mild-mannered he may appear, but Joseph was obviously no stranger to violent death.

'She's here,' he said softly.

Nikki shivered. She really wasn't sure how she would cope, but she had a damned good idea it would not be well. This was all too familiar. Too close to home.

'Who is it?' she whispered. Joseph's body was still between her and the dead girl.

'Can't say. It's like the farmer said, she has one of those damned masks over her face.'

'Kerry was wearing hiking boots.' Nikki moved closer, but still could not bring herself to look directly at the girl's body. Then she saw two white, straight-toed, bare feet protruded from the end of the rotting hay bale. *Oh dear God! The poor child!*

'We have to get that filthy mask off her,' said Joseph.

'No,' she snapped. 'We'll compromise the crime scene. They'll need to photograph it.'

Joseph's voice was calm. 'Ma'am, we *have* to know who she is. I'll take every precaution.' He pulled a large evidence bag from his pocket.

He was right. 'Then do it, Sergeant.'

All Nikki wanted to do was run away, but this was something she knew she had to face. So she set her jaw and pulled on a mask of her own; the professional face. With her stomach churning, she stepped forward and began to clinically appraise the scene.

The girl, clothed only in a short blue skirt and a thin, cap-sleeved T-shirt, lay on her back across two mouldering hay bales. The hideous rat-like death mask concealed her face, and from the blotchy discolouration of the skin, she had been dead for a while. Nikki had seen her fair share of unnatural deaths and she guessed at maybe two days. There was no obvious cause of death.

'Right. Are you ready?' Joseph had carefully moved around to the back of the grotesque tableau, and with gloved fingers prepared to remove the mask.

95

'Just do it,' she muttered.

With a deft movement, the sergeant peeled back the mask, and as he did so, a cascade of brunette hair fell gently over the girl's shoulders.

Nikki tried to stifle it, but a low moan escaped from her slightly parted lips. And in that moment, the years fell away and she was back in a filthy cellar, cradling a dying girl in her arms. 'Oh no! Oh please, no!' She stepped backwards, almost tripping in her haste to get away. She knew that her breathing was becoming erratic and she felt horribly light-headed. Then her heart began to pound like a hammer against her ribs and she knew immediately what was happening. She had not had a full blown panic attack for years, and the intensity of it was terrifying.

'Breathe! Come on now, Inspector! Look at me, and breathe with me.'

Joseph was in front of her, holding her by the shoulders and demanding that she watch him. His face looked weirdly distorted, but she heard his voice echoing as if they were underwater, and she tried to do as he asked.

'Can't!' A roaring noise filled her head and her chest tightened.

'You can! Concentrate on me! Now, in, and out. Slowly, calmly, you can do it. In, and out.'

After a while, her desperate battle for breath began to ease, but she still couldn't focus properly or talk to him.

'It's okay, it's okay. It's not Hannah. Do you understand me, Nikki? It's not Hannah.'

Hannah? What did he mean? She sunk down onto a storage box, and tried to understand. What was he talking about? 'What . . . ?' She gasped, still trying to control her breathing. 'What the hell . . . do you know . . . about Hannah?'

'I've seen her. I saw you with her, at the hospital.'

Even through her own discomfort, she knew that he sounded horribly miserable at the admission.

'I never mentioned it, because I wanted to respect your privacy. No one at work mentioned the fact that you had a sick daughter, so I gathered they didn't know.'

Anger burnt through her, then almost immediately it abated, and was replaced by a cathartic kind of relief. She stared at him, then sighed, 'I wasn't thinking of Hannah. It was another girl. Her death was . . .' she paused. She *never* talked about the death of Emily Drennan. '. . . just too much of a waste to bear.'

Joseph sat beside her, and with no hint of embarrassment, placed an arm firmly around her shoulders. 'An old case? A bad one?'

'The worst.'

'There's always one that takes your world and tears it to shreds.'

Nikki nodded numbly, then had the saddest of thoughts. It was irrelevant to the case, but she could not remember the last time that someone had held her. A tear formed in her eye, and she sniffed it back. When she'd had attacks in the past, and there had been quite a few just after Emily's death, they had always been immediately followed by a period of black depression. It didn't last long, but during that time she felt unnaturally aggressive and was best left alone. Today was different. She just felt sick, tired and vulnerable. And there really was no time for all this. She straightened up. 'We should contact the station. Let them know . . .'

'Not yet. You take a minute to calm yourself before they get here, hey? They are already on their way, and this is one heck of a backwater.' He paused for moment then said, 'The dead girl? It's Lisa Jane Leonard, isn't it? I saw the tiny scar beneath her ear.'

Nikki nodded. 'Archie and his family will be devastated.'

'Everybody's family gets devastated at one time or another, doesn't it?' The arm remained gently across her shoulders and his hand squeezed her reassuringly. 'How long has Hannah been in a coma?'

'She's not in a coma,' replied Nikki. It seemed odd to talk about herself. So odd that she almost didn't know how. 'She was, but now she can breathe for herself.' She looked down. 'But that's about all she can do. She's in what they call a persistent vegetative state.'

Joseph puffed out his cheeks. 'Phew, how long?'

'Eleven months.'

He turned to her and his gaze was full of honest admiration. 'How on earth have you coped?'

'That's all I ever do, Joseph.' She gave him a sad smile. 'I cope. I just cope. I don't live, I don't enjoy anything. I exist, I work and I manage. I *have* to because one day I'm going to get my daughter back.'

'I hope you do, really.' A terrible sadness crept across his handsome face. 'Because I'm certain I'll never see mine again.'

'You have a daughter?' she asked incredulously. Somehow the fact that he may have a family had never even occurred to her.

'Had. She's abroad somewhere with her mother. I haven't seen her for six years.'

A quiet descended on them both, as they fell into a sort of personal reverie and thought about their lost daughters.

After a while, Nikki said, 'I guess there is nothing we can do for Lisa Jane now, not without disturbing anything. We'd better ring the station and check how long it will be before forensics can get out here. It's no longer a missing person's case. It's murder.'

'Shall I do it, ma'am?' asked Joseph.

Nikki slipped, rather reluctantly from his arm, and stood up. 'I'm okay now, Sergeant, thank you. And I could do with some fresh air.'

'You and me both.'

Together they made their way back out into a watery sunshine, and Nikki flipped open her phone and reported their findings. 'They reckon about five minutes, then they have to get across the fields, of course.' She looked across the acres of flat farmland. 'Why did her killer pick this place, I wonder?'

Joseph leaned against the quad bike and shook his head. 'And how did he get her here without Nigel Grieves or one of his family or workers seeing them?'

'I'm pretty sure he, or maybe they, used the dyke.' Nikki pointed to the narrow waterway that ran close to the barn. 'With all the summer rain we've had of late, you could easily get a small boat along there.'

Joseph walked across to the edge of the dyke. 'I think you're right. The bank is pretty well trampled down. The SOCOs may find something.'

'Let's hope.' Nikki sat down on a stone bollard that had probably once been part of a wall, and looked up at her sergeant. 'Why haven't you seen your daughter for so long?'

'Because she hates me.' He swung himself onto the quad bike and sat back in the saddle. 'Well, actually she hates the person I used to be, but Tamsin refuses to believe that that man is dead and gone.'

'And who was that man?'

'A soldier. A highly trained special forces operative. One who killed people for a living.' He threw Nikki a resigned look. 'So I can hardly blame her for disowning me, can I?'

'Soldiers don't kill for fun.'

'If you ever meet Tamsin, perhaps you might tell her that fact.' He scratched his head. 'But if I'm honest, I can see where she's coming from.' He gave a humourless laugh. 'You know what some young people are like these days, full of passion and determination — to save the whales, the polar bears, the rainforests, the planet! Tamsin spent all her childhood collecting orphaned animals and mending broken wings. To her, all life is sacred. Her father's job just didn't gel with her concepts of what made a good person.'

'So did you give up your career for your daughter's sake?'

'No.' Joseph shook his head sadly. 'Like you, I had a bad mission.'

Nikki looked at him, her head tilted to one side. Her natural curiosity wanted to hear about it, but she of all people knew when not to push.

'Let's just say the intelligence we were given was wrong. People died. The wrong people.' He shuddered. 'Afterwards, I threw my assault rifle in the river and told my commanding officer that I was going home, for good. He knew they'd cocked up, and he never tried to stop me. I was given an honourable discharge. What a joke!'

'So then you joined the police?'

'Not for a long while. I knew I was damaged, so I went away. I travelled, then I spent a year in an ashram, and finally the healing began.' He smiled at her. 'Please don't tell the mess room, but I've never been religious. I've just spent a lot of time listening to people who lead truly spiritual lives, and now I can embrace the good things in life, and try to forgive the bad ones.'

'Oh I wish it was that easy, Joseph! I don't think I could ever forgive some of the bad people that I've come across in my life.' Nikki closed her eyes and saw Frankie Doyle's wicked eyes twinkle maliciously at her. 'No, never.'

Joseph gave her long look. 'I never said it was easy. One day you may be surprised at what you are capable of.' He smiled again. 'But right now, I see the Cavalry approaching.'

Nikki stood up. Across the fields, two Land Rovers were churning up the fertile soil as they made their way towards them. She looked back to her sergeant. Somehow she knew that she did not have to ask him to be discreet about her panic attack.

For a moment she just stood and stared at him. For the first time in a very long while, DI Nikki Galena actually trusted someone.

CHAPTER FIFTEEN

'Do we know how she died?' asked Superintendent Bainbridge.

Joseph bit his lip. 'Unofficially, sir. It's strangulation.'

The super nodded slowly, 'I hope they manage to get her off that marsh before night fall.'

'She's already here, sir. She was taken into the hospital mortuary a few minutes ago. Professor Wilkinson will do the post mortem this evening.'

'Rory Wilkinson? He's from your neck of the woods, isn't he, Sergeant?'

'Yes, sir, he's covering while your own man is up at the Old Bailey as an expert witness. Wilkinson is a brilliant forensic scientist.'

'*If* you can put up with his weird sense of humour. I know him, Sergeant. And you're right, he is very good.'

Nikki felt relieved. She had known the girl, and wanted her treated respectfully. If his reputation was to be believed, Professor Wilkinson would do just that.

'Now,' the super ran a big hand through his iron-grey hair, 'we have to break the news to the Leonard family. Lisa Jane needs to be formally identified.'

'I'll do it,' said Nikki. Then she looked across at Joseph, and corrected herself. 'I meant w*e'll* do it, sir.'

The super stared at her for a second, his expression mildly confused, then he nodded. 'Okay, but do it quickly. This is one bit of news I do *not* want him coming by on the underworld grapevine.' He sat back in his chair, and Nikki saw deep worry lines etched all over his already craggy face. 'And be careful, Nikki. I know you have a particular rapport with Archie, but the situation itself could be like lighting a fire-cracker under a powder keg. The Leonard family *will* want revenge.'

'I know that, super. And we'll do whatever it takes to keep him from starting a blood-bath, I promise.'

'How much are you prepared to tell him?'

She thought for a moment, then said, 'Everything, sir. I need his help, so he has to know all the facts.'

The superintendent pursed his lips. 'You trust him more than I do, but I'll support you in whatever you decide, Inspector. Now, you have a job to do. I suggest you go do it.'

* * *

As they drove towards the Carborough Estate, Nikki was forced to wonder just how good her relationship with Archie would be after this god-damned meeting was over. The only thing she knew for sure was that her sorrow for his loss was genuine, and he would realise that. She began to rehearse what she would say, then gave up. There were no right words at a time like this. You just had to hope that what you did say came from the heart, and didn't finish up sounding like a load of tawdry platitudes.

'What happened to Hannah?'

Joseph's voice broke into her thoughts, and for a minute she felt like telling him to mind his own sodding business. Then she remembered his kindness earlier, and the fact that he had shared some pretty painful memories with her.

'Drug overdose,' she said quietly. 'After Emily died I was really screwed up, and in the end it wrecked my marriage. Robert went to live abroad, and refused to take Hannah. She was gutted by his rejection, and blamed me for everything.'

'And went off the rails?'

Nikki gave a short, barking laugh. 'Oh no! Not Hannah! She was far too clever to do that! She had a master plan. Her one aim in life was to make me suffer. Every day, in every way.'

'So she dabbled with drugs, just to piss you off?'

Again Nikki shook her head. 'No, but she did start mixing with some seriously dubious characters, just for my benefit. Then she made the mistake of confiding in someone who hated me even more than she did. Someone who was much cleverer than Hannah, and totally unscrupulous.'

'Don't tell me,' breathed Joseph. 'Frankie Doyle.'

'Got it in one, Sergeant.' Nikki pulled into the Carborough and made her way confidently through the maze of streets. 'And it was Archie Leonard who helped me find out what had happened, and gave me the name of Frankie Doyle.'

'What *did* happen?' asked Joseph.

'I believe Doyle got hold of a bad batch of drugs.' Nikki faltered for a second, then she took a deep breath and said, 'And she spiked Hannah's drink with enough junk to fell an ox.'

'She meant to kill her?' Joseph's voice rose an octave.

'I'm sure she did. What better way to get at me, but I could never prove it. Even the info that Archie managed to get hold of was obtained through a dozen backdoors. Only one man could ever help me, and that was the dealer who sold Frankie the junk, so, you can see where that led me, can't you?'

'You've been on a one-woman witch-hunt ever since.' Joseph exhaled loudly. 'But why did Archie help you? You may have had some weird good guy/bad guy relationship, but you're still the Old Bill.'

Nikki pulled into a space, switched off the engine, then looked up and almost gasped. 'Another time, Sergeant. Take a look at that!'

In front of them was the end wall to one of the smaller blocks of flats, and painted across it in giant multicoloured letters, were the words, *MASK WARS*.

'Shit!' Joseph jumped out of the car and ran over to the uncommissioned art work. 'Graffiti artists sign their work with a tag.' He searched the bold swirls and slashes of vivid colour. 'Yeah! Got it, look.'

Nikki caught up with him and peered at the strange hieroglyphic. 'What's that? Looks like P-I-E-T to me. Ring it in, Sergeant, get Cat or Dave to run a check for us.'

Joseph pulled out his phone, spoke briefly to Cat, then flipped it shut. 'She's going to run it through the computer, not that I think it'll get us far. I can't see this being the only one, can you? The estate's probably covered in them.'

They walked across the road towards Archie's house, and Nikki paused at the gate. 'This is not going to be easy.' Her voice was low. 'A hell of a lot rests on how we deal with this. Are you up for it?'

Joseph nodded. 'I haven't needed my negotiator's skills for a while, but I guess you never forget.' He opened the gate and held it back for her. 'Shall we go?'

* * *

Archie Leonard sat on a cream leather sofa, and stared, granite-faced at Nikki. 'Whoever did this is going to pay. My God, they'll pay!'

'Oh they will, Archie. You have my word.' Nikki chose her words carefully. 'But right now, you know what I have to ask you, don't you?'

'The identification?'

'I'm afraid so. And I'm sorry you have to go through it. There is no doubt that it is her, but we need either you or her mother as next of kin to formalise the process.'

'I'll go. I'm her guardian,' he paused, 'I *was* her guardian while Frank is inside. And Margaret is in no state to see Lisa Jane, not like that.' The man drew in a deep shaky breath and looked back to Nikki. 'The family will not take this well, you know that, don't you?'

'Archie, you *have* to convince them to leave this to us. We have another girl to think about. Another Carborough family is also going through hell. A vendetta on the estate could seriously hinder our enquiries about Kerry Anderson, *and* about your niece. It's bad enough with the gangs and the masks, don't make it even more difficult for us, please.'

'I care about you, Nikki, you know that, but I went against the family when I walked through that door to the nick. It was not a move that they appreciated, so . . .' He shrugged. 'So, they may not be in any frame of mind to listen to me right now. And frankly, I think I would actually *like* to be first to get my hands around the neck of the animal who killed my girl.'

'Of course you would,' said Joseph quietly. 'That's natural for any loving man.'

Nikki watched as Joseph fixed Archie Leonard with a penetrating stare. 'But Lisa Jane was not your only responsibility. As I understand it, you have three more girls to consider. Your own two daughters and Frank's other girl, Melissa. *And* you have boys, there's nothing to say that one of them may not be targeted. Surely you'll want to channel all your considerable resources into protecting *them?*'

Archie did not flinch under the unblinking gaze. 'Ah, we're a big family, Sergeant, with a lot of friends. Since the moment my niece disappeared, my other children have been watched as carefully as newborn babies. There will still be plenty of time and personnel to sort out our problem.'

'Then help *us*, Mr Leonard.' Joseph leaned forward. 'Think what a combined team could achieve. You have the knowledge on ground level, and we have a whole army of experts and equipment in every field.'

'He's right, Archie. We've got the technology, and you've got street intelligence. And don't give me that old crap about the family not listening to you. They love and respect you, and the bottom line is, what you say, goes.' Nikki looked earnestly at him. 'Work with us. I promise I'll hold nothing back, if you and the other Leonards keep us in the loop here on the estate.'

Archie rubbed his forehead, but said nothing.

'I suppose there might be something else we can do, sir.' Joseph sat back and looked thoughtful. He looked to Nikki more like a successful plastic surgeon discussing a nip and tuck, than a detective on a murder case.

'And that is?'

It was Joseph's turn to remain silent for a moment, and Nikki wondered what plan he was hatching.

'We may, we just *may* be able to keep Lisa Jane's name from the media. If you could see your way to assisting us, that is.'

Nikki let out a loud breath. 'Hold on, Joseph! How the dickens do you suppose we're going to manage that? Promising something that's damn near impossible is a big mistake!'

'I never said the word *promise*, ma'am. But we could try, couldn't we?'

'Could you?' asked Archie solemnly.

'Would you help us, if we did?' came back Joseph.

'Before you answer, Archie, there'd be no guarantees,' butted in Nikki. 'If the grapevine gets hold of it, or if someone offers a hefty backhander, well, it's all over, you know that.'

Archie Leonard looked thoughtfully at her. 'I'll speak to the family. No promises, but I'll try, and you do all you can to keep her name from the press. Deal?'

Nikki took the outstretched hand. 'Deal.'

It wasn't the first time she'd formed a liaison with this particular part of the underworld, but such a gamble often came at a cost. She looked at Archie Leonard's troubled blue eyes and hoped the risk would be worth it. Then, as she released Archie's hand, a picture of Kerry Anderson swam before her, and she knew it was.

'Now, I'm afraid we have to ask you to go to the hospital. As we need to keep this under wraps, I suggest you make your own way there. It's visiting time until 8 p.m., so it won't look odd, and I'll meet you. I'll take you to her through the back corridors.'

'I understand.'

'I'll be in the hospital shop in half an hour,' said Nikki. 'Don't acknowledge me, just buy something, a magazine or some flowers, then follow me out, okay?'

Archie nodded.

'And, I know it goes without saying, but I'm so very sorry.'

The man dropped his head. 'I know, Nikki. And part of me says that it's my fault, if I'd come to you sooner, maybe . . . ?'

Nikki shook her head emphatically. 'Don't even begin to think like that. I know we're still waiting for the official reports, but from what we do know, *no one* could have helped her. We are sure she was killed when she was first abducted. What we don't know, is why.'

'Then we have to find out what's going on, before some-one else dies.' Archie straightened up, and a steely expression of determination swept over his face. 'I'll call the family immediately, and I'll see you at the hospital.'

CHAPTER SIXTEEN

'I'm knackered!' Niall swung the cell door shut on a scream-ing teenage girl and leaned against it heavily. 'I swear the girls are worse than the boys!'

Yvonne grinned at him. 'I have to admit that one was a particularly feisty specimen.'

Niall pulled a face. 'It would be funny, if Greenborough wasn't becoming more like a war zone than a peaceful market town. Let's grab a coffee before we get sent back out there again.'

As they approached the coffee machine, they saw Cat Cullen waving to them.

'Hey, guys! Got a minute?'

'Sure, want a coffee?' answered Niall.

'No, thanks all the same.' Cat's eyes looked abnormally wide. 'I've had so much caffeine in the last twenty-four hours that there's a good chance I'll never sleep again! Now, what do you two know about this tasty little geezer?'

She pushed a photograph at them.

'Oh dear, those ears make him look like the FA Cup, don't they?' Yvonne held the picture at arm's length, then smiled. 'This is Petey Redfield. Tag name, Piet. Lives on the Carborough with his married sister, Rene. Mum in Rehab, Dad in the Scrubs.' Yvonne handed back the photo to Cat. 'He's no real trouble, and he has no convictions, which is something of a miracle considering his family. His only problem is that he can't keep his grubby little finger off the nozzle of a spray can.' She pulled a face. 'I've felt his collar a few times *and* had a word with his headmaster. Shame really, his school reckon he could be a top art student. He's got the flair and the ability to learn, but . . .'

'Yeah, I get the picture,' said Cat. 'No attention at home, no parental guidance and no support. So he goes out and gets noticed by using an aerosol can. So who does he hang out with?'

'A few other graffiti kids. No one heavy.'

Niall made a slurping noise with his coffee. 'Actually, he's got real talent. If I could paint like he can, I wouldn't be hanging off a railway bridge somewhere, I'd be trying to get myself into college.'

'Yeah, well, that's where the difference lies, mate, and why you're in gainful employment and he's hanging off a bleedin' bridge with a paint can gripped between his teeth! Got an address for the sister?'

'43 Tennyson Buildings. Her name's Rene Wilson,' Yvonne replied immediately.

'We really don't need a Police National Computer with you around!' said Niall shaking his head incredulously. 'Is there anyone you don't know in Greenborough?'

'I don't know who abducted Kerry Anderson, and that's the only name we really need, isn't it?'

'And that of whoever killed the other girl,' whispered Niall. 'Is it true she was wearing one of those rat-masks when they found her?'

'Seems that way,' said Cat. 'But no one is talking about it, so I suggest you belt up and keep it to yourself.'

'This one has a very big gob,' muttered Yvonne. 'One day it'll get him into deep shit.'

'Nah!' Niall grinned broadly. 'I'm just enthusiastic, that's all. Now, if you've finished that drink, let's go nail some bad guys!'

Yvonne raised her eyes to the heavens. 'Any room in your department, Cat? I'd pay good money to get in! In fact . . .'

'Collins! Farrow! Get your arses into that car of yours! There's been a serious attack on a youngster.'

'Where, Sarge?' called out Yvonne, as she ran towards the door.

'Just around the corner, in the recreation ground by the river.'

'Show us committed, Sarge! We're on our way!'

* * *

'Do you think Leonard can be trusted, ma'am?' Joseph perched on the edge of Nikki's desk.

'*I* trust him. If he says he'll help, then he will.' Nikki sipped her coffee, then glanced at her watch. 'Shit! I need to be at the hospital.'

'Shall I come with you?'

'No, Sergeant. It won't take two of us for this miserable job. And I'll try to grab a private word with Archie after he's seen Lisa Jane.' She stood up and grabbed her jacket. 'You catch up with Cat and check out the graffiti kid lead. Go find him if you want, although I doubt he'll be sitting at home playing Scrabble with granny.'

'Probably not, but I'll give it a try, ma'am.'

'And if you can't find him, ride around the estate, see how many new artworks have sprung up with a connection to the masks.' She paused at the door. 'Then get yourself home and grab some sleep. Today has had its fair share of traumatic moments.'

Joseph looked at her intently. 'Will you be all right seeing Lisa Jane again? I'll go, if it helps.'

'I'll be fine. It wasn't the girl that upset me, Sergeant.' She thought for a moment, wondering how much of herself she was prepared to share with this unusual man. 'It was just that whole scenario. That gloomy half-light, the filth everywhere, the . . .' she shuddered, '. . . the way her hair fell.' Then she knew that she'd said enough. Maybe too much. She shook her head trying to rid herself of the horrible returning memories of Emily Drennan's death. 'In the mortuary, it won't affect me at all. And if I keep Archie waiting, we may not have a deal any-more.' She moved quickly out of the door, then called back, 'And nice one with Archie, by the way. I'm sure he realised that it's very much in our own interests to keep the news of the death of a gangster's girl quiet, but you put it over beautifully, even I believed that you were only thinking of him!'

She flashed a rare smile, and raced off down the corridor.

* * *

Joseph went to his desk and logged on to his computer.

'Got that info you wanted, Sergeant.'

He looked up to see Cat grinning down at him. She was a strange one, but take away the tarty clothes, the make-up and the spiky hair, and there was something almost childlike and appealing about her.

'Great! What do we have?' Joseph took the photo and the print-out that she was handing him.

'Just a freaky kid really. His sister looks after him, and she's clean, too. It's the parents you don't want to meet. Two really nasty characters. One's inside and one's drying out.'

Joseph skimmed through the history, raised his eyebrows in surprise over the kid's school report, then said, 'Fancy paying Rembrandt here a visit? I need to know if this latest masterpiece was his idea, or whether someone paid him to do it.'

Cat pulled a face. 'Sorry, Sarge, but I'm stuck here wait-ing for news on the mask factory.'

'Oh well, I'm getting to know my way to the Carborough by now. Thanks for this, anyway.'

'Pleasure.' She gave him an elfin smile and went back to her desk.

Joseph closed his computer. He really should get over to the estate, but if he were honest, he was worried about his new boss. He'd seen panic attacks before, he'd even experi-enced a couple in the past, but the DI's had been a bad one, and he wondered what the hell had happened to her.

Joseph abruptly stood up. Whatever it was, it was not his business. No way should he be prying into Nikki Galena's nightmares. He had enough of his own to deal with. He pushed his chair under his desk and grabbed his car keys. He couldn't put off his trip to the Carborough any longer. He called out a brief goodbye to Cat, then made his way down stairs.

As he passed the station desk the duty sergeant called out. 'Excuse me! Is DI Galena still around?'

'Sorry, no. She's at the hospital.'

'Oh, now that could be advantageous. We've got something that I think she should see.'

'Can I help?'

'There's been an attack on a young boy. He's in a pretty serious condition.'

'On the Carborough?' asked Joseph.

Jack Conway shook his head. 'No, not far from here. There's a kid's recreation ground down by the river. A dog walker found him in the bushes. I thought the DI should know because from what my officers report from the crime scene, it's mask-related again.'

'Oh, what a surprise!' Joseph puffed out his cheeks. 'Look, best not to ring the inspector, she's carrying out an identification so she'll probably have her phone switched off. I'll go down to the hospital and tell her myself then we can go directly and check on the victim.'

'That's fine, sir,' said Sergeant Conway. 'If it's no trouble.'

'Do we have a name for the boy?'

'Not yet. He had no identification on him.'

'And what's the mask connection?'

'He was wearing one.' Jack Conway's expression darkened. 'And I'm afraid that's all he was wearing, sir. He'd been stripped.'

Joseph gritted his teeth. 'Poor little sod! How old do your officers think he is?'

'Hard to say, he's taken one hell of a beating. Maybe twelve, thirteen?'

'What the hell is going on here?'

Jack Conway looked almost grey with tiredness as he shook his head and said, 'I wish I knew, Detective Easter, I really do.'

CHAPTER SEVENTEEN

As night fell, Nikki and Joseph sat outside the Intensive Care Unit and waited for news on the unidentified boy.

'Why don't you go home and get some sleep, ma'am? I'll ring you if there's any change.'

Nikki yawned. 'Tempting, but I need to be here.'

Joseph stared through the glass section of the door at the small figure on the hospital bed. Tubes snaked everywhere around his thin body, and to Joseph, the child seemed almost overpowered by the bank of monitors and equipment that surrounded him. 'I don't think that lad will be talking to anyone for a while.'

'I agree, but in the absence of a mother or a father . . .' she left the sentence unfinished and he filled in the gaps.

Joseph flopped down on the chair next to hers. 'I drove through the estate on the way here, ma'am. There is more Mask Wars graffiti, but not as much as I'd expected, then I saw they were all courtesy of Petey Redfield.' Joseph stretched and leaned back, his hands interlocked behind his neck. 'He'll probably be out there again tonight, so maybe,' he sat forward again, 'if you are dead set on doing the night watch here, guv, why don't I go over to the estate and try to nab the little shit, spray can in hand?'

'Not a good place to be after dark, Sergeant. Especially on your own.'

Joseph gave her an exasperated look. 'Believe me I've been in far worse places than that! And on my own is how I like it.'

Nikki said nothing for a moment, but Joseph knew that she would agree with him in the end. There really was little point in both of them wasting time in a hospital waiting area when they needed to be out finding Kerry, and Lisa Jane's killer. *Or,* considering that they seemed to be tied up with everything; something concrete on those damned masks.

'Okay,' she said finally. 'But if you get into trouble, don't bank on the wooden tops bailing you out. They are still out searching the marshes for Kerry Anderson. And we're pretty thin on the ground even for routine stuff, so . . .'

'I'll go careful, I promise, ma'am. And if I find anything of interest, I'll come straight back and fill you in, okay?'

'Oh, bugger off, Sergeant, I can see you're itching to meet up with Piet and his paint cans. Just nothing gung-ho, you hear?'

Joseph tried to look affronted. 'Moi?'

'Yeah, you.'

* * *

On his earlier trip, Joseph had earmarked four possible targets for spray paint boy. Each area was moderately hidden from prying eyes, and each offered a nice blank canvas for Petey's gaudy graphics.

Leaving his car parked well away from the danger zone, Joseph changed his shoes for a pair of black trainers, and slipped on a black zipper jacket with a deep hooded collar. There was no point in making himself obvious. He'd just blend.

The air around him felt heavy. Like when a thunder storm was imminent. He hoped it would hold off, as a downpour would not provide the greatest conditions for decorating the council's exterior walls. And he would dearly like to meet young Piet.

With his hood pulled up, he sauntered silently through the streets in search of his four likely spots. On the third, he got lucky.

He did not so much see his mark, as hear him. That singular sound of a can being shaken. The tinny rattle of the bearing inside was unmistakable.

'Perfect,' he whispered, as he slid like a shadow along the side of a darkened building. He was careful, because there could be a whole gang waiting around the corner, but somehow Joseph doubted it. If money was at the heart of Petey's new venture, he probably wouldn't want to share it. Not only that, graffiti kids usually worked solo. He just hoped Petey was a loner.

For a while, Joseph hung back in the darkness and watched the artist at work. If he hadn't been defacing public property, Joseph would have been full of admiration.

Petey Redfield worked on stilts. The sort you see plasterers wear to enable them to reach higher without the use of ladders. They strap to the legs and give the arms freedom of use.

Very neat, thought Joseph, although probably not too clever if you need to make a run for it. The kid worked fast and with considerable skill, it was almost a shame to interrupt him. But as the guv'nor had already said, this was not a nice area to hang around in, so he really needed to deal with young Petey as speedily as possible.

'Evening, Mr Redfield, not quite good enough for the Academy, but close,' Joseph grabbed a firm hold on the boy's wide belt. ''Fraid I need a quiet word.'

'What the fuck . . . ?'

Without another word Joseph yanked him backwards, caught him, and laid him on his back on the ground.

'Just a few words, then I'm going to disappear into the night, and you can continue to paint the town red, or sky-blue-pink, for all I care.' He tightened his hold and Petey yelped.

'Okay! Okay! You the Fuzz?'

'Not tonight.' Joseph leaned over the boy. 'Now, I really don't want to hurt those talented fingers, but if I have to, I can arrange it that you never paint again, unless you use your toes, of course. Catch my drift?'

'I said, okay, man! What do you want?'

Joseph caught a strong whiff of sweat. Petey was scared, and he had every right to be. Only Joseph knew that he had no intentions of hurting him. With a boy like this, the simple suggestion that he might, should do the trick.

'Now, how much are you getting paid to do this?'

The boy swallowed. 'Not enough.'

Joseph smiled. 'Probably not. But now that we've ascertained that you *are* getting paid, I asked how much?'

The boy thought for a moment, but sensibly decided not to be a hero. 'A hundred smackers a night, for three nights.'

'And as many walls as you can cover, I suppose?'

'Yeah.'

'And who is it that is willing to cough up £300 for a bit of graffiti?'

'No idea, and before you break my fingers, that's the God's honest truth.'

Joseph nodded. 'Funnily enough I believe you. So how did you get the money?'

The boy shifted uncomfortably, but Joseph just leaned a little closer and stared intently at his long, narrow fingers. 'Come on, Petey. Tell me, and your sweet little pinkies will live to paint another day.'

'Okay, but just get away from my hands, man! I dunno when, but someone shoved a Griffyx into my school bag.'

Joseph was startled to hear the name being used, but kept his interest hidden under a blank expression.

'There were two fifties stuffed inside it, and a note telling me to scribe a wall with the words 'Mask Wars.' If I did it, and promised to go out for three nights, I'd get two hundred quid more.'

'Nice work if you can get it! And how did they get the remaining money to you?'

Petey shivered. 'I found it on my bed when I woke up this morning. Some freaky creep had gotten into my fucking room and left it there.' He pulled a face. 'That's why I'm out here now. No way am I going to piss off someone like that. They are seriously scary people, so I really need to get on.'

'Patience. You can, just as soon as you tell me where the tag 'Griffyx' came from?'

'Check out Lyco's blog and follow the link to the game, then you'll see. Now, please, mate, can I go earn my money?'

Joseph helped the boy up, then raised both hands in the air and stepped back. 'Go do what you have to, Petey. But keep away from those guys, whoever they are. I get the feeling that they would be happy to do far worse than break a few fingers.'

Petey Redfield stared at him. 'Who the hell are you?'

Joseph pulled up his hood and started to walk away. 'No one, son. I was never here, and I never saw you or your aerosol cans. Just lock your doors at night. It would be a real sin to waste all that talent.' He glanced over his shoulder and called back. 'And I like your tag. Fan of Mondrian's 'Wall Works,' are you?'

Petey was adjusting his stilts, but he stopped and looked incredulously at Joseph. 'Most people think I can't even spell my own name. I dunno who you are, man, but respect! You're the first one to make the connection.'

'Your teacher reckons you're a smart kid with a passion for Bauhaus. You could go far, Petey. Do yourself a favour and use your new wages to buy some art books and maybe a proper canvas.'

As he slipped back into the shadows, he heard the familiar rattling sound, and he smiled to himself.

* * *

Back at the station, Joseph found the office empty, but as he switched on his computer, his mobile rang.

'Joseph? DI Galena. Look, if you were planning on coming back to the hospital, I'll be getting away shortly.'

'How's the kid?'

'Not good. He had some sort of fit. They've got him on a respirator.' She paused. 'It wasn't nice to watch, Joseph, I can tell you.'

He thought about what she must have gone through with her own daughter, and knew that it could not have been easy for her. 'No, I'm sure it wasn't, ma'am. So, are you going home?'

'Shortly. As I'm here, I'll call in on Hannah for a few minutes, then I'll go grab some sleep. I suggest you do the same.'

'I've one more thing to do. Petey gave me a lead on the Griffyx. I'll check it out, then go back to my digs for a few hours kip.'

'I'll be calling a meeting for the whole team at 9 a.m. tomorrow. Bring whatever it is that you come up with, and I'll see you then. Goodnight, Sergeant, and don't work too late. Remember what you told me, we need to stay sharp.'

'Roger. Night, ma'am.' Joseph closed his phone and turned to the computer. Now, what was it? Lyco's blog and follow the link to the game?

He tapped the name into the search engine, yawned, and went to the coffee machine.

On his return he found 1,890 results, and decided that he should have been a little more thorough in his interrogation of young Petey. He hadn't even clarified the spelling. With a sinking feeling, he sipped the hot coffee and tried again.

After fifteen minutes searching, he found what he was looking for. And quickly came to the conclusion that the link had led him to just the kind of game site that parental control locks had been invented for.

Joseph started to play, but soon gave up, made a few scribbled notes, then shut down the computer. It may be clever, in a macabre, puke-making kind of way, but the bit he'd seen both turned his stomach and made him boiling angry. Tomorrow he'd pass it over to Cat. She'd handled this sort of crap before, and if the Griffyx was there, she'd find it. Well, he sincerely hoped so. Because they were getting nowhere fast, and Kerry Anderson was still missing.

CHAPTER EIGHTEEN

The general noise in the CID room ceased the moment she entered.

Nikki moved to the front of the room and faced them. 'There's no good news this morning, in fact things are going from bad to worse. I think it's time we recapped on what we know, throw in anything that has come to light in the last few hours, and make sure that we are all up to speed.' She looked across to Dave Harris. 'Could you give us the latest from uniform regarding the hunt for Kerry Anderson?'

Dave stood up, his face drawn and his eyes tired. 'Along with the volunteers and the dog handlers, three main areas have now been covered. The seabank and the marsh, for four miles in each direction from where we believe Kerry Anderson was abducted, the surrounding farmland and buildings in a three mile radius, and the area surrounding the university. The Coastguards have patrolled the Wash banks, the estuary and the river. Nothing of note has been found.' He looked apologetically at Nikki, and sat heavily back down.

'Thank you, Dave. What about the other major incidents that have occurred?'

'Well, there's a cordon in place around the spot where the unidentified youth was attacked, ma'am. The recreation ground is closed and boards have been put up to ask the public for assistance. And with regards to your particular find out at Amber Fen, the barn and the farm land is off-limits to everyone until a full forensic examination has been conducted and the crime scene released.'

'Okay, right. Let's take these occurrences in order, shall we?' Nikki walked across to where a large glass evidence board was in place. 'Here,' she pointed to the right hand side of the board where the title, *Unknown young white male*, had been written. 'We have the brutal attack on a youngster. For those of you who were not here late yesterday, the boy, who we believe to be around twelve years of age, was found at around 7 p.m. last evening. He had been beaten and stripped of his clothes. All he was wearing when he was discovered was a mask. His status is critical, but despite all our enquiries, a local radio station alert, and a slot on television news this morning, no one has come forward to identify him.'

'CCTV cameras, ma'am?'

'The only two in the vicinity had been disabled prior to the attack.'

'What about the schools, ma'am?'

'That's our best hope, WPC Collins. I've already sent a general description out to the schools in the area. We just have to wait and see.'

'He could be a runaway, ma'am.'

'He looked too clean, Constable, but we are running a missing persons check for that age group.' She looked back at the board. The only information they had was a photo of the area where he was found, and a list of his injuries, and that made Nikki feel both angry and sad. It seemed all wrong. *Someone* must have missed their son by now, after all, he'd been missing all damned night.

'What are his chances of recovery, ma'am?' asked Yvonne Collins.

Nikki paused, and saw again the battered child convulsing on the hospital bed. 'Not good, I'm afraid. We have officers there with him, and the hospital are keeping in close contact regarding his condition. Swabs have been taken from him for DNA testing, but it will be a while before we get any results. So, anything you guys can pick up off the streets regarding a missing friend, sibling or relative, check it out immediately, okay?'

There was a murmur of assent.

'Moving on, the stabbing of Callum Lodge requires no more attention at present. He is recovering well, and his family are sending him to stay with an aunt somewhere miles from the Carborough. The incident was witnessed by myself and several other officers, and the weapon used was confiscated at the scene. Forensics will sew that up nicely and the suspect has been detained, so forget that for the time being.' She took a deep breath. 'Now, what we need to be working on is our other major worry; the finding of the body of Girl X at Amber Fen.'

Nikki looked in turn at each of the grave-faced officers.

'I don't have to tell you how important it is that we keep this girl's identity a closely guarded secret. Last night she was positively identified by Archie Leonard, and it's time you all knew that he has pledged his support to us, in order to help facilitate the catching of his niece's killer.'

A ripple of surprised voices echoed around the room.

'Yeah, I know this is irregular, but Greenborough is in a shit state right now, and I'm taking help from every available source. Even the Leonard family.'

'Does he have any leads for us, guv?' asked a young detective constable.

'Not yet. The Leonard family are as much in the dark as we are. But, Archie is not just going to support us regarding Girl X, he's offered to make some street level enquiries about both Kerry Anderson and the Mask Wars.'

'Are we quite sure he's not involved with that in any way?' asked Niall suspiciously. 'The masks seem to emanate from the Carborough, and we all know that Archie is the big daddy there.'

'Sorry, PC Farrow, but Archie Leonard is as sincerely pissed about the troubles that they are causing as we are.' She drew up a chair and sank back into it. 'So, what have we got on the masks? Sergeant Easter? Any luck last night?'

Joseph stood up. 'I managed to have an informative chat with the graffiti artist who has recently been decorating the Carborough. It's fair to say that he's been pretty badly frightened by whoever commissioned him. He really does not know who it is, but he gave me a web site to check out regarding the name *Griffyx*.'

'Well, bugger me! I've been working on that for days!' muttered Cat Cullen. 'So what's the story, Sarge?'

'I need your help with it,' said Joseph. 'The site is some sort of online game. All weird fantasy stuff.'

'What sort of fantasy?' Cat's eyes lit up.

'Violent and pornographic. Not one for the kiddies, that's for sure.'

'Ooh, I bet that upset the good *Reverend* Easter,' whispered an anonymous voice.

'Whoever said that,' hissed Nikki, 'should keep their stupid mouth shut until they have something worth saying, do you understand?'

She did not expect an answer, and she didn't get one. Which was fine, she'd made her point. It wasn't until she looked around afterwards that she noticed a lot of mildly surprised expressions. Apparently it must have been some while since anyone had heard Old Nick spring to the defence of a second in command.

Cat broke the silence. 'So, Sarge, just pass all that computer stuff my way and I'll take a look at it for you.'

'I'll bet you will!' said Niall with a grin, and the awkward atmosphere dissipated.

Nikki rapped on the desk top. 'Okay, anything else? Anything sensible, that is.'

'Figures from control show that mask-related crimes have increased to around ten a day, ma'am,' said Yvonne. 'And that doesn't include the serious issues.'

'And I've temporarily hit the wall regarding the manufacturing of masks, ma'am,' said Cat. 'I'm not giving up, but my main line of enquiry has gone AWOL, which leads me to believe that at least I am on the right track. It's just getting trickier.'

'Keep on delving, Cat. Discovering where they come from would be a major breakthrough.' Nikki looked at the clock. 'One last thing, does the tag 'Fluke' mean anything to anyone?'

There was a low buzz of discussion, but the consensus of opinion came up only with a vague 'It sort of rings a bell.'

'Then ask around. Speak to your snouts. This tag is cropping up too regularly for comfort. I want his or her name, and I want it soon. Right, back here at four o'clock, and I know I don't have to tell you this, but Kerry Anderson is still, above all else, our major priority. Off you go!'

Nikki leant back in the chair and exhaled.

'What now, ma'am?' Joseph sat down next to her.

'I'm going to ring ITU about the boy, and then I think it's time we completed the journey that we were on the other day, don't you?'

'Barnby Eaudyke?'

'Barnby Eaudyke and our creepy Night Watcher.'

Joseph nodded. 'I'll go introduce Cat to my computer game while you talk to the hospital.'

* * *

'I can't believe that you've got a lead on the Griffyx when I've been working my butt off looking for a connection.' Cat sounded mildly miffed.

'If you'd come with me to see Petey last night you'd probably have it all figured by now.'

'Yeah, and if I'd known my lead on the manufacturers was going to bugger off, I wouldn't have wasted my time waiting on a phone call.'

Joseph grinned. 'Bummer, but that's the way it goes.' He handed her his notes. 'This is the pathway I was given.' His tone turned serious. 'It's pretty disgusting stuff, Cat, and I mean by anyone's standards, not just mine.'

'Bet I've seen worse. I worked the Vice Squad for two years.'

'Oh.'

'Had it's up side,' said Cat, as her fingers flew deftly over the keyboard. 'At least I got the chance to remove a lot of human garbage from the streets.' She stared at the screen, 'Here we go. It's loading.' She looked across at him. 'If you'd like to avert your delicate eyes, I *can* take it from here.'

'My eternal thanks.' He stood up. 'I have an appointment with the guv'nor, so I'll catch you later. Best of luck.'

* * *

Cat watched as he left the room. Nothing had changed her earlier opinion of him. Sergeant Easter was sincerely hot.

She shook her head and tried to stop her hormones going into free-fall. There was work to be done, and it would help if her mind was actually on the job and not on luscious, fit detectives!

Suddenly the monitor screen went black, then a small red dot appeared in the centre. It slowly increased in size until it was about two inches in diameter, then morphed into a blood-shot eye. A leathery, heavily veined lid blinked a few times, then a strangely echoing voice asked if she would like to enter the Kingdom of LycoRapture.

'If I must,' she mumbled and hit Enter. A new screen, full of light and unimaginably colourful flowers filled the monitor. Waterfalls cascaded into crystal pools and eagles flew over snow-covered peaks. The voice told her that this was her home, and she was the guardian. She would need a name and a physical appearance before she could play.

'Oh, I don't know, what . . . ?' She turned around and called over to Dave. 'Give me a name to use on this computer game.'

'What sort of name?'

'Anything! Just think of something quickly.'

'Bumtilda?'

'Lovely! Can't you think of something a bit more, well, attractive?'

Dave grinned across at her. 'Considering that magazine you were looking at, how about 'Rubbatitti'?'

'Oh, get a grip! That's from a *Carry-on* film! Oh just forget it, Bumtilda will do.'

She typed in her 'name' and was given a selection of body types to adopt. She chose tall, athletic, scarlet hair, and incredibly sexy.

'Can I watch?' asked Dave.

'No, you can't. It's very difficult to get dribble marks off a silk blouse. Now shut up, I have to defend my new kingdom from the Lyco-monsters.'

Cat sat engrossed for almost twenty minutes, then saw Dave placing a coffee next to her mouse mat. 'How's it going?' he asked.

'I've reached level 6, and if this is anything to go by, I don't think I want to get to level 10!'

'Is it as bad as the sarge reckoned?'

'Worse,' said Cat, and exited the programme. 'And from his description I'm pretty sure he never got past level 1. It's all about going to extremes for something you care about, then getting rewards,' she paused, 'or punishments as the case maybe.'

'And the Griffyx?'

'It's there alright. You don't meet it until you reach level 5. It's one of the monsters, kind of half rat, half human, and it dispenses the most unpleasant retribution, if you are unlucky enough to cross it. It also has the biggest dong I've ever seen.'

'Thanks for sharing that.' Dave grimaced. 'And does it look like the masks?'

'I'd say they are based on it, yes. What I need to do now, is find out who the devil Lyco is.'

'Do you reckon he's connected to the mask war?'

Cat stretched and massaged her shoulders. 'We won't know until we meet him, Davey-boy. And if I'm honest, I'm not sure that I'd want to be in the same room as the twisted mind that devised this.'

She had needed to deal with some pretty hard-core material while with the Vice Squad, but this particular game had shocked her. There was a vicious ruthlessness there, that made her believe that its inventor had already lived out one or two of his sadistic fantasies for real. She shuddered. Sergeant Easter had said that a school kid had told him to view the site. If *she* felt physically sick, what the hell would a vulnerable youngster feel like? A wave of anger burst through her. She hated injustice, and just for a moment, she changed her mind about being in the same room as Lyco. Only she'd make sure she took a pepper spray and a meat cleaver with her.

* * *

'His mother says Kris is out' Nikki put the phone down and pulled a face. 'She reckons he's been scouring the marshes, day and night, looking for Kerry. Even his dog's been chasing all over the fen trying to find her. No point in driving all the way to Barnby Eaudyke if he's not there. I've asked her to get him to contact us when he gets back.'

'I've just had the report from the officers who searched his cottage.' Joseph unsealed an envelope and removed several sheets of paper.

'Anything interesting?'

Joseph skimmed through quickly. 'Nothing really. No sign of his missing phone, and nothing to indicate anything untoward had happened there. Apparently both Kris and his mother were pretty unhappy about his observatory being searched, and when the officers saw two heavy padlocks and a mortise on the door, they wondered what they'd find, but the whole interior is packed with computers, telescopes, cameras, tripods and accessories. "Like Jodrell Bank." is the comment made.'

'And that is relevant in some way?'

Joseph shrugged. 'It indicates he's obsessive. And stuff like that costs big money.'

'How big?'

'Hundreds, maybe thousands.'

'So where the devil does a twenty year old get that kind of dosh from?'

'Pass.' Joseph placed the papers on her desk.

Nikki glanced at them 'I'm more concerned about his being out day and night. He could well be spending time with his captive.'

'But the neighbour gave him an alibi for when Kerry was taken.'

'Not good enough for me, Sergeant. The dog may have been there, and Kris may have made quite sure that his potty old neighbour saw him at certain times, but in between times, he could have gone out, to abduct Kerry.' Nikki grimaced. 'Sorry, but I think that alibi has enough holes in it to strain cabbage.'

'Mm, maybe,' Joseph gnawed on his bottom lip. 'But I have a different kind of concern about young Kris. For someone who is so averse to mobile phones and texting, he seems to be very comfortable with a computer console that sounds like it's previous owner was NASA. It doesn't add up.'

'If you ask me, not much about that lad does,' growled Nikki. 'And another thing, do you remember when his mother spoke to us about him, she said he 'treasured' his friends. Isn't that odd terminology when describing a young bloke?'

'Yes, that does have an unhealthy feel to it, I agree.' Joseph frowned. 'Although I really don't think Kris has any connection to Lisa Jane Leonard. His mother would have mentioned a girl as stunning as that, wouldn't she?'

'If she ever saw her. Mummy's boy may have had good reason not to bring her home for tea and cakes.'

'You really don't like him, do you?' said Joseph.

'Until you can show me someone else who fits the bill.' Nikki narrowed her eyes. 'Galileo is still my number one.'

CHAPTER NINETEEN

'Bingo!' Cat pushed her chair away from the computer and gave a little whoop of delight.

'That sounds more promising,' said Dave, putting down the phone.

'Got a trace on Lyco.' She stood up. 'Coming with me? We could do with some fresh air.'

'From what you told me about that creep, the air would probably be fresher in the men's karzy.'

'So bring a peg. Let's go make a house call!'

'What house call?'

'Oh, hello ma'am,' Cat calmed her enthusiasm. The boss didn't always go a bundle on frivolity. 'I've been hunting, guv. In cyberspace. I've located the pervert who designed the computer game.'

'The one with the Griffyx?'

Cat nodded. 'Dave and I were just about to drop in on the sleaze-ball.'

The inspector held up a hand. 'Before that, what's the connection with the masks?'

Cat filled her in as concisely as possible, then added, 'And this Griffyx character really likes to maul beautiful women.' She paused, 'well actually he likes to do a lot more than maul them, but I guess here is not the place or the time . . . ?'

'Precisely.' The guv'nor threw her a dark look. 'But you can forget about the two of you tackling this creep alone. I really don't think you've thought this through, Detective.'

Cat sat back down and stared up at her boss. A small "thank you, good work, Cat." would have been nice.

'If this man, what's his name?'

'Terry James, ma'am.'

'Right, well, if this James has a direct link to the masks, he could be very dangerous, apart from being a pervert.' She paused, 'Where does he live?'

'Rydell Street, ma'am. Over the Off Licence.'

'OK, we'll all go and we'll take uniform with us. And wear your stab-proof vests. As we have no idea what the agenda is behind the masks, we can't be too careful.' She stood up, then smiled at Cat. 'And good work, Detective. It's the first proper lead we've had on those damned rat-faced masks.'

Cat said nothing, but could not contain the satisfied grin that was spreading slowly across her face.

* * *

The door of 42 Rydell Street was opened by a plump, middle-aged woman with brown cow-eyes and an instant smile. The smile faded swiftly when she saw police officers, and her hands flew to her mouth.

'Oh no! Something's happened to my Terry, hasn't it? He's had an accident!'

'Please, Mrs James, don't distress yourself.' Joseph stepped forward and with his most sincere smile, said, 'We just need his help with something, that's all. There's no accident, okay?'

The woman heaved a great sigh. 'Oh dear, well, I'm sorry but he's out visiting a client. That's why I thought . . .' she allowed the sentence to trail off, then added. 'He's due back any minute, you'd better come in and wait.'

Nikki sent Dave and the uniforms back to their cars, then she, Joseph and Cat went inside. The living room was big and airy, with large sash windows and a high ceiling. Everything was scrupulously clean, tidy and minimalist. So spotless that Nikki felt the urge to check the soles of her shoes for specks of dirt.

'What sort of work does your husband do?'

'He's a web designer.' Mrs James announced with pride. 'And he's very good. Got lots of satisfied customers.'

Nikki didn't dare look at Cat, who was making a strange coughing sound. From what Cat had told her about the computer game, the people who used it were after a very particular sort of satisfaction.

'What is this is about, Inspector?' Mrs James had begun to look worried.

'We just have a few questions for him.' Nikki looked at the woman shrewdly. 'What sort of people does your husband work for?'

'Small businesses mainly. So many people shop online these days that it makes economic sense to have a mail-order side to your business, if it's appropriate. Terry designs sites for them.' She stood up. 'I can show you some of his work, if you like?'

'That would be helpful.'

The woman led the way out into the hall, down a narrow corridor and into a large room used as an office. Two computers sat idle, and shelves full of books, CD-ROMs and office equipment neatly lined the walls.

'Here.' She moved the mouse on one of the computers and a vivid desk top appeared. She double-clicked on one icon and a very professional cookware site appeared. Not quite the sort of thing that Nikki had expected.

'This is his latest design.' She closed the site and opened another. 'This is the company he's working with today. They are a floral postal service. Nice, isn't it?'

Brightly coloured bunches and bouquets of flowers filled the screen.

Joseph leaned towards the screen. 'Must be quite difficult work, what with all the different options, shopping baskets and checkouts, etcetera?'

'Oh yes. But Terry's worked with computers for years.'

'And you, Mrs James, what do you do?' he asked.

'I look after the accounts. You could say I'm Terry's general factotum.' She smiled. 'I work harder now than when I was employed by the university.'

'The Fenland university?'

'That's the one.'

'Bella?' A voice echoed down the hall. 'What on earth is going on?' A tall, receding and bespectacled man, accompanied by Dave, was hurrying towards them.

'Don't worry, it's alright, dear. These officers just want to talk to you. Let's go back into the lounge.' Mrs James led the way.

'What is it you want?'

Nikki's heart sank. This man, with the buttons on his jacket done up wrong, looked more like an absent-minded professor than a pornographic high-tech gamester.

'Does the name Lyco mean anything to you?' asked Joseph.

The man turned the corners of his mouth down and frowned. 'Lyco? Can't say it does.' He swung around to his wife. 'Bella? Have we a client with a name like that?'

'Definitely not,' she said emphatically.

'Mr James.' Cat stood up. 'Would you mind if I take a look at your computers? You can come with me, of course.'

'Be my guest. The older one has my basic designs on it, and Bella uses it for our invoicing and banking. The newer one has the finished articles, and a data base of all my business accounts. There's nothing on there that you can't look at.'

'Do you encrypt anything, sir?'

'No need. Only my wife and I use them, and we have no secrets.'

'Thanks, I won't be long.' Without waiting for Terry James, Cat slipped out of the room.

'So what kind of company is this Lyco?' asked Bella James.

'It's not a company, Mrs James,' said Nikki. 'It's an alias for someone we want to talk to.'

Mr and Mrs James looked at each other with puzzled glances, then Terry James said, 'And you think this Lyco person has used our company?'

'If he did,' cut in his wife, 'he must have done it under another name.'

Nikki drew in a long breath. With every minute that passed she was closer to thinking that Cat had made a massive error over these people.

'How big is your customer data base, Mr James?' interjected Joseph.

James thought for a moment. 'We have about fifty clients in all. Twenty are main clients, who have had full web designs and follow-up maintenance. The rest are companies and individuals who have used us for consultancy or for troubleshooting.'

'Could you let us have a print-out of them, please?'

Bella James gasped. 'Oh no, Sergeant! We hold our clients details in the strictest confidence. I don't think it would be very ethical if we just handed information like that out, do you?'

'Do it, Bella.' Terry James shrugged. 'We have nothing to hide. Just the names and addresses won't hurt.'

'Well, if you think so, dear. I'll get them.'

A few minutes later both she and Cat returned to the room.

'Here they are, Officer.' Bella James passed a sheaf of papers to Joseph. 'But I'd appreciate it if they were destroyed once you've looked at them.'

'Of course, and thank you.'

'Are we through, DC Cullen?' asked Nikki, rather icily.

'I've seen everything I need to, ma'am.'

Nikki noticed a look of something like excitement on Cat's face, but whatever the detective had unearthed, she clearly did not want to share it with the James family.

'Then we are sorry to have taken up your time,' said Nikki with a fake smile. 'You've been most helpful. If we need anything else we'll be in contact.'

Back in the car, Nikki turned to Cat. 'Okay, spill the beans.'

'I think I know what's happened, ma'am. I saw this with another case, a paedo ring that we busted.'

'Then share it with us, for heaven's sake!'

'Have you heard of an evil twin?'

'No. And try to use English when you explain what the hell you are talking about,' said Nikki impatiently.

Cat rubbed her temples. 'Right, well, we're talking Cyber Crime, right? Now, most people use Wi-Fi, that's wireless high speed net, and that needs a hotspot to . . .'

'Lost! I said English!'

'It's like this, the evil twin poses as a real hotspot, and when you use your computer, it steals your information, all your personal stuff, everything.'

'Right. I get that, but how does it fit in with Terry James and the Lyco computer game?'

'There's another scam, just like the one that I was telling you about, but the cyber-thief steals your domain. If he's done something that he doesn't want traced, he uses the stolen domain, and the shit lands on your head, not his!' Cat shook her head. 'One of those two computers has been hacked into by Lyco. There's nothing more scary on the James's hard drive than a game of Spider Solitaire.'

'Great, another dead end.'

'Maybe not,' Cat grinned. 'If I ask the IT section to help me, I think I can still track Lyco. That's unless Sergeant Easter feels like leaning on graffiti boy, the one who gave him the lead in the first place.'

'I don't think Petey Redfield would have a clue who Lyco was. I'm sure it's just a dirty game that one of the gang stumbled on, now everyone wants to play it,' said Joseph.

'Then we go down the IT route. Cat, get onto it as soon as we get . . .' Nikki's phone interrupted her. 'Hello, DI Galena here.'

133

'Sorry to bother you, Inspector, but it's Sister O'Keefe from Greenborough ITU.'

'Hi, Leah. How's the boy?'

'Showing signs of improvement. We will be taking him off the respirator shortly, and we wondered if you'd like to be here?'

'I certainly would. Thanks for that. We'll be straight over.' She closed her phone and looked at Joseph. 'We'll drop Cat off at the station and get straight over to the hospital. They're going to try to bring the lad round. If he says anything, I want to know what it is, first hand.'

CHAPTER TWENTY

As Nikki entered ITU, she was met by familiar faces. This was one of the few places where she was rarely known as a detective inspector, but simply as Hannah's mum.

'We almost lost him,' said the sister shaking her head. 'But he's a tough little devil. The doctors are pretty certain that we can keep him stable this time.'

'Is he off the ventilator?' asked Nikki.

'Yes, and he's holding his own. We are just waiting for the anaesthetist, then we'll bring him round.' Leah looked at Nikki, her eyes full of compassion. 'And considering your previous involvement with this procedure, it's our joint decision that you wait outside for that bit. We'll call you when he's compos mentis, okay?'

'You're all very thoughtful,' said Nikki, 'and I really appreciate it, but I'm here with my police hat on today. It's imperative that I hear everything that he has to say.'

'It could still be very traumatic for you.' Leah looked worried. 'It's bad enough without all the bad memories that you have.' She squeezed Nikki's arm. 'I'll come and get you immediately he's stable, I promise.'

Nikki raised her hands in silent surrender, and secretly felt a rush of relief. After the panic attack in the barn, she still didn't quite trust her own emotions.

'I suppose you've had no luck finding out who he is, have you?' Leah was asking.

'Nothing as yet. Beggars belief, doesn't it?'

'Beautiful looking child, too. Well, he *was* before someone decided to re-sculpture his face.'

Nikki shuddered. 'I cannot begin to wonder what he could have done to warrant such a brutal beating.'

'Hopefully, we'll know soon, then you can get the animal that did this.' The sister looked towards the door. 'I have to go. The anaesthetist is here. Keep your fingers crossed, Nikki, and I'll be out as soon as I can, all right?'

Nikki watched as the nurse hurried away, then went back to the family room to find Joseph.

He stood up as she entered, and somehow that simple gesture touched her. It may have been just inbred good manners, or an army-indoctrinated respect for a higher ranking officer, whatever, it made her feel somehow worthwhile. And that was a welcome change to the kind of treatment she generally received.

'How's the lad?'

She slumped into a chair. 'They are about to bring him around. It's a critical time, anything can happen, and not all of the options are good.'

Joseph sat down beside her. 'This must be hell for you.'

Nikki looked around the empty waiting area. 'Put it like this, I'd never want to go through what I did with Hannah with anyone else, especially a loved one.' She gave him a sad smile. 'But right now, all I can think about is that little kid in there.'

'How long does this procedure take?'

'Not long. The anaesthetics they use these days are carefully patient targeted, so they can bring him out of sedation quite easily. It's just that boys often fight for some reason, and they'll want to know that he's safe and calm before we see him. Luckily, apart from the bleed that they drained, they didn't find any severe legions on the scan,' Nikki paused, '. . . but until they wake him up and do some tests, they'll have no idea of how the damage will have affected him.'

'Have they told you what other injuries he sustained?'

'Broken nose. Deep laceration to the right cheek. Three broken ribs and a cracked sternum, plus extensive bruising to the abdomen and groin areas. And that's without the head injury.'

'Then dumped naked in the bushes, presumably to die.' Joseph's face hardened. 'What drives some of these animals?'

'Drugs.' Nikki almost spat the word out.

'Yes, I guess so. *And* alcohol, and hate, and abuse, and neglect.'

'But mainly drugs.' Nikki sank further down in her chair. 'I know that back at the station, the others think I'm obsessed, and maybe I am. But when you see the damage they do, the families ripped apart, and the abysmal waste of young lives, can you blame me, Joseph?'

'No, I can't. But whereas we see it every day out on the streets, it's far worse for you, because it's hurt you on a personal level.'

'It's not just Hannah. Although, God knows, that was enough to drag the heart from any parent.'

'Your *bad case*?' asked Joseph tentatively.

Nikki nodded. 'My bad case.' She looked at her sergeant, and saw a face full of compassion. Not a condescending kind of pity, just a simple understanding, from one injured soul for another. 'Why don't you go grab us a coffee, and I'll tell you about Emily Drennan.'

When Joseph had sat back down, Nikki leaned back, legs outstretched, closed her eyes, and allowed a chestnut haired teenage girl to fill her thoughts. 'Emily Drennan was highly intelligent, came from a good family with no money troubles, and was absolutely beautiful. She was the daughter of a local GP, and had secured a place at Durham university. But that was before she met the love of her life.'

Joseph sipped his coffee and stared at her over the top of his polystyrene cup.

'Stephen Cox was known to most as a successful Greenborough Town footballer. We knew him as an aggressive little thug, skilled with his feet certainly, but also pretty skilled with his fists.'

'I don't like where this is going,' murmured Joseph.

'Cox got a signing for a big league team, and the money started to roll in. Get the picture? Sponsorship deals, fast cars, all that was missing was the pretty girl on his arm, and funnily enough, Stevie boy never seemed to keep his girlfriends for long. Until he met Emily.' Nikki stared into her coffee. 'I have no idea what happened when they met, but something did, some weird attraction of opposites, maybe. She was totally infatuated with him, and he saw something in her, something he could control, something he could own.'

'You knew her, before she met this Stephen Cox?'

'Oh, I knew her. She was three years older than Hannah, but the Drennan's lived in the same village as we did. The girls played together as children. Emily was the most sweet natured kid I'd ever met. Hannah was always the feisty one, the one who questioned every damned thing you asked her to do, but Emily would just smile and nod and get on with it.'

'Did she marry Cox?'

Nikki waited for a moment before replying, and watched through the glass door panel as two nurses hurried into the ITU. 'No, they never married. I don't think that was ever in his game plan. He convinced her to move in with him, then he began the long, slow process of destroying her.' Nikki stared impassively at the door to the Intensive Care Unit. 'I hadn't seen her for almost a year, then one evening, I was just going off-duty when a call came in, someone had heard crying coming from a derelict building near the docks. Everyone on the incoming shift was committed, there'd been a major RTC, so I volunteered for the shout.'

'Emily?'

This was not easy. Nikki had only twice spoken about what she found, once for her statement, and once, over a very large Scotch, to Rick Bainbridge. She had refused counselling, and had never allowed anyone to broach the subject again, including her family. Which, a long way down the line, she knew to have been a big mistake.

And now, here she was preparing to bare her soul to a stranger. But was he a stranger? She looked at Joseph thoughtfully, and wondered how this had come about. She'd decided from the moment that the super had told her about him, that they would not get on. She had wanted to hate him for intruding into her domain. Part of her couldn't wait to find an excuse to send him scurrying back to Fenchester. But now . . .

'You don't have to do this,' he said gently. 'The longer old pain has been buried, the harder it is to dig up.'

'But you shouldn't leave someone as beautiful as Emily Drennan buried in a cellar, should you?' said Nikki. 'She deserves to be brought into the light.'

And thinking about those words, Nikki steeled herself and slipped back into the past.

'Is there anyone there?' Her voice echoed back to her from the high, cavernous basement of the old warehouse. 'It's the police. I'm here to help.'

At first she heard nothing, except the dripping of water and the occasional scurrying of a rat. Then she caught the faint sound of a sob. Picking her way carefully through the debris of the deserted building, she moved towards the area where the sound had come from. 'Don't be afraid, I won't hurt you! Can you hear me?'

The sobbing was getting louder, but swinging her torch beam around, Nikki realised that she was walking beneath dangerously rotting timbers. The floor above had collapsed in several places, leaving splintered wood and chunks of masonry everywhere. Perhaps shouting loudly was not such a good idea.

Nikki stopped to get her bearings, and looked around. Shafts of late evening sun were filtering in from the ground floor, through the gaping holes, and into the cellar. They criss-crossed the dark, gloomy basement like a giant cat's cradle of golden light. If it were not so treacherous, it may have been beautiful.

'Over here.' The voice was tremulous and weak.

Nikki sprang forward. 'Where are you? Are you badly hurt?'

For a second she thought she heard a laugh. But it was not a happy laugh, or a laugh of relief that help was finally at hand. It was a sound that made Nikki's blood run cold, and a sound she was to hear for years to come, in the dead of night, when sleep evaded her.

'Help me.' It was a girl's voice.

'I'll get help, don't worry.' Nikki pulled herself around a pile of broken brickwork, and saw her.

The girl was lying, curled up in the foetal position, in the dirt and rubbish on the cellar floor. One ankle was twisted in an unnatural position away from her body, but she didn't even seem aware of it. She cried softly, whispering one name, over and over. Stevie. Stevie. Stevie.

'You're safe now, sweetheart,' Nikki dropped down beside her. 'Can you tell me your name?'

'Stevie? Oh, I knew you wouldn't leave me.' The voice was little more than a hushed sigh.

Nikki tried her radio but couldn't get a signal. 'I've got to find a spot where my radio works. You just hold on, I'll be back, okay?'

She scrambled towards one of the holes in the ceiling, and managed to get a weak, stuttering message across for an ambulance and some assistance.

When she got back the crying had stopped. She sank down on the floor beside the girl and gently rubbed her wrists. 'Come on, sweetheart. The paramedics will be here soon. You'll be out of here in no time. I'm Nikki, can you tell me your name?'

The girl turned a little, and in the hollow eyes and the gaunt face of the heroin addict, Nikki saw the fleeting hint of a smile. Then she said, 'I'm so cold.'

Nikki slipped off her jacket and wrapped it around the girl's thin shoulders. Junkie or not, this kid was going to be lucky to make it. She needed to do all she could for her. 'There you are. You just hold on for a bit longer.'

'Thank you, Mrs Galena.' The girl gave a shudder, then whispered, 'I'm Emily. Emily Drennan.'

Nikki's eyes flew open and she saw Joseph's concerned expression.

'I never recognised her!' Nikki shook her head violently. 'It was horrible! Not until she said her name, then I saw something in that ravaged face that I knew. That bastard had taken a beautiful, beautiful child and annihilated every lovely part of her.'

'And the ambulance didn't get there in time, did it?' said Joseph.

'That RTC I mentioned? Everything was jammed up. She died in my arms,' said Nikki with a long, painful sigh.

'And did you get Cox?'

'It's amazing what money can do, Joseph. He played the part of the grieving partner, and managed to get some cheap tabloid newspaper editor on his side. Vomit-making stories of how he'd tried to get her off the drink and the drugs.' Nikki's face screwed up with distaste. 'But the worst thing of all, was the fact that she had loved him. She died believing that he'd come back for her. How could you build a case when Cox produced a dozen witnesses to say how much he loved her?'

Joseph took a deep breath, then raised one eyebrow. 'But I'm guessing that you didn't leave it there?'

'I hounded him. Every way he turned, he found me watching him. I spent every moment, on and off-duty, haunting that evil little murderer. And then I hit on his dealers, and I hit hard. In the end, he moved out of Greenborough. Last I heard, he was in rehab and his money had run out.'

'Good. That's how karma works. What goes round, comes round.'

Nikki picked up her cooling coffee and drank it back. 'And now, I wonder. If I'd known that my vendetta would wreck my marriage and ultimately leave my only child in a High Dependency Unit, would I have just let him go?'

'I doubt it. Given the circumstances, we do what we think is right at the time. That's all we *can* do. The fact that we agonise and moralise over it afterwards at least means we have a conscience, and that separates us from the ones who don't give a toss.' He shrugged and gave her bitter smile. 'Believe me, there are things that I would have done differently in hindsight, but you can't live your life constantly wondering about repercussions that *may* occur.'

'I'm sure you're right, but why do I still feel so guilty?' Nikki looked out through the glass. 'At last! Leah's giving us the thumbs up. We can go see the boy.'

* * *

'He's sleeping naturally now, and his breathing is fine,' said the sister, her fingers gently pressing on the boy's pulse. 'You can stay with him until he wakes up again.'

'Has he spoken, Leah?'

'Just to tell us that his name is Mickey. He knows that he has been attacked, that's all so far. His throat is naturally sore from the tube.'

'He gave you no surname?'

'No, he stuck at Mickey. And strangely, he didn't ask for his parents.'

Nikki looked down at the sleeping boy, and her heart went out to him.

Half his face was a mottled purplish, red, with a long row of stitches and steri-strips holding together the torn flesh of his cheek. His corn-blond hair was still streaked with dry-ing blood, and a wide band of dressing covered the bridge of his nose. Whatever reflection the lad had seen in the mirror that morning, had gone for ever.

Leah O'Keefe saw her looking at the child's face. 'We've let the maxillofacial surgeon take a look at him, and luckily his jaw is okay. Plastics will sort that scar out later, although he'll always have a mark there.'

'Sounds as though a scar should be the least of his wor-ries,' remarked Joseph grimly. 'He's lucky to be alive.'

'Maybe that depends what his life is like in the first place,' Nikki mused. 'Whoever did this is still out there, maybe waiting to finish the job.'

'That's if Mickey here was actually the target, and not just a wrong place, wrong time kid.'

'Sorry, Sergeant, but something tells me my theory is the correct one. Now, pull up a chair and we'll wait and see, shall we?'

Mickey slept for half an hour, and when he came round and saw his two visitors, he remained abnormally quiet. His frightened eyes darted from one to the other, but he said nothing.

'You're not in trouble, Mickey. Honestly. *You* are the victim here, so you can talk freely to us, I promise,' said Joseph.

'Absolutely,' added Nikki. 'We just want to get the people who did this to you. They have to be punished for hurting you.'

'We only want to help you, Mickey, do you understand?'

The wild eyes continued to dance around, as if he were looking for a way out of the small room, but still he refused to speak.

Nikki sat back, trying not to crowd or intimidate him. He'd been through too much already to wake up and find himself pressured by a couple of pushy strangers. 'What's your surname, son? I'm sure that your parents are worried sick about you.'

For the first time Mickey showed some sort of expression. And it wasn't one of pleasure. Through split and bruised lips, he rasped, 'That's a laugh! They couldn't give a flying fuck about me.'

Nikki sighed with relief, at least he was fully aware of his situation, even if it wasn't a good one.

'Come on, Mickey. We have to let your mum know where you are,' said Joseph amiably.

'You'd have to find her first.' He shifted uncomfortably, then groaned in discomfort. 'Shit! My ribs!'

'Just lie still. The doctor will give you some more pain relief soon. Now, if you'd just tell us your name.'

Mickey closed his eyes and said nothing.

'Do you know who did this?' asked Joseph.

The boy didn't reply.

'Because sadly, until we get some answers from you, we are just going to have to sit here and bug you.' He smiled down at the lad. 'And we possess endless patience.'

Still Mickey chose to keep silent, but after a while, he sighed shakily, and Nikki noticed a tear creeping slowly down his cheek. 'Please go away and leave me alone.'

'We can't, my love,' said Nikki gently. 'Just let us help you.'

'I'm scared.' His voice was small, and all vestige of his earlier bravado had disappeared.

'We won't let anyone hurt you again, Mickey. We'll have someone with you, day and night.'

'It won't matter. He'll get me, even if you had a bloke with an Uzi outside my door, he'd still get me.'

'Who is *he*, Mickey?'

'I'm not saying.'

Nikki and Joseph looked at each other, then Nikki nodded and indicated her head towards the door.

Joseph reached across and very gently touched the boy's hand. 'Okay, you need some rest now, Mickey. You sleep, and we'll come back later. And there will be two police officers outside your door until you're well enough to move. Understand?'

The boy gave an imperceptible nod, then closed his eyes.

As Nikki and Joseph left the room, she saw the tears begin to flow, and his narrow chest rise and fall with soft sobs.

'Poor little sod. He's exhausted.'

'And terrified.'

Nikki's eyes narrowed, 'With good reason. He knows his assailant, and he knows he hasn't finished with him yet.' She closed the door. 'I want our best officers on duty here, with no sneaking off for a fag break or spending ten minutes in the bog. This kid needs us to give him one hundred per cent.'

Joseph nodded. 'And he'll get it. With your permission, I'll take the first shift, ma'am, and if anyone wants to hurt him, they'll have to get through me first.'

Nikki agreed. 'Right, then I'll go back and organise a rota, and I must check out any progress being made on Kerry.' Her face hardened. 'I don't want to think like this, but with every hour that passes, I fear the worst for that poor kid.'

CHAPTER TWENTY-ONE

'I'm holding off the media-fest, but I don't know how long I can keep Lisa Jane's death secret.' The superintendent paced restlessly up and down his office. 'Have you spoken to Archie?'

Nikki leaned against the wall with her arms folded. 'I'm going to see him when we've finished here.'

'Where's your sergeant?'

Nikki grinned. 'It's okay, I haven't bought him a single ticket back to Fenchester. He's at the hospital, with Mickey.' She chewed on her lip. 'I think the boy may respond better to Joseph, kind of like a man-to-man thing.'

The super stopped pacing. 'Is it my imagination, or are you and Sergeant Easter,' he stopped, almost scared to voice the words, 'getting on?'

'I'm saying nothing, sir, But I do concede, there is more to the man than the mess room gossips would ever dream of.'

Raising his eyes upwards, the super said, 'So, there is a God! Hallelujah!'

'Whoa! Don't count your chickens, sir. There's still plenty of time for him to right royally piss me off.' Her smile faded. 'The thing is, time's running out for Kerry Anderson, and frankly, we both know the gravity of that. I'd make the effort to work alongside Vlad the Impaler if it meant we found that missing girl.'

'I know Nikki, and I won't hold you up. Keep me posted on all levels, okay?'

'Yes, sir. Oh, and we need a Victim Support Officer allocated for Mickey. He's terrified, and I want exactly the right person to get the best out of him.'

'Okay, let me know when you've assessed him, and I'll sort that out.'

Nikki thanked him, then went to the CID room to find Cat. What she found when she got there was an empty room and a memo telling her that Kris Brown was in the foyer waiting for her.

'Wonders will never cease!' she muttered to herself, and ran down the stairs.

* * *

'No, Inspector. I've never heard of either of those women. Are they missing too?'

Kris Brown looked haggard. He had three days stubble on his face, and his eyes were red and sore.

Nikki stared at him and tried to decide whether his rough look was due to honest concern, or guilt. Finding no sure answer, she sidestepped his question about Lisa Jane and Frankie Doyle, and continued with her interview.

'And do you know of a student, a guy named Lewis?'

'Lewis is another third-year on the photography programme. He's a pod neighbour to Kerry.'

'You've met him?'

'Once or twice when I've been visiting the Hub.'

Nikki looked down at her notebook. 'He said you'd been mugged. Is that true?'

Kris looked up with interest. 'Yeah. But how . . . ?' He shrugged and answered his own question. 'I suppose Kerry must have told him.'

'And did you report it?'

He shrugged again. 'No point. I wasn't hurt. And although they nicked my wallet, it didn't have much in it, and I found it again, in the gutter about 100 yards down the road.'

'Would you recognise them if you saw them again?'

'Oh sure. Attractive faces, part rat, part cadaver, I'd say. I'd recognise them anywhere.'

Nikki's mind raced. Was it just another mask-related petty crime, or was there a connection somewhere, between the masked gangs and Kerry's abduction? Whatever, she was in no mood for Kris Brown's sarcasm. 'Don't be clever with me, Mr Brown,' she hissed. 'In case you've forgotten, your little friend is still missing, and I'd rather be spending my time looking for her than listening to your snide digs! Now stick to answering the questions, all right?'

'Sorry.' Kris looked as if he were about to cry. 'But I'm as worried as you! I've been to *every* place that we used to go together. *Every* place that she liked for atmospheric pictures. *Every* place that I can think of. I've walked half the length of the coastline, and nothing! I'm exhausted, but as you say, she's still missing, and I *have* to find her.'

His outburst caught Nikki off guard, and for the first time, she wondered whether Kris Brown was genuine.

She thought for a moment, then changed the subject. 'Where did a young bloke like you get the money for all that super-fancy star-gazing equipment?'

He frowned. 'If it's any of your business, Inspector, that's what happens when someone dies and leaves you twenty grand in their will.'

'Very nice!' said Nikki. 'That really enabled you to indulge in your pastime on a grand scale, didn't it?'

When Kris spoke, his voice was cold and his words clipped. 'Oh sure, it's very nice. But frankly, Inspector, I'd rather have my father back. Now, are we done?'

* * *

Nikki met Archie in a small café on River Walk. He sat at the back, concealed from the windows, and stirred an over-sized cup of cappuccino.

'I hoped to be handing you your Fluke character on a plate, but it seems I was wrong.' Archie's face darkened. 'My boys have been up more blind alleys than you could believe. And,' he paused and gave her a long pondering look, 'I hate to tell you this Nikki, but one name has cropped up rather regularly as the family have been making their enquiries.' He sipped his coffee, winced, then tore the top from another packet of sugar and tipped it in. 'A name you won't like.'

'I'm supposing it's Frankie Doyle,' said Nikki sombrely.

'You suppose correctly.'

'In what context does she appear.'

'Well, my sister-in-law Margaret tells us that Doyle visited Lisa Jane a few days before she went missing.'

'I didn't know they were friends,' said Nikki, unable to keep the surprise out of her voice.

'They weren't,' said Archie, his jaw set forward. 'We've had nothing to do with that piece of shit since we found she was responsible for your daughter's, uh, unfortunate accident.'

'My daughter's attempted murder, you mean?'

Archie nodded sadly. 'How is she?'

'Some days I think there is improvement, and others, well, you know.' She drew in a breath, she didn't want to think about Hannah right now. 'But back to Frankie Doyle, does she still live on the Carborough? She slipped off our radar a few months ago, then I was told she was back and running with the big boys.'

'She will never run with the big boys. She's evil, but she's not clever. She's a maverick, a disturbed one. No one with any sense would trust her.' He frowned. 'And I'm sure she's not living around here anymore. One of my nephews is trying to get you an address. If he succeeds, I'll ring straight-away.' He took a big gulp of coffee. 'Do you have anything for us?'

Nikki told him about Mickey, but did not mention that the boy had regained consciousness. She trusted him, but still knew when to be tactful.

'If he's the boy I'm thinking of, he's not the luckiest kid on the block. He's an only child, and takes the brunt of his father's drunken rages. His mother, as I recall, spends more time with her sister in Peterborough, than she does at home.'

'What's the boy's surname, Archie?'

'Smith.'

'And where does he live?'

Archie thought for a moment. 'Cavendish Buildings. Not sure of the number.'

'Thanks. Let's just hope he pulls through.' She leant forward and lowered her voice. 'We may have a lead on the masks, or at least something about the name they've given them.'

'Ah, the Griffyx.'

'That's the one. Our techies are checking out some violent porno computer game, there's a definite link, and they're trying to trace its inventor. We know he's local, and he stole some poor unsuspecting website designer's identity to do it.'

'Sounds probable, it's just the sort of thing some of the young yobbo's around here would love. Anything brutal, vicious or nasty.' He shook his head. 'I think I'm getting old, Nikki. I don't have the stomach for all this anymore.'

'You never did, my friend. Well, not gratuitous violence for the sake of it.' She smiled at him. 'As you rightly said, you needed brains to get to the top, not just skill with a flick knife. But I really have to go. We'll speak later.'

She stood up and pushed her chair back under the table. 'Take care, Archie.'

'And you, Nikki. Especially if Frankie Doyle is back.'

* * *

The 4 p.m. meeting brought them no closer to finding Kerry, and the enquiries regarding the elusive Fluke were inconclusive, in fact there was considerable disagreement between the reports.

Afterwards, Nikki sat with Joseph in her office and tried to make sense of it.

'Conflicting descriptions, and nothing concrete at all,' Nikki grumbled. 'I'm beginning to wonder if this Fluke is a figment of our collective imagination.'

'Mm, the Carborough's own urban myth.' Joseph absent-mindedly picked a speck of fluff from his jacket sleeve. 'And it's frustrating to only have an out of date picture of Frankie Doyle. Young women, and please excuse the generalisation, have a tendency to follow fashion and alter their appearance every time they step outside.'

'No offence taken. I totally agree with you. Our Cat is a prime example. What I find amazing is that a wicked bitch like Frankie has managed to stay out of our clutches for so long.'

'Maybe she decided not to dirty her own doorstep. She could be working another county, under a different name.'

Nikki wasn't convinced, but left it there. 'How did you get on with young Mickey Smith after I left?'

Joseph's face lit up. 'I reckon that boy will open up a treat. I didn't push him, but he's starting to relax with me. And I get the feeling he could be a chatterbox, which would be useful.'

'Who's with him now?'

'Two wooden tops, until I get back. I promised I'd get him a couple of his favourite comics and drop them in when I finish.'

'I need to get a dedicated Victim Support Officer over there soon. Got any ideas about who would be suitable?'

'I'll sound out his relationship with his family, then we'll see what he needs, if that's okay?'

Nikki nodded. 'Well, I've just received the preliminary post mortem report on Lisa Jane from your pet pathologist, so I'm going to be tied up for a while. Rather than hanging around like a bad smell, why don't you get yourself back to the hospital?'

Joseph stood up. 'Sure, and if he tells me anything interesting, I'll ring you.'

'You do that,' said Nikki, opening the folder. 'And by the way, what *are* Mickey's favourite comics?'

"Fraid it's the *Beano* and the *Dandy*. It seems not all twelve-year-olds are the violent thugs we believed.'

'Excuse me, but have you ever taken a good look at Denis the Menace?'

'Not for about twenty-five years,' Joseph grinned. 'But I'm secretly hoping to get a sneaky peek before I give them to Mickey. Bye.'

As he left, Nikki smiled. If anyone was going to get Mickey Smith to talk, it would be her new sergeant.

* * *

By eight o'clock that evening Detective Sergeant Joseph Easter and Master Michael Nathan Smith, were on first name terms. Joe, as he now was, had read both comics to his captive audience, and although he wouldn't have admitted it, thoroughly enjoyed himself. Mickey had hardly noticed the carefully interspersed questions about himself, and as the boy dozed for a while, Joseph summed up what he had discovered.

Dysfunctional family with a father who used his fists when he'd had a drink, and the benders sometimes lasted for a week. Mother regularly disappeared, apparently to a sister, but from the way Mickey spoke, Joseph suspected she actually went to other arms for comfort. No siblings and Mickey was very young for his age. Joseph wondered if he was trying to use his status as a child to protect himself from his father's violent outbursts. That, or he was just not terribly bright.

He stared at the battered child in the hospital bed. It was strange, because kids who were treated badly often grow up quickly, learn fast to fend for themselves. It was a bad world out there and they needed to survive. It seemed that Mickey had gone the other way.

'Sergeant?' The sister in charge beckoned him to the door. 'We are happy that he's stable enough to move him from this unit now. His observation can continue in less frightening surroundings. We would appreciate your help with the transfer.'

'Where is he going, Sister?'

'There's a private room in the general surgery ward. It's next to the nursing station and would provide plenty of privacy, but also it would be easy for you to watch him.'

'Sounds perfect. What floor?'

'Top floor, Sergeant.'

Joseph nodded. 'Even better. When is this going to happen? I need to keep my boss up to speed.'

'In about an hour. The Bed Manager is breathing down our necks, I'm afraid.'

'Fine. I'll ring in, then tell my colleagues here what we're up to.' Joseph looked at the sister. 'Sorry to ask this, but did all of your tests on the lad come back okay?'

The woman's lips tightened. 'We wouldn't be moving him if we were not completely happy, Detective.'

'Oh, I didn't mean that! I'm just concerned that he seems to have a rather erratic concentration span, and he talks very quickly, almost as if he's hyperactive.'

The sister softened. 'That's very perceptive of you. Some old notes did mention a suspected learning difficulty when he was younger.' She smiled. 'It's not his head injury, Sergeant, I'm afraid the childish behaviour is quite normal for Mickey.'

Half an hour later, Mickey was ready to go.

'You are coming with me, Joe? You won't leave me, will you?'

'I'll be right by your side, no fear.'

'Promise? I mean I like the thought of a police guard. Your men are armed, aren't they? I mean they're not much use if they can't shoot anyone who threatens me. And what if . . .' The boy's agitation was becoming almost alarming.

'Hey! Slow down, partner! This isn't a scene from *Lethal Weapon*! It's sleepy old Greenborough, remember.' He reached across and held the boy's hand. 'No one is going to get to you, understand? You've got Sergeant Joe right here with you.'

'Yeah, yeah, I have, haven't I?'

'Now, listen. If you just stay calm until we get you settled into your private room, then when the doctors have checked you over, I'll tell you a secret, right? A really big secret!'

'What is it?' asked Mickey, temporarily forgetting his fear.

'You be a good lad, and you'll find out. Deal?'

'Deal, Sergeant Joe.'

The trip was uneventful, and in no time Mickey Smith was being made as comfortable as possible in his new room.

'Very nice! Even I've never had a private room before,' said Joseph in mock awe. 'Look, Mickey, they've even got pictures on the walls! And your own toilet! How snobby is that?'

A tall, stick-thin nurse threw him a conspiratorial grin and whispered. 'You're a natural with the lad. If you ever need a new vocation, I'd seriously consider paediatric nursing.'

Joseph raised his eyebrows and whispered back. 'You have to be joking! This is really hard work compared to catching criminals!'

Finally, one by one, the nurses left, the last one saying. 'He's very tired, officer. I suggest you let him sleep now.'

Joseph checked that his uniforms were in place outside, then drew up a chair.

'So what's your big secret, Joe?' muttered a sleepy voice.

'You won't ever tell, will you?'

'Cross my heart and ho—'

'I believe you, Mickey,' interrupted Joseph, not wanting to hear the unfortunate child say that he'd *hope to die*. 'In the job I had before this one, I used to have to guard people. Very important people just like you.'

Mickey yawned. 'So who did you protect?'

Joseph leaned across and whispered a name in the boy's ear, then he moved back to see the child's dark eyes widen and the lips form an amazed 'O.'

'Never!'

'Yep. I really did.'

Mickey's eyes began to close, but the smile stayed on his face. 'I got secrets, too.'

Joseph stiffened, but kept his tone soft. 'Really? Big as mine?'

'Bigger.'

'Wanna share them?'

'Maybe.'

As Joseph watched, the child's breathing changed, and his ravaged face relaxed into sleep.

'Great timing, Mickey.' He sat back and tried to make himself comfortable. 'But I'll still be here when you wake up, believe me!'

* * *

Nikki closed the folder and let out a long, audible sigh. The forensic findings showed that Lisa Jane had been grabbed from behind, and throttled to death with great force. The whole horrible incident would have taken only minutes. She hoped that Archie and his family might take some sort of consolation from that fact. She could just as easily have been incarcerated somewhere and tortured. Nikki tensed. Which could be the fate of Kerry Anderson, if they didn't damn well find her.

'Ma'am. May I have a word?'

She looked up to see WPC Yvonne Collins, dressed in civvies, waiting in the doorway.

'Sure. Problem?'

'I hope not, but I've got bad vibes about something, guv.'

Nikki pointed to a chair, and realised that Collins, a woman who had never been her greatest fan, had just called her 'guv,' and her tone had none of its usual rancour.

'What's worrying you, Yvonne?'

'Earlier today Niall and I went to see an old snout of mine. We'd asked him about Fluke, and he said he'd get us some information and meet us at five.' Yvonne rubbed her forehead. 'Thing is, we waited at the rendezvous, but he didn't turn up.'

'And he's normally reliable?'

'I've known Vic longer than some of my work colleagues, and he's never missed.'

'Do you drop him anything?'

'Just a token amount, guv, from my own purse.'

'I'd do the same. It keeps them coming back.'

Yvonne looked miserable. 'It's not just that, I like the old boy. He's harmless, and very intelligent. I'd hate something to have happened to him. I'm off-duty now, and I'd like to go look for him, but I thought I should check with you first.'

'I'm not sure that the Carborough at night, and out of uniform, is good move.'

'It's far worse with your uniform on, believe me! But Niall has offered to go with me.'

'Okay, but keep your enquiries low-key and your phones switched on. I don't want two damned good officers getting hurt for the sake of an old wino whose liver finally gave up on him. He may be a good old boy, but you know what I'm saying. Any sign of anything amiss, call for help, understand?

'Absolutely, ma'am, and thank you.'

Nikki sat and watched the officer leave, and quietly wondered about herself. That was the second time today she had praised her staff. Maybe she was like Archie, getting too long in the tooth for all the agro. Then she thought about Kerry, and her heart hardened. No sodding way! Nikki Galena was as tough as ever, and ready and waiting to do battle. She would clean this town of the drug dealers, if it were the last thing she ever did.

CHAPTER TWENTY-TWO

Joseph had dozed on and off, while still keeping an eye on the slumbering boy. The slightest movement or whimper from the direction of the bed, and he was wide awake in a nanosecond. If you wanted to stay alive on Special Ops, you learned to cat-nap but remain vigilant, and in his year away from the world, he had learned how to meditate, which refreshed him more than an hour of sleep could ever do.

Outside on the ward he could hear the nurses coming and going, buzzers bleeping and the occasional voice, but in the single room, it was quiet. The last few days had been an unexpected rollercoaster, and it was good to take a breather.

He watched as the boy's chest rose and fell rhythmically, and decided that his move to Greenborough had been a good one. He liked his new team, even if the boss did call them dysfunctional. And then there was DI Galena herself. She was not what the jungle drums had warned him about. Yes, she had a vitriolic tongue, and yes, she could put people's backs up in an instant, but she was a complicated woman. There were deep, dark and tangled parts to her, but there was also intelligence, shrewdness and above all, compassion. It didn't show itself too often, but it was there all right. Joseph smiled and thought about Dave. Generally he was considered a scruffy, lazy bastard, but DI Galena had made it her business to look deeper, and that was why Dave was working with her right now. Joseph didn't know the details, his guess was a disabled wife or mother, but the man had serious family commitments which left him exhausted and with no time to look after himself. If the DI had been the hard-hearted harridan that so many thought her, she would not have taken the time to rescue Dave Harris. Then, of course, there was Cat Cullen. The DI took the piss out of her, but openly respected her strengths, and Joseph had seen the effect that a word of praise from the boss had had on the girl earlier that day. It had really meant something to her. Okay, so they *were* a dysfunctional bunch, and he included himself in that statement, but he would prefer them over most of the people he'd worked with. He took a deep breath, let it out slowly, and wondered if he might have a chance to stay in Greenborough. Strangely, considering the havoc that surrounded him, he was beginning to like it.

At around ten thirty he stuck his head out of the door and asked one of the officers to get him a strong coffee. For some reason he'd suddenly felt unnaturally twitchy about Mickey Smith, and wanted to keep as alert as he could.

He sat back down and sipped the scalding liquid tentatively. Maybe it was the fact that he knew that Mickey had secrets that made him so edgy. If *he* knew, others would as well. Maybe it was those secrets that had put him into Intensive Care in the first place. And if it was, what the hell did he know that was worth going down for murder for?

The boy moved uncomfortably, then cried out, in fear and pain.

'No! I'm sorry! Don't hurt me! I'm sorry!'

'Hey, it's alright, Mickey. You're safe now.'

'Sergeant Joe! Don't let him hurt me again.'

'I won't let anyone hurt you, son.'

The cries faded into sobs.

'Who hurt you, Mickey?'

'The man my friend works for,' he whispered.

'What friend is that?'

'Marcus. Marcus Lee.'

'And do you know the name of the man Marcus works for?'

'He calls himself Fluke.' He paused and stared mournfully at his new friend. 'I dunno his proper name, but I know where he lives.'

Joseph took a deep lungful of air. No wonder the boy was in danger! 'And Marcus, did he help Fluke to hurt you?'

The tears welled up again. 'No, Sergeant Joe. He tried to stop him. I think he thought Fluke would just give me a good thrashing for being so stupid about the masks, but when he saw what the man was doing, he tried to help me.'

A shiver crossed Joseph's back, from shoulder blade to shoulder blade. 'And what happened to Marcus?'

Between gulping air and trying not to cry, Mickey said, 'Fluke hit him with something. Something heavy. He went down and he didn't move again. Then the man came back to me . . . and he had . . . a knife . . .' Mickey began to shake uncontrollably.

'That's enough now. You try to rest. It's all over. You can leave it all to us. Just tell me where Marcus lives, then we'll find your friend and we'll make sure that we find this Fluke too.'

Joseph went to the door and called one of the constables inside. 'Stay with him. Don't leave him for one second. I have some urgent calls to make.'

* * *

Nikki picked up the phone on the first ring. 'He said what!' she exclaimed.

'Yes, he doesn't know Fluke's actual address, but he said he could take us there.'

'Shit! We can't wait for that. Could you could get him to describe where it is?'

'I'll try, ma'am, but he's asleep again and the nursing staff are not too happy that he got so upset earlier. His last outpouring really floored him, poor kid.'

'But we have to find this Marcus Lee, whoever he is. He could be badly injured, maybe dead or dying. Damn it! Is this never going to end?'

'If he's got form he'll be on the police computer, but not if he's clean, why don't you save time and ring Archie. Ten to one he'll know exactly where the Lee's live.'

'Good thinking, Sergeant. Now get back to your charge. Apart from keeping him safe, he's worth his weight in gold right now. And do all you can to discover Fluke's address. Mickey can sleep for days and have all the comics he wants, *after* he helps us nail his attacker.'

'I'm onto it, ma'am.'

* * *

Nikki caught the super just as he was leaving. She briefed him and promised to call him if anything of note happened. He had offered to stay, but Nikki had not liked the unnatural pallor of his face, and decided the man badly needed some sleep.

Having done that, she rang Archie, got an address for Marcus Lee, then after thanking the man profusely, she phoned Yvonne Collins on her mobile.

'Any luck with that snout of yours?'

'No one's seen him since lunch-time, ma'am.' The constable sounded both tired and worried.

'Look, sorry to add to your problems, but would you two make an unofficial call on 201 Bristow Street? We are anxious to locate a young man who lives there named Marcus Lee. We believe he may be injured, possibly severely. Softly, softly please, Collins. We don't want to alarm his family if this turns out to be unreliable information, okay?'

'We're quite close to there now, ma'am. I'll ring you back. Oh, and ma'am, there's an ugly feeling on the estate this evening.'

'Like what?'

'Hard to put our finger on it, just feels really uneasy.'

'I'll pass on those good tidings to your sergeant, as if he wasn't stressed enough already! Hear from you soon.' She closed her phone and strode along the corridor towards the lift. If Mickey was correct, this was the first time Fluke had shown his hand and actually been identified. Not that he believed Mickey would be around long enough to point the finger. Nikki stopped in her tracks. It was imperative that Fluke did not find out that Mickey had survived the attack! She thought for a moment. This whole case had been riddled with deception, would one more hurt?

Picking up her step, she went down to the main office to report Yvonne Collins observations regarding the mood on the Carborough, then hurried back to her office.

It was a big and risky chance to take, but if Mickey Smith's home life was as bad as she'd been led to believe, then it could just be the answer. She sat back and considered how she would go about it. The one thing she was pretty certain about, was that Sergeant Easter would back her to the hilt. Yes, to save the boy's life, she would allow a rumour to spread that Mickey had not survived. Then she would spirit him away to safety, until she had fucking Fluke banged up.

A small smile spread across her face. She could feel it in her bones that they were getting closer to him, and if they found him, please God, they'd also find Frankie Doyle.

* * *

'He's not at home, ma'am. And his family didn't seem unduly worried about him. Marcus is nineteen, and he's a law unto himself apparently. We've left a message for him to ring the station, if and when he gets back, but I suspect my card is already in the dustbin.'

'Thanks for trying, Yvonne. Are you continuing with your search for your snout?'

'Word says he's been frightened off, guv. And there are more urgent issues when you look at the big picture, plus we both need sleep.'

'Sensible. Get yourselves home, and thanks.' She hung up, and wondered about Marcus Lee. Had he run off, and was he licking his wounds somewhere? Or had Fluke decided not to leave any more loose ends lying around? They really needed Fluke's address.

She flipped open her phone, then closed it again. Joseph would ring as soon as he had something to tell her, there was no point bugging him, and putting the hospital staff's back up in the process.

Nikki began to pace the floor. She felt about as happy as a newly caged tiger. She needed to be out there, doing something, not stuck in her office waiting for the damned phone to ring. She glanced at her watch. She had missed the tea-time television news, and the super had organised the Anderson family, well Mr Anderson, to make an appeal for Kerry's safe return.

She logged onto her computer and found the television station's catch up channel. While she waited, she may as well find out how it went.

Five minutes later she closed it down again. Anderson had been eloquent and seemingly devastated. His wife had sat silently beside him, and for the full interview had managed to look like a frightened rabbit caught in a headlight. The super was grave-faced and every bit a senior officer with the weight of the world on his shoulders. And why wouldn't he be? There had been no confirmed sightings of Kerry right across the region, and nothing from any other county force.

Kerry Anderson had walked out into the night, and disappeared without trace.

Nikki wandered out to the CID office and stared at the glass evidence board with the words 'unidentified young white male' written on it.

Mickey Smith. He could be their Golden Child. He was young, into everything, inquisitive and lonely. He spent as much time out of his house as he could, and Nikki was pretty sure that he knew more about the Carborough and the folks who lived there, than Archie Leonard.

Her gaze moved across the board and settled on a picture that caused her to shiver every time she saw it. It was of a young woman, approximately five-eight not skinny but certainly not overweight. Her hair was short, a non-descript mousy brown, and her eyes were evil, whatever colour that was. The name under the photograph was Frankie Doyle; the woman who had taken her daughter's life and put it on hold, possibly forever.

Officers were still working in the big room. Phones were still ringing, and printers clattered and whirred, but Nikki was lost in a private place with only Hannah occupying her mind. She knew the grim facts about persistent vegetative state, and she knew that if it went on much longer the hospital would be coming to her and asking that terrible question. The question that she could not even bring herself to contemplate.

There had been miracles before, so why not a miracle for Hannah? Surely where there was life there was hope? That's what everyone said, and she was sure that Joseph would be the first to embrace that old adage. Although he didn't seem to think it applied to his own daughter, Tamsin.

Joseph. Nikki frowned, and wondered why his opinions mattered to her? She had known him for such a short time, yet, no, this was not the time. She turned from the board and swiftly walked back to her office. As she opened the door, the phone screamed into life.

'DI Galena here. I hope that's damn well you, Joseph Easter!'

'Funnily enough, it is, ma'am.'

She could hear the excitement in his voice. 'So, what have you got?'

'First; a clear description of Fluke.'

Nikki scribbled down everything he said, 'And what else?'

'I've narrowed down his address to within two or three houses.'

'Brilliant! Fire away with that and I'll get uniform and an armed unit straight round there.'

'Okay, this is what Mickey says. From the traffic lights on Main Ridge, go down Haltoft Lane, then into Fishmere Crescent. There's a small dead end street down there, he can't remember the name, but there's only six or seven small terrace houses. Fluke is staying in one of the middle terraces. It has a blue front door.'

'He's talking about Carson Villas. Quiet, tucked away, perfect!' Nikki sighed with relief. 'If that kid were here now, I'd hug him!'

'With three broken ribs, he wouldn't thank you for it.'

'Joseph, I need your thoughts on something.'

'Fire away, ma'am.'

Nikki sank back in her chair and told him about Mickey Smith's 'faux demise.'

For a while, Joseph said nothing, making her wonder if she'd been wrong about him, then he said, 'I'll get an idea from the doctor of when he'll be safe to move. It's not just a good idea, ma'am, I think it's critical to get him to safety.' He paused, then added, 'And to be honest, I don't think that's here.'

Nikki's shoulder's tensed. 'Why?'

'Gut feeling, ma'am.'

'Right. That's good enough for me. Get his name changed on the hospital records, and talk to his doctor, in the strictest confidence, understand? There must be no reports to the press on his progress. As far as the media are concerned, he's still in a serious life-threatening condition, and we have *no* name for him. It must be believed that we do not know who he is, that's vital.' She paused, 'and Joseph, I know you feel something of a personal responsibility for this boy, but you *have* to get some sleep yourself. We'd like to believe otherwise, but we're only human.'

'Speak for yourself, ma'am. I'm off to find his doctor.'

CHAPTER TWENTY-THREE

Nikki took the information that Joseph had given her, and went directly to the CID room. Within minutes the officers on duty had identified the correct property.

It was time to go visiting.

'This is the description of your target, Sergeant. We have no name, just the tag of Fluke. We know the property is let, but the agency is closed and we can't locate anyone to give us the name of the tenant.'

The uniformed sergeant nodded. 'The armed unit should be with us in minutes, then we go in. I've held off scrambling the chopper, I think we'll have enough personnel covering back and front, don't you, ma'am?'

'Yes. If this turns out to be bad information, the powers that be would probably hang me out to dry for wasting money on the helicopter, as well as the firearms boys. We'll rely on your troops on the ground, Sergeant.'

'Very well, ma'am. Are you coming along?'

'Try and stop me! I've been waiting to see this elusive villain for too long to miss out on this.'

* * *

It had only taken one swing of the heavy metal enforcer to shatter the front door of 9 Carson Villas.

'Front room, clear, sir!'

'Kitchen, clear!'

Men stormed through the property checking room after room, and as each call of 'clear' came back, Nikki's hopes of finding Fluke sunk further and further.

'Sir! Back bedroom! We have a white male, not responding!'

Nikki ran up the stairs two at a time.

In the small room, huddled on his side on the floor was a dark-haired youth. Drying blood was caked around his ear and in his hair, and had soaked down into the soft material of his hooded jacket.

She dropped down beside him and felt the side of his neck with her fingers. 'Get an ambulance! Quickly! There's a faint pulse, but he needs help, and fast!'

From what she had seen on the police computer, the teenager oozing his life-blood into the cheap nylon carpet was Marcus Lee.

'Hold on there, son. Help's on the way. Can you hear me, Marcus?' There was no answer and although Nikki was pretty sure they were going to be too late, she continued to talk to the boy.

Calls were still being shouted from around the house, but after checking the loft space and the cellar, the place was declared safe. Nikki still sat on the worn carpet with her hand across the boy's shoulder, and cursed the day she had ever heard the name of Fluke. The raid may have been a success from the point of ascertaining the whereabouts of Marcus Lee, but they had lost their main man.

She looked around the filthy room. Well, at least, if Marcus had been brought here, then Fluke must have been here too, and forensics would have a good chance of picking up some DNA, once they had managed to discount twenty sets of policemen's boots that had stamped all over the place.

'Paramedics, ma'am.' A PC looked over her shoulder at Marcus' still form. 'Are they too late?'

Nikki shrugged. 'I'm no expert, but I hope the Ambulance Service have sent their best team, because this kid is going to need them.'

Half an hour later the ambulance pulled away. There were no sirens or blue lights. The crew had fought to stabilise him, but Marcus Lee had sustained a catastrophic head injury from which there was no coming back.

Nikki closed up the house, saw it was cordoned off and arranged with the sergeant to organise a police watch.

'No one goes in or out. I've already sent for the scene-of-crime officers, and until they are through, this is off-limits to absolutely everyone.'

She walked back out into the night, and to her car. She felt tired, no, she felt exhausted, and for a moment she wondered how Joseph kept going. She just *had* to get her head down, if only for a few hours. She turned on the ignition and looked at the time. Two o'bloody clock!

With a long, noisy yawn, she pulled out of Carson Villas and headed for the station. She would write a swift report for the superintendent, then ring him early morning. He had asked to be kept updated, but as there was nothing he, or anyone else, could do right now for Marcus Lee, she'd allow him a few more hours of precious sleep.

She parked badly, cursed, then locked the car anyway. Just a few more minutes work and she could go home. Young Mickey was safe with his own personal and very professional bodyguard, and her energy levels had just plummeted to rock bottom. She craved sleep. Joseph Easter may be supercop, but she really was only human.

* * *

Nikki awoke at five, with her alarm clock beeping in ever increasing volume close to her ear. For the first time in years, she had slept soundly and dreamlessly.

She switched off the alarm and lurched unsteadily to the kitchen. Two and a half hours solid sleep should have

166

refreshed her, but she felt like shit. All she could think about was that Kerry had now been missing for three days and four nights, and that was not good.

As she automatically made coffee, she went over the happening of the day before, and briefly wondered how old the cornflakes were. She tried to concentrate, but her mind felt fuzzy and her head ached as if she had a god-awful hangover.

We have to be sharp, she heard herself saying, and this morning she felt anything but. She ate a few spoonfuls of the stale cereal, then threw the rest in the bin. She'd call in and get a Danish on her way to the station. Or maybe . . . ? What had she said to Joseph on their trip to Barnby Eaudyke? *When I'd had a bad shift, I would go up to the seabank, be on my own, and get my head back together.* If ever there was a time for that, it was now. She showered and dressed hurriedly, then locked the front door and headed for the station, and her badly parked car.

In twenty minutes, she was standing on the high bank that looked across the marsh to the Wash. For once there was little wind, just a light warm breeze, and apart from the call of a skylark above her, it was completely silent.

She walked along the uneven track and down a narrow path to a spot where she knew there was an old wooden seat. It was a little known place, rarely used even by birdwatchers, and being some way down the bank, it was partially hidden by weather-beaten shrubby bushes.

Nikki sat down and gazed out across the salt marsh. It looked deserted, almost like a still photograph, until you really studied it. Then you realised it was teeming with life. A water bird dipped its beak in a shallow lagoon of brackish water. A hare stretched up, sniffed the morning air, then sprang off in search of breakfast. A heron, grey and prehistoric, flapped its great wings and rose laboriously into the air, only to be chased by a pair of rooks that had materialised out of nowhere. And all around, the song of the skylark rose and fell, like an anthem to the dawn.

She breathed in the salty ozone and closed her eyes for a moment. It was so peaceful, and she knew that when she opened them, she would see only nature surrounding her. No police uniforms, no decomposing bodies, no masks and no dying teenagers.

A sharp bark brought her from her reveries, and when she looked, she saw the shape of a small dog, nose to the ground, running sure-footed across the marsh paths. Caught the scent of a hare, she thought. Which is more than we seem to be able to do.

Nikki stayed for another fifteen minutes, then as she walked back to her car, she realised that the seabank had worked its wonders. She felt calmer and far more in control of her thoughts. Before she started the engine, she took out her phone and rang the super. She told him there was a report on his desk that he should look at before anything else. She didn't go into detail, there would be time for that when he'd read it.

With one last look across the marsh to the silver-grey horizon, Nikki started the car and went back to face the music of another day at Greenborough nick.

* * *

Joseph rang her at seven thirty. She needed to get to the hospital as quickly as possible. His expression, "There are things I'd rather not talk about on the phone." had her gulping back her coffee and heading for the door with a half-eaten Danish still gripped between her teeth.

He met her in the corridor outside the surgical ward. His hair was ruffled and dishevelled, but his eyes were bright, and she wondered again how he managed to keep going.

'There are two officers in his room with him, and they won't budge until I get back, ma'am. Would you mind if we talk in my car?'

'No problem.' She turned back and headed for the lifts. 'How is the lad this morning?'

'I think the gravity of what almost happened to him has hit home, ma'am, and he's in a lot of pain, poor kid.' The lift doors closed, and Joseph said, 'Between short bouts of sleep, he's talked off and on all night long. He knows more about mask war than you would believe!'

The lift sighed to a halt and the doors opened. They hurried from the building and across to where Joseph's car was parked.

When the doors were shut, Joseph sank back in his seat and exhaled loudly.

'You need some rest, Sergeant.' She looked at him severely. 'But I get the idea that if I stuck an SAS squad in there with him, you'd still not be happy.'

'I'm glad I stayed.' He smiled at her. 'And so will you be, ma'am. But first, let me tell you what his doctor said. Doctor Langley is a smart guy, he won't compromise his patient's health, but he understands fully the danger he's in, so,' he stretched, then went on, 'Langley is on the board of a small private hospital here in Greenborough. It's about a half mile from the nick, so it couldn't be more convenient. He's prepared to 'leak' the news that their unknown young victim is being transferred to a city hospital, where they have better facilities. They do have patients legitimately being transferred to both Nottingham and Leicester later today, so ambulances will actually be leaving on transfer runs.'

'While our boy is sneakily moved to his private facility?'

'Absolutely. He'll go under a pseudonym, into a care-fully designated private room.' Joseph smiled. 'Langley's used to rich people needing to maintain their privacy, you know, celebrities, politicians etc.'

'That is perfect!' Her elation suddenly cooled. 'But there's something I have to tell you before we go on. Mickey's friend, Marcus? He's dead. And I don't think the lad should be told, do you?'

'Damn it! No, I certainly don't.' Joseph's face creased into worry lines. 'There's only so much a kid can take on board without lasting damage.'

Nikki quickly explained what had happened the night before in Carson Villas.

Joseph's expression softened when she told him about Marcus' death. 'Tough on you, ma'am. All things considered.'

'A lot tougher on Marcus and his family, Sergeant.' She threw him a weak smile.

'And I was fine, thank you. Different situation, different altogether. It was just another gruesome aspect to police work, and one I can handle.' Nikki turned towards him. 'Now, what does this boy know that we don't?'

'Phew, where do I start?' He pushed his floppy fringe of dark blond hair from his eyes. 'Most importantly, he knows all about the masks, well, pretty well all about them. Marcus and Mickey were the distributors of the damn things! And Mickey, who is slightly hyperactive, didn't just do as he was told and get on with the job, he nosed around, trying to discover what was going on.'

Nikki rubbed her eyes and massaged the bridge of her nose. 'I now see why you are practically phobic about him. Keeping him safe is absolutely vital.' She looked up. 'But getting everything he's told you recorded is almost as critical.'

Joseph reached into his inside jacket pocket and handed her a folded sheaf of papers. 'While he slept, I got it all down, ma'am. It makes interesting reading. And I've also written down the address and contact number for Dr Langley's clinic.'

'Excellent. Now, I just need to decide what to do about his loving parents.'

Joseph pulled a face. 'Loving mother left home the night before last, for good. No forwarding address. Doting father went banzai, tore up the house, then went on yet another bender. Mickey has no idea, or gives a toss, where he is.'

Nikki shook her head. 'Archie said he wasn't the luckiest kid on the block. But this makes things easier for us, at least temporarily. They'll have to be found, but frankly they're the least of my worries right now.'

'And I'd better get back in there.'

'*You* need a break, Sergeant.'

'Once we've got him to safety, ma'am. Let me stick it out until then?' He looked at her with those infuriatingly sincere dark eyes, then added. 'I'd never be able to rest, now would I?'

'Okay, have it your way, but the moment he's settled in, you go home, understood?'

'Perfectly, ma'am.' Joseph opened the door and stepped out. 'And thank you. I appreciate it.'

* * *

Nikki was met in the CID room by Cat, who was remarkably, an hour early.

'Something's bugging me, guv.' She ran her hand through her spiked up hair and looked earnestly at Nikki. 'I want permission to go back to the home of Terry James, the web designer, with a search warrant.'

'What have you found on his computer, Cat?'

'It's what I've *not* found, guv. Something isn't right and I've got a hunch that all is not what it seems in Rydell Street.'

Nikki looked carefully at her. It was unlike Cat to stick her neck out on a hunch, so her gut feeling had to be pretty strong. 'Have you got enough evidence for us to convince a magistrate to sign a warrant?'

'I believe there is a third computer in that flat, ma'am. We know that one of the ones we've seen has been hacked, and we assumed from an outside cyber-thief. Now I think it's a double bluff. I reckoned they've set this up themselves.' She shrugged her shoulders. 'I don't know quite know how to put that over to the magistrate, but IT agrees with me. The web design bit is kosher, but we suspect it's a cover for something darker than pretty bunches of flowers and cake tins.'

'Then I'll do all I can to get it organised for you. And when you go, take Dave and couple of uniforms, unless you think it's more serious than that?'

'No, that should be fine, ma'am.' She turned back to her computer, then paused and looked up, 'Oh, Dave asked me to tell you he's down in the control room, ma'am, trying to trace Lisa Jane Leonard's last movements on CCTV footage.'

171

'Right. Any news on the mask makers?'

'I've got a crew checking out an old unit on a small trading estate on the outskirts of town, ma'am. I found a supplier who had delivered goods there quite a bit recently, but he reckons they've done a bunk, owing him a small fortune.' Cat grimaced. 'Which coincides nicely with my disappearing lead.'

'Well, keep at it, and I'll go sort out this warrant.'

Nikki went down to the front desk, got a statement typed out and signed it, then authorised a WPC to go disturb one of the local magistrate's breakfast.

Her mobile rang just as the WPC was heading out of the station.

'It's Archie. Can we meet, Nikki?'

'Hell, I'm up to my armpits! Where are you?'

'I'll drive down to the riverside car park, five minutes is all I need.'

'Give me ten and I'll be there.' Nikki closed her phone and leaving a message on the desk to say that she would be out for half an hour, hurried from the building.

* * *

'My boys, along with some of her friends, have traced the first fifteen minutes of Lisa Jane's movements since she left her home on the night she died. Then we lose her. If I give you specific times and locations, would your CCTV cameras be able to pick her up from there?'

'We can certainly try, Archie, although Greenborough's equipment is hardly state of the art. Dave is actually working on that now, I'm sure he'll be pleased to have some points of reference to help him.'

She scribbled down everything he told her, then shut her notebook. 'Marcus Lee is dead, Archie. This Fluke character is favourite for his murder, although we have no proof.' She paused then added, 'yet.'

'Ah, the mysterious Fluke again. I wanted to talk to you about him, Nikki.' Archie leaned back against the bonnet of his old Mercedes, and stared down the river. 'I may be wrong, but since my family has been paying particular interest in this vermin, we have come across several very contradictory descriptions, and as my boys have been quite, eh, how shall I say? well, forceful in their methods, I do not believe any of our informants are lying.'

'We've had exactly the same.' Nikki narrowed her eyes. 'So what does that say to you?'

'That there is more than one Fluke.' He raised his hands, palms up. 'What else can it mean?'

'Unless he's a wizard at disguise, I totally agree. Although,' it was her turn to stare thoughtfully down river, 'I have no bloody idea what these bastards are playing at.'

For a while neither spoke, then Nikki said, 'One of my officer's said there was a bad feeling on the estate last night.'

'Mm, and I expect we haven't helped much either.' He gave Nikki a slightly apologetic look. 'We have offered to help you, and we appreciate your help in return, but it doesn't mean that the family isn't at boiling point. Some of the younger ones, Lisa Jane's peers, are wanting blood.'

'Hardly surprising, Archie, but for God's sake rein them in! I don't have to tell you what more violence erupting on the Carborough would mean.' Nikki paced up and down angrily. 'What with this bloody Fluke, masked gangs, the stabbing, the attacks and the death of Marcus Lee, added to your own tragedy and the missing student! We are at our fucking wits' end!'

'I'm sorry, Nikki, and I'll do what I can with the young guns, I promise. We'll continue to track Fluke, if you'd help us with that CCTV footage?'

'Yeah, I'll do that, never fear.' She went to move away, then said, 'And Frankie Doyle? Any news of her?'

Archie Leonard shook his head. 'So far we haven't located her, but she has been seen in the last few days, and I've heard her name has been tenuously linked to Fluke.'

'What does she look like now, Archie?' asked Nikki, thinking of the old photo on the CID room wall.

'Sly as ever. Short cropped, boyish-style fair hair and stick thin, is all I can say.' He looked at her with a chilly expression. 'But, believe me, Nikki, the minute she shows her head above the parapet, you'll be the first to know.'

* * *

Mickey's midnight confessions certainly did make interesting reading, but as far as Nikki could see, the boy had done nothing serious enough to warrant an attempt on his life. She read it again. Mickey had stolen a mask from a consignment, worn it to impress his cousin Liam, then nicked six more from the next delivery and sold them to Liam. Enough to get him chucked off the team, and maybe a good thumping, but to strip him and almost beat him to death? No way.

Nikki placed the handwritten document on her desk and stared at it. The boy had given them the exactly locations of the mask drops and a concise list of the places where they were to be distributed. Plus he had sneakily followed Marcus, listened into private phone calls and even managed to track Fluke to his rented property, which was more than the police and Leonard family combined had managed. So, what more did the boy know? A street-wise kid like that may well have heard of Frankie Doyle, and if could get an address for one slime-ball, maybe he could get an address for another?

'Ma'am?' The WPC that she had sent to obtain the warrant, popped her head around the door. 'Got it for you. The magistrate wanted to know the ins and outs of the proverbial duck's whatnot, but he has signed it.'

'Good, leave it on the desk, Constable.' Nikki went back to Joseph's notes, then looked up as the woman walked back to the door. 'Oh, and on your way out, would you ask DC Cullen to come to my office.' She paused, then said, 'And thank you, good work.'

The constable glanced back, with a slight rise to her eyebrow, then smiled. 'No problem, ma'am.'

Cat almost ran into her office. 'You've got it, ma'am?'

'All yours.' Nikki held the document out to her. 'And as much as I'd like to come with you, I've got more than enough on already this morning.'

'Don't worry, guv, I'll report in as soon as we're through.'

'You're pretty sure you'll find something, aren't you?'

Cat nodded. 'Oh yes, the more I think about that squeaky clean, "we have no secrets" attitude, and that clinically clean and clutter free home, the more I think they're hiding something.'

'People *are* allowed to be fastidious in their habits, Cat. And you do know that we can't arrest them for overkill on the magnolia paint, don't you?'

'Mm, pity. But I'm dead certain there's dirt of a different kind in Rydell Street.' She grinned mischievously. 'And I can't wait to dig it up!'

'Just be careful.' Nikki threw at her as she made to leave. 'We seem to know very little about anything or anybody.'

'I will, ma'am.' Cat's smile was replaced by a more serious expression. 'These masks are beginning to freak even me out. A group of young thugs, all wearing the damned things, jumped out in front of my car when I was going home last night. I nearly crashed the bloody thing!'

'The day we get those friggin' things off the streets, I'll stand a round for the entire station.'

'Could we have that in writing, guv?'

'Just bugger off, and be careful.'

CHAPTER TWENTY-FOUR

Nikki spent over an hour in the superintendent's office bringing him up to speed on the occurrences of the night before, but all the time they spoke, her mind kept returning to Kerry Anderson and Mickey Smith. Finding Kerry was paramount, but keeping the boy from further harm was also vital. She didn't know how or why, but her gut was telling her there was a link between them. She had nothing concrete, but she was certain that Mickey Smith was the one person who could not only help them solve the riddle of the masks, but lead her to Frankie Doyle.

The superintendent had wanted to go over everything in detail, and Nikki finally used the excuse of expecting an urgent phone call to get herself free. She then hurried down the corridor to her own office, closed the door and rang Joseph.

'He's safe,' said her sergeant, with considerable relief. 'Transfer went off like a charm, ma'am. Have you managed to read my report?'

'Who needs intelligence when you've got the Carborough Kid?'

'Oh, he can talk for England! My ears ache! But it was worth taking the time to sort the wheat from the chaff, wasn't it?'

'Certainly was. I'll be calling in on him myself later, when he's had chance to settle in.'

'Why not wait until I've grabbed a few hours shut-eye, and I'll come back with you. That boy is an acquired taste.'

Nikki's hackles rose. 'Meaning?'

'Meaning only that you asked me what I thought about a Victim Support Officer, and I'd definitely say send a male. I've seen him with some of the nurses, and he does not respond well to women.'

Nikki festered quietly for a moment. She had been hoping to follow the Frankie Doyle route privately, but the last thing she wanted to do was upset their main source of information.

'Right. I'll get onto sorting that, and when you're rested we'll go speak to your young oracle.' She paused then added, 'Together.'

'Great.' Joseph sounded either unaware of her irritation, or he was magnanimously ignoring it. 'I'll get back to my digs for bit then. See you this afternoon, ma'am.'

'Joseph?' Nikki softened. 'You did really well with the boy. Take as long as you need to recharge, okay?'

'Thanks, ma'am, but a few hours will do. Once I'm awake I'll want to get back to work.' She heard a smile spread through his voice. 'You haven't seen my digs. The wallpaper alone could bring on epilepsy.'

Before Nikki could reply, her office phone rang. 'Gotta go. And *you*, get some rest.' She flipped her mobile closed and picked up the desk phone. 'DI Galena.'

'This is Rory Wilkinson, your totally exhausted and run-ragged locum pathologist.'

'Professor Wilkinson! Well, we've never met, but I have to say that your reputation precedes you.'

'I'd say the same about you, but I suspect I may be brought to task, and possibly flogged publicly, but hey-ho! It's a pleasure to talk to you, ma'am.'

Nikki smiled. This man made a refreshing change from their own, stick in the mud forensic pathologist. 'What can I do for you, Professor?'

'Several things. I'll start with the attack on the unknown young male in the recreation ground. We've identified two separate blood samples, and although I'm awaiting confirmation from the lab, one is almost certainly from the dead teenager that you so kindly sent me by over-night delivery. Let's see . . .' there was a rustle of paperwork, '. . . that would be, Marcus Lee. Which would seem to confirm that he was attacked in the same place as the injured child, then moved to the house in Carson Villas where he subsequently died.'

'That fits in with what we believe, Professor. Do you think you'll be able to isolate some DNA from the Carson Villa crime scene?'

'Oh, by the bucket load, I should think! The residents there were perfect candidates for a visit from Kim and Aggie! I didn't need to even see the place to tell you it was a filthy hovel, and if the samples are anything to go on, their personal hygiene was far from meticulous.'

'It wasn't good. I spent some time sitting on the carpet with that unfortunate boy.'

'Oh, you poor woman! But I can recommend an awfully good dry-cleaner.'

Nikki laughed out loud, and marvelled at the unusual sound. 'Thanks, but I think I'll survive. What else have you got for me?'

'Ah, now, this next point is not so jolly.' His voice changed. 'That lovely young woman, Lisa Jane Leonard? Sadly, whoever strangled her, and I'm sure you saw in my preliminary report that from the height and sheer strength of her assailant it was most certainly a male, left no traces of DNA, but,' Nikki felt him frowning. '. . . there was saliva on the side of her face.'

'Someone kissed her?' asked Nikki with surprise.

'Nothing so pleasant. Someone spat on her. And having fast-tracked the DNA results, I can tell you, it was a woman.'

Nikki's brain threw up an instant picture of Frankie Doyle's evil eyes.

'So . . .' continued Rory Wilkinson, '. . . if you just happen to come up with an accessory to murder, and you suspect she has a heart as cold and hard as a gravedigger's shovel, then I'd be more than happy to prove you correct, if I can only get her onto my dissecting table, that is.'

'If it's the woman I think it is, I couldn't think of a more fitting place for her,' muttered Nikki through gritted teeth.

'Spoken with sincere venom, Inspector. I *like* that,' said the pathologist appreciatively. 'Now finally I have to say, and please don't think I'm complaining, but just because I'm filling in while your own eminent professor is boring the pants off anyone who's still awake in the Royal Courts of Justice, don't feel that you *have* to pack every moment of my fun-filled day with new forensic challenges. Strangely I actually find the odd hour or two of sleep quite acceptable, and I've seen very few of those since I arrived.'

Nikki had heard about this pathologist many times, seen a few photographs of him, and even read some of his work on police-related cases. He was a tall, gangly man with a drooping fringe, a beak of a nose and thin wire-rimmed glasses. His weird wit was legendary, and he was happy to tell the world that he was as camp as a row of tents, but over the years he had proven himself to be one of the finest Home Office pathologists in the country. Nikki had just not realised that in the strangest of ways, his black humour when dealing with such a gruesome job, was almost a breath of fresh air. 'Believe me, there is nothing I'd rather do than give you a peaceful life, Professor, but sadly, my lovely Greenborough market town has turned into something more akin to a twenty-first century location for *The Night of the Living Dead!*'

'I have to agree, and because of that, dear lady, I must let you get on, and I shall return to my homely little chamber of horrors, of which by the way, the door is always open if you care to visit.'

'I'll remember that, and thank you.' Nikki hung up the phone and her recent amusement faded.

Frankie Doyle had contacted Lisa Jane a few days before she was killed, and a woman had spat on the girl's dead or dying body. Nikki's eyes narrowed to little more than slits. It had to be Doyle. But why the hell couldn't they find her! She had half the police force and most of the local villains out looking for her, and zilch! Nikki cursed. She didn't want to pin too much hope on the kid, but Mickey Smith was looking like her last hope. Fluke was linked to Doyle, and Mickey knew Fluke, ergo, Mickey may well know Doyle too.

She glanced at her watch. Almost mid-day, and Joseph wouldn't be in for a while yet. It was very tempting to just ignore his advice and go see the kid on her own. But did she dare risk it? She flopped down in her chair and stared at her sergeant's report. The answer was probably not. Apart from shooting herself in the foot if her plan backfired, it was hardly fair on Joseph if she cocked up all the hard work he'd done gaining the boy's trust. Oh, but finding Frankie Doyle was a very strong incentive. No, Nikki closed the debate she was having with herself. Like it or not, she'd wait, and use the time to catch up on the latest reports from Kerry's search.

* * *

An hour later Cat Cullen came striding through the door from the CID room with Dave Harris puffing along behind her.

'From your expression, I gather your 'Policeman's nose' was correct?'

'Was it ever, guv,' said Dave easing himself into a chair. 'She's got good instincts, our Cat.'

'So, from the beginning, please.'

'The bad news is that the Terry's are not directly connected to the case,' Cat scratched her cheek, 'which is something of a bummer after all the work we've done tracing the mask design back to them.'

'So why are you two looking so bloody pleased with yourselves,' asked Nikki impatiently.

'Because there *was* another computer in the house, in a very interesting attic room,' answered Cat.

'Blimey, guv! I've never come across the like in all my life!' said Dave, his eyes wide in almost childlike incredulity.

'Sadly I have,' added Cat. 'When I worked Vice. The thing is, ma'am, 'LycoRapture' *is* the brainchild of Mr and Mrs Squeaky-Clean, only the dirty bastards are far from that, and that particular perverted game is just one of many. The pretty web design stuff is legit, but they keep it up purely as a front.'

'So they *are* the originators of the rat death masks?' Nikki felt mildly confused.

'No. Some sleaze-bag downloaded the game, saw the hideous creature, nicked the character's design for the masks, and named it Griffyx.'

'So, it's another dead end?'

'Not exactly,' Cat leant back against the wall. 'James and his wife are both top IT boffins. I checked her out after she said she worked at the university, and she did, she taught high level computer studies. He's a graphic designer, moved on to web design, and the other thing they have in common, is weird sex. The more perverted the better.'

Nikki's mouth dropped. 'You *are* talking about the same couple that we met the other day?'

'Oh yes, guv. Mr and Mrs Prim-and-Proper have produced some of the worse pornographic computer games I've ever seen in my life.'

'And they charge extortionate money to download them, ma'am,' added Dave. 'One of them costs nearly five hundred quid!'

'And as you can imagine, guv, it is not one to play with your mum or your dad around!' Cat screwed up her face in distaste. 'We've got them both downstairs in custody, guv, and frankly I think we are only scratching the surface with these games. If it's okay with you, I'd like to hand the whole thing over to a specialist unit to deal with.'

'Considering what we're trying to handle at present, I whole-heartedly agree.' Nikki frowned. 'But you said something about it not being a dead end?'

'Ah yes, well, before the masks materialised on the streets, you had to pay to get hold of LycoRapture, and the James' may be a pair of pervs but they are painstakingly precise on their book-keeping.'

'They have copies of all their transactions for the last three years,' said Dave.

'How does that help us?'

Dave leaned forward. 'Because a few of their customers were particularly interested to know if they had any other games that had the Griffyx in them, and the James' made notes to that effect. When they produced a follow-up game, they contacted the interested parties and told them.'

'And they kept the contact details?' Nikki was beginning to understand.

'Yup,' smiled Cat. 'But when they saw kids suddenly wearing Griffyx masks, dear Terry and Bella nearly shit a brick! It didn't take too long to realise that the masks were going to be big trouble, and they may be implicated.'

'Which could scupper their very lucrative sideline,' Dave interjected. 'So they ran a blog, with a link to a free download of the game, then hacked into their own business computer to make it look like *they* were the victims of a cyber theft.'

'And we'd have swallowed that, if it hadn't been for you, Cat. Well done.' Nikki gave her a rare smile. 'So, have you got the list of names?'

'I've sent their hard drive to IT to retrieve the data. Terry James offered to get it for us, but I didn't let him within touching distance. I suspected he'd installed some ingenious destruct programme.'

'Smart thinking.' Nikki sat back in her chair and looked enquiringly at Dave. 'So tell me about this attic room of theirs?'

Dave's eyes widened again. 'Well, part of it was like some high-tech recording or photographic studio, more equipment than it would take to launch the space shuttle, but the rest was more like a home cinema.' He swallowed noisily. 'Big, big screen, and a row of seats, but they weren't like normal armchairs, they . . .' His face reddened and he looked helplessly at Cat.

'They were electronic, guv, and the coverings were made of thick rubber. They enabled you to relax and play along with the game. They reclined and had certain accoutrements to assist with one's pleasure. Need I say more?'

Nikki shuddered. 'You've said too much already, thank you. But it's my fault, I did ask the question, didn't I?'

A soft knock on the door made her look up.

'What am I missing?' Joseph's benign smile entered the room before he did, and he was greeted by a roar of laughter.

'Bagsy you tell him, Dave!' called out Cat, and Dave blushed even deeper.

'Come in, Sergeant,' said Nikki. 'And believe me, you've missed nothing of importance. Well, nothing any of us are pre-pared to share with you right now.' She turned to the others. 'Okay, you two get onto those contact details, and let me know what you come up with. The sergeant and I are going out for a while.'

CHAPTER TWENTY-FIVE

The private hospital was concealed at the back of a small industrial estate. From the front it looked like an upmarket office block, nothing like a fancy clinic, and that was perfect as far as Nikki was concerned.

Mickey, now known as Jonas (from his favourite group) Lincoln (his favourite football team), was in a small private room on the first floor. When he saw Joseph, his eyes lit up. Then a sullen look spread across his face when he saw that his hero had not arrived alone.

'Hi, champ! How's the pain?'

'Okay, I s'pose,' he mumbled. 'Who's she?'

'Well, that's a nice way to talk to my boss!' He grinned at the boy, then leant down and whispered something in the child's ear. After a moment or two, Mickey gave her a half-hearted smile, and Joseph continued. 'Right, let's start again, shall we? Allow me to introduce Detective Inspector Nikki Galena. Guv'nor, this is Jonas Lincoln.'

'Hello, Jonas. Do you like your new room?'

'It has TV, loads of channels, look.' He pressed a handset and the screen shot dizzily from programme to programme.

'Mm, good stuff, and they tell me the food is ace, as well,' said Nikki, hating the small talk, and desperately wanting to get on and grill the child.

'I guess,' he said miserably. 'But everything tastes weird to me. The doc says I swallowed a lot of blood.'

'It'll pass and you'll soon be enjoying whatever you want, you'll see,' said Joseph with a grin. 'Now, are you up to answering just a few questions for us?'

'I'm pretty tired.' He closed his eyes, and blinked a few times for effect.

'Then we'll get it over very quickly, and you can rest,' said Nikki. 'Now, I've heard from my sergeant here that you're a really smart kid, and I'm wondering if you know something about someone, something that no one else seems to know.'

Mickey drew himself up on his pillow and looked at her suspiciously. He reacted to the compliment, but was obviously wondering who she was talking about.

'Ever heard of Frankie Doyle?'

Mickey didn't even need to consider his reply. 'I don't like her!'

'You know her?'

'I've seen Marcus talking to her, and, hey, have you guys found Marcus? Is he okay?'

'Sorry, sport, we've got no news for you yet.' Joseph looked apologetic, then turned to Nikki and with a tiny wink, said, 'See, ma'am, I told you this was the boy to ask! Not much gets past Jonas here! So you've actually met this Frankie Doyle?'

Mickey/Jonas visibly inflated when he heard Joseph's words of praise. 'I know her well enough to stay clear of her, and the people who do mix with her say she's not right.'

'Not right about what?'

'Not right in the head, is what I mean.' He shifted uncomfortably and clutched at his damaged ribs. 'I don't want to talk about her.'

'Has she ever hurt you, Mickey?' asked Nikki.

'Don't call me that! My name is Jonas! Sergeant Joe said so.'

'I'm sorry, Jonas, but I have to know about her. Does she live near you?'

'No. She moved away, but she's been hanging around again.'

Nikki had a strong feeling that the boy had had some kind of dealings with her at some point in his young life, and she had not exactly made a good impression. 'Does she hang around with Fluke?'

'Maybe, but I've never seen them together.' He looked at Joseph pathetically. 'I'm really tired, Sergeant Joe. Can we leave it at that, please?'

'Sure. One last question and we'll be off. Have you seen her with anyone in particular?'

The boy shook his head slowly. 'No. No one. But they say she's hooked up with a drug dealer. Someone from out of town. That's all I know. Honest.'

'That's cool, Jonas old buddy. You get some rest, I'll check in on you later. Okay?'

As they left, Nikki spoke briefly to the two officers outside, then walked down the corridor to the lifts. Behind her she heard the ever-changing background noises from a dozen different television channels.

'Oh my God!' She clasped Joseph's arm in horror. 'What if he sees the news about Marcus' death!'

'It's okay.' Joseph touched her hand reassuringly. 'I've already thought of that. I've tuned it in to specific channels, cartoon, film and kid's stuff. It's all pay-as-you-go, so I've set it up myself. He'll get no nasty surprises from that particular television.'

Nikki relaxed, and he released his hand.

'Oh yes, and what exactly did you whisper to him when we went in?'

'Oh that! I told him that you were the really big cheese, and if I didn't impress you, you could send me back to Fenchester.' He gave her a rueful smile, 'I told him to make me look good, or I'd be history.'

'Mm, many a true word, and all that, Sergeant Joe. Maybe you should remember that for the future.'

* * *

On their return the station yard was packed with vehicles, and Nikki had to drive with great care through the crowds of officers and volunteer helpers.

'What, more reinforcements? This looks like organised chaos!' Joseph said in surprise.

'The super said they were going to send us help from other forces.' She looked around at the sea of uniforms. 'At least they'll be able to extend the search for Kerry out to the fen villages.'

'About time,' said Joseph gravely. 'This is day four, if we don't find Kerry soon, we'll be searching for a body, not a survivor.'

They made their way up to the relative peace of the CID room, where they were met by a disconsolate Cat.

'The officers who went out to my possible site for a mask making factory have found it totally cleared out, ma'am. It was definitely the right place, they've found odd pieces of rubber and a few damaged masks, but the trail ends there, I'm afraid.' She looked down at the floor, clearly angry at herself. 'It was gutted. All the equipment, the moulds and the basic ingredients have gone. If I'd just got on top of it a bit quicker, we may have got them.'

'You did better than most, Detective. Don't beat yourself up over it.' Nikki stared at her thoughtfully. 'I suppose they paid their rent in cash, and under a bogus name?'

'Naturally. And scarpered owing most of it.'

'No one saw them go? No one could identify their vehicles?'

Cat sighed. 'Nope, and the area is dead seedy, no cameras, no security. They just disappeared into the night. It's like they'd never existed.'

'Cheer up. You did your best,' said Nikki. 'What are you working on now?'

'Helping Dave to trace Lisa Jane's movements on the CCTV.'

'Good. Stick with that for the time being.'

As Cat left the room, Nikki was suddenly hit by a frightening thought, and one that left her mind reeling.

'Something wrong, ma'am?' Joseph stared at her.

For a moment she could only look at him, then she said, 'I'm not sure. Grab us a drink, if you would. Something's just occurred to me, and I could do with a hefty shot of caffeine to help me get my head around it.'

As Joseph went to the coffee machine, Nikki carefully removed a large map of Greenborough from the wall, took it into her office and tacked it up where they could see it.

Joseph placed the mugs on the desk then threw her a puzzled glance, but remained silent.

Still trying to rearrange her thoughts, Nikki pulled a tin of coloured marker pins from her drawer, and began to stick them in various parts of the map.

'Think about this, Joseph, and tell me what it says to you. One, the mask factory shuts down. Two, the distributors of the masks are both disposed of. So?'

'They've finished with them. No more use for them. Whatever they set out to do, has either been achieved, or for some reason they've given up,' he paused. 'And I don't think it's the latter.'

'Nor do I.' She fixed him with a steely stare. 'And I'm pretty sure they have done *exactly* what they planned.'

'Which was?'

'You answered your own question as we drove into the car park. Chaos. Organised chaos, you said.'

Joseph stared at her uncomprehendingly.

'What if . . .' Nikki rubbed hard at her temples with her middle fingers and tried to concentrate. 'What if this whole damn manic scenario, is just a smoke screen for something else? Something bigger!' She began to pace the room, and suddenly felt other things start to slot into place in her mind.

'Oh my God!' She stared at the map. 'Why didn't I see this before!'

'What?' demanded Joseph. 'What the devil have you seen? And what could be bigger than multiple murders and abduction?'

Nikki grabbed another handful of coloured pins. 'Where do we believe Lisa Jane met with her killer?' She stabbed a pin into the map. 'Somewhere close to this area, right? Now,' she didn't wait for an answer, 'we have the university, here.' Another pin. 'Kerry walked off from here, and was accosted on the seabank, at this point where her phone was found.' A red pin. 'Lisa Jane's body was left in the barn way out here.' She jabbed a blue pin into a spot close to the coastline. 'And all those pins I'd already placed indicate Mickey's list of where the masks were delivered and the specific places where the boys were told to take them.' She drew in a deep breath and pointed at the map. 'Notice anything, Joseph?'

For a moment, he frowned and stared unblinkingly at the pin-spotted map. Then his eyes widened, and his mouth made a silent 'O'.

'Exactly.' She slowly circled her finger around the one area that was pin-free. 'The docks! The *only* location in Greenborough that isn't either heaving with flat-footed policemen, or being patrolled both day and night by vengeful criminals. *Something* is going to happen at the docks!'

Joseph sank down onto a chair. 'I don't believe it! You mean all these petty crimes, the gang fights, the mask war, the murders? All orchestrated just to keep us chasing our tails and tearing our hair out?' His face paled. 'Dear Lord! Even Kerry Anderson's abduction?'

'What better than a missing girl to tie up every man and woman on the force? And even our natural enemies, the Leonards, have been thrown into disarray while they hunt for the killer of one of their own. As you said, total chaos!' She picked up her coffee, and drank it back. 'And another thing,' she picked up Joseph's earlier report of his talks with Mickey and leafed swiftly through them. 'I know exactly why they tried to kill your boy!'

She found what she was looking for, then flung the folder on the desk. 'I thought so! Mickey Smith was selling masks to his cousin, who lives here.' She stabbed a finger on the map. 'In a small estate of cottages, *right* on the edge of the docks.'

Joseph puffed out his cheeks. 'That's why they were so specific as to where the masks were distributed! And why they chose the Carborough! The damned place is located way across Greenborough, at the farthest point from the docks.' He leant forward, head in hands, 'And Mickey, the silly little sod, was introducing the masks straight into their *mask-free zone.*'

'And where there's masks, there's coppers, so he may possibly have corrupted their whole plan.' She grimaced. 'No wonder Fluke lost his rag. He could see the whole operation going straight down the pan.'

'And the whole operation is . . . ?'

'Drugs.' Nikki almost whispered the word. In her world, it always came back to drugs. 'Listen, I have to go speak to the superintendent. Meantime, do you have any mates in Peterborough CID? Someone both in the know, and that you trust implicitly?'

Joseph thought for a moment. 'Yes I do. What do you want me to ask them?'

'Word from the city street. Rumours of an incoming consignment, probably cocaine. A big one, and I mean really big. To go to all this trouble, it has to be massive.'

Joseph jumped up. 'I'm onto it, ma'am.'

With her head still spinning, Nikki ran up to the superintendent's office and told him everything that she suspected.

'Would you ring that friend of yours, the one in the Met, sir? He helped me once before with information regarding a big drugs ring.'

Before she'd even finished speaking, Rick Bainbridge had picked up the phone and asked to be put through to

London. Five minutes later, he carefully replaced the receiver on the handset, and looked at her squarely.

'It looks like you are right, Nikki Galena! The undercover drugs squad have intercepted information that a huge amount of cocaine will be hitting the streets in the next few days. They just have no idea where or how it's coming in.' He ran a hand through his iron-grey hair and shook his head. 'You really mean all this . . . this carnage, is a distraction?'

'I do, sir. What would focus us more than a murder enquiry? What would stretch us to the limits more than a hunt for a missing girl?'

'And what would use up our remaining manpower more than trying to quell a gang war? What's the old saying? Divide and conquer?'

'Well, sir, they've divided us, but I'll be damned if they'll conquer!' Nikki's brain was moving into overdrive. 'The drop is obviously imminent, isn't it? They've stopped making the masks, and killed off their distributor.' Her eyes lit up. 'But they have no idea that we have sussed what they are up to, and that puts us in the driving seat, sir! We need to get onto HM Customs and Revenue, and the Port Authorities and see what ships are due to berth in Greenborough Port.'

'And we'll have a very big and extremely well-armed reception party waiting for them.' The superintendent seemed to have suddenly shed a few of the years that he had put on over the past days. 'I'll get onto that immediately, and I'll involve the Special Drugs Squad, they have a protocol for dealing with something as big as this.'

'It's my guess that the gang who have arranged all this will think it's going to be a walk in the park.'

'Well thanks to you, it'll be far from that.' Rick Bainbridge smiled warmly. 'Well done, Nikki. If we pull this off, your job will be safe and secure until you decide to draw you pension!'

'Or just until I ruffle a few more feathers, sir. But thanks, I appreciate all your support recently. I know I've been a total pain in the arse.' She stood up abruptly. 'But this can wait,

Kerry Anderson is still out there somewhere, and I *have* to find her.'

'One more thing, Nikki. All co-operation with Archie Leonard stops here. I know you're fond of him, for reasons that I really don't want to know about, but this could be the biggest drugs bust of the century, and like it or not, the Leonard family are criminals. We can't afford for a single slip up and the talking to him constitutes an unacceptable risk. Do you understand where I'm coming from?'

Nikki nodded. 'I get on with him, but I'm one hundred per cent copper, and I'm not stupid. Although,' she added, 'I really believe he's been used just as much as we have.'

'By this Fluke character?'

Nikki shrugged. 'Fluke may not even exist, sir, but there's someone lurking out there in the shadows, and when we find him, I'm willing to bet that Frankie Doyle will be draped decoratively across his arm.' An icy smile twitched at the corners of her mouth. 'Which would be something of a bonus for me. There's someone I'd *so* like her to meet.'

The superintendent looked mystified, but Nikki's smile just widened. 'Sorry, sir. Private joke between Professor Rory Wilkinson and me.'

CHAPTER TWENTY-SIX

Joseph hurried back to the DI's office with his news. Peterborough was on high alert for an imminent shipment, and the estimated street value was in excess of three million pounds. Something that some evil shits would consider well worth killing for.

He knocked on the door and hearing no reply, stuck his head round. The room was empty and he decided that she must still be with the super. He walked away, then heard her phone ring. With a little shrug, he went back inside and picked it up.

'I need to speak to DI Galena. It's urgent.'

The voice was female, and sounded to Joseph as being distinctly odd.

'Can I take a message, or get her to ring you back?'

There was a long pause, and he thought the woman had rung off, then he heard her say. 'I *have* to speak to her, and there's no time left.'

Joseph tensed. 'Who is this please?'

'My name is Frankie Doyle, and there are things that she *has* to know.'

The name alone sent a shiver coursing down Joseph's spine. Was he actually talking to the woman who had deliberately tried to kill Nikki's daughter?

'Listen, I'm DI Galena's sergeant. Tell me what it is she needs to know, and I'll make sure she gets your message the minute I see her.'

'No good. It's her who needs to hear this, and she needs to hear it from me.'

'Then give me your number, I'll go find her now.'

There was a strange sort of hollow laugh from the other end of the phone, then he could have sworn he heard the woman start to cry.

'Are you hurt? Do you need help?'

The answer was a muted sigh. 'Yes, I need help, but it's too late.' There was a pause, then the woman said, 'You sound nice, whoever you are, just tell her that she's got it all wrong. Everything she ever believed about me, it's all wrong.'

'Where are you?'

'Hiding.'

'Why?'

'There are some very bad people out here. They kill pretty girls.'

Joseph froze. 'What do you know about that?'

'Everything. And I have to see DI Galena about it.' Tears broke through. 'Don't you understand, I have to see her!'

'Look I'll get her, okay? Just stay on the line!'

'No, I can't. It's not safe. I made a big mistake, and now,' another pause, 'now I'm scared, Mr Policeman. You probably don't know what that's like, but I'm really scared!'

'I *do* know about being scared, Frankie. Honestly I do. But I want to help you, just tell me how I can do that.' Joseph looked frantically out of the door, but no one was in sight, and he was running out of things to say to keep her on the line.

'If I can, I'll be at the old cattle market in one hour. The river end. No promises, but I'll try to get there. Tell her to come, but no other rozzers, understand? Or I'll disappear, got it?'

'Sure, sure, I understand. But Frankie? Can I go with her?'

There was a long pause. 'If you must. But only you, Mr Policeman. No others.'

The phone howled in his ear. Frankie Doyle, if indeed it had been Frankie Doyle, had gone. Joseph tapped the receiver swiftly and asked for a trace. Two minutes later, Joseph uttered a word that rarely escaped his lips, and went to find his boss.

* * *

'Joseph!' Nikki's voice echoed down the corridor. 'There's a Dutch cargo vessel docking in two hours' time, then nothing for two days. It has to be the one!' Nikki stopped and stared at Joseph's confused expression. 'Aren't you pleased? It looks as though we are right!'

'I'm sure we are, ma'am. Peterborough confirms that they have heard the rumours, just no time or location.'

'So, why the long face?'

'Because you just missed a call from Frankie Doyle, on an untraceable 'pay-as-you-go' mobile.'

'What!' Nikki's voice rose several octaves. 'When? Are you sure it was her?' With her mind in turmoil, she pushed her office door open and pointed inside.

'Close the door.' Nikki spun round. 'What the hell did she want?'

'To talk to you.'

'About what exactly?'

Joseph relayed the conversation, word for word, then leant heavily against the door and stared directly at her. 'I know you hate her, and with damned good reason, ma'am. But I think she's in trouble, real trouble.'

'Fucking good luck!' spat Nikki, 'with all my heart, I hope she is!'

'She sounded terrified.' Joseph stared at the floor. 'And I mean, terrified.'

Nikki felt as if her head could explode at any moment, but she fought for control and grittily said, 'She's a con artist,

Sergeant! Even your pet kid said she's not right in the head, for Jesus Christ's sake!'

Joseph gave her a disparaging look at the blasphemy, and once again, her original anger at him welled up. 'Get real! Sergeant Joe! You've just been talking to a cold-blooded, heartless psycho! Do you honestly think she was telling you the truth? Are you really that gullible? Because if you are, I don't think I want you on my team.'

Joseph clamped his jaw tightly, but said nothing in his defence.

The pressure in her head was building, and without pre-meditation, she grabbed at her desk lamp, picked it up and flung it against the wall.

The crash echoed around the small office, and shards of glass scattered across the floor. Then everything went quiet, and the crushing force inside her head slowly abated.

She looked across at Joseph, who was still standing immobile and silent, by the door, and said, 'I'm so sorry. That was unforgivable.'

'Smart move, actually. It's what they teach you in Anger Management.'

'What the hell do you know about Anger Management?' she whispered, still trying to understand why that dreadful, evil woman could evoke such violent reactions in her.

'Plenty. I've screamed into more pillows, and smashed more plant pots than you've had hot dinners, but that's another story.' He looked at the pile of mangled cheap metal and glass in the corner. 'Hope that wasn't one of your favourites?'

Nikki looked at it and shook her head. 'I don't think I've ever even noticed it, until I picked it up.' She sat down heavily in her chair. 'And when I said that was unforgiv-able, I was referring to what I said to you, and I apologise.' She looked up at him. 'What on earth are we going to do? The ship is arriving in under two hours, and now this! What should we do?'

'At the risk of endangering more electric light fittings,' Joseph raised his hands in the absence of a white flag, and said, 'I have to say that I would meet with Doyle, even if just to see what the hell she's on about.'

Nikki took a deep breath. 'And I suggest that this is just another ploy to keep us occupied, to keep us away from the docks.'

'And if that *is* the case, the gang would be even more complacent if we *did* turn up. They would believe we know nothing about the consignment.' He turned his head a little, then looked at her sideways. 'And what if, just possibly, Doyle is out of her depth? You told me once that she was evil, but she wasn't clever. What if she has pissed off the wrong people. We know what they are capable of, look at Marcus and Mickey.'

'We should go to the docks. This could be the biggest thing you've ever been involved in.'

'Those guys are professionals, they can manage very well without us.' Joseph perched on the edge of her desk and looked down at her thoughtfully. 'You've been hunting this woman at the expense of all else for a very long time. This is your one chance to find out what really happened to Hannah.'

Nikki bit down hard on her bottom lip. It was true. She had waited all this time, and now she was going to let the opportunity slip away? She closed her eyes and saw her daughter, her lovely girl, as she was before she went out for a drink one night, with a deadly friend.

When her eyes opened again, they were completely focused, and as cold as ice. 'So, where exactly are we meeting her?'

CHAPTER TWENTY-SEVEN

'What is this place?' asked Joseph in a low voice. 'It's got a bad atmosphere.'

'It is what it says, a cattle market, only we haven't had a livestock market here since the first outbreak of foot-and-mouth disease.' Nikki looked around. 'They are gradually demolishing it. They've taken most of the stalls away, and the hard standing is being utilised as a temporary overspill car park.'

'Looks like the kids use it too,' remarked Joseph. 'I think I recognise some of my friend, Petey's artwork over there.'

One wall, in front of which were a few randomly parked cars, was completely covered in graffiti.

'Yeah, we try to keep them out, there's a lot of junk and old wood around. What's left could go up like a tinderbox if they decided to have some fun with a box of matches.' Nikki's eyes were continually watching for movement. They were early, but she did not feel at all comfortable about this meeting. The place was secluded, but not completely unused. People took shortcuts through it to the town centre, and although not many felt confident enough to park their cars there, it was frequented on a fairly regular basis. She looked around again and shivered. She could hardly believe that she may be meeting her nemesis after all this time. 'Where did she say again?'

Joseph watched as a man with a scruffy dog skirted around a derelict wooden office and sauntered slowly towards the riverside path. 'The river end, that's all she said.'

Nikki didn't like it. Every nerve ending was screaming out that something was wrong, but Joseph, the ex-special forces officer seemed strangely oblivious to the dangers.

'There are no guarantees that she'll come,' he said softly, 'But I hope for your sake that she does.' He moved a little closer to her. 'You need to talk to this woman, you *need* to know.'

Nikki nodded. Yes, she did need to know. But what would she do then? Doubts clouded her usual confident, no-nonsense belief that Frankie was responsible for her daughter's terrible state. What if she'd got it wrong? Most of her information had come via a villain. Maybe Archie wasn't the friend that she thought he was. Nikki stared around at the boarded up offices and partly dismantled buildings, maybe today was the day that she would find out.

Joseph was edging forward, glancing this way and that. Nikki looked at him and tensed. He had suddenly switched to a more heightened state of awareness.

'Something moved.' He swung towards a stack of planks of wood, piled high and waiting for collection by the demolition company. 'Someone's there.'

For a second, Nikki was glad that she had told Dave Harris what was happening at the cattle market. Not the full details, just a sighting of Doyle that she and Sergeant Easter considered worth following up. Because right now, Nikki was a bubbling cocktail of anger and anticipation with a splash of fear thrown in for colour. 'Can you see her?'

'Someone's behind those wood piles.' Joseph inched forward. 'I don't know if it's her or not, but I'm going to check it out.'

He moved forward again, with Nikki close behind. They passed a deserted shell of a wooden office, and began to circle the stack of old timber.

'Frankie sends her apologies.' The voice was low and slightly muffled, but its intent was crystal clear. 'She got tied up at the last minute, Inspector Galena.'

Nikki turned slowly, to see a stocky, broad-shouldered man standing beside the debris of the old office, and the reason for his distorted speech, was the dead rat mask that covered his features. 'Neither of you even think about making a move! I'm not alone.' He gave a short, husky laugh. 'Let me introduce my friends. This is someone you've been looking for recently,' he gestured to a taller, skinnier man who had just emerged from the back of the office to stand unmoving in the shadows. 'Say hello to Fluke.'

The masked man gave a small stiff-backed bow, and passed a heavy iron bar slowly from one hand to the other.

Nikki felt, rather than saw, Joseph stiffen in the presence of the man who had killed Marcus Lee and tried to beat Mickey Smith to death.

'It would be polite to take off those masks! You filthy cowards!' growled Joseph.

'All in good time. But what right do *you* have to shout the orders, you weren't even invited to this party, Sergeant Easter!'

As he spoke, two other masked men silently materialised on opposite sides of them. 'Ah, my other brothers. This is Fluke.' He pointed to one of the other men, a small man with a large knife clasped tightly in his right hand. 'And that one over there, you guessed it, is also Fluke.' He laughed. 'I hope I'm not confusing you, officers. But you see, to be able to be in more than one place at a time, gives one a wicked reputation.'

'Where's Doyle?' Nikki's voice held nothing but contempt. 'You and your freaks don't interest me one bit. I want Doyle.'

'Don't be a fool, Inspector, Frankie was never going to be here. It's me you should be worried about. It always was.'

As the man ranted at her, Nikki half heard his words, and half watched Joseph, as she saw him glance back along the narrow avenue that they had just innocently walked down, and visibly pale.

To her horror, she looked past him, and saw the reason why.

Across the concrete parking area, a young woman was just unlocking her car, and extracting a child's pushchair from the boot.

Her knowledge of the area automatically kicked in, and she saw in her mind, the children's play-school, situated at the end of the river walk. She even saw the rainbow coloured sign above the doors. *'Bizzy Little B's.'* She swallowed hard and tried to think of a way of alerting the girl to the dangers that lay ahead of her.

'One word from either of you, and I'll let one of my freaks have her! For as long as they want her, if you see what I mean?' The voice had a sibilant quality and Nikki imagined snake's eyes beneath the mask.

'Then just let her go on her way,' she hissed back. 'She has nothing to do with any of this! It's me you want, isn't it? Well, you got me, so let her be!'

'Then you better be as quiet as the grave! Her life, or maybe just her sanity, depends on it.'

As they spoke, the click-clack of the woman's shoes got closer. Nikki's mouth was dry as chaff, but she managed to whisper to Joseph. 'Say nothing. Do nothing.'

'Wise words, Inspector,' came softly from behind her.

The silent masked men had blended back into the shadows, and as the girl got closer, it took all of Nikki's strength to stop herself screaming out loud for the woman to run for her life or she may never see her child again.

At that point, her helplessness, her inability to change this terrible situation, caused the world to slip into slow-motion. All Nikki could see was the girl's long, auburn hair swaying from side to side as she walked, handbag casually over her shoulder and pushing the bright blue buggy ahead of her. And for the first time, since Emily Drennan had died in her arms, Nikki prayed.

Oh dear Lord, don't let this happen. Just don't let this happen.'

And it seemed that her prayer was answered, until the woman was almost past them, and she hesitated, and looked uncertainly back at Joseph.

Whether she was suddenly spooked, or had been in a daydream and realised that a handsome man was looking at her strangely, Nikki didn't know, but the world came crashing back like a hurricane hitting.

Faster than she would have believed, the masked man leapt out and grabbed the young woman. The buggy fell over, and the woman screamed in surprise and horror when she saw the hideous masked face so close hers.

'Help me!' was all she could say before a big hand clamped itself roughly over her open mouth. The girl's eyes flew wide open, and she looked directly at Nikki.

Those eyes! In that single second, Nikki knew they had been tricked.

She swung round to Joseph, but he was no longer there.

In the time it took her to scream out to him, Joseph had leapt on the masked man, wrenched the terrified girl away from him, and grabbed her to safety.

But there was no safety. Not for Joseph.

As he opened his mouth to calm her, no doubt to utter some soothing words of comfort, as he prepared to rush her away from her assailants, his face changed.

Shock and disbelief fought for recognition, then distress screwed his handsome face into a knotted mass of pain.

'Joseph!' Nikki's cry echoed high above the deserted market place, and she lunged forward to catch him as he fell.

Above him, with a long bladed knife still in her hand, stood Frankie Doyle.

Nikki took Joseph's weight and went to the ground with him, holding him and trying to roll him away from the woman who was standing there laughing at them.

All she could think of was protecting him from any further thrusts with that wicked knife.

'Ah, touching! Don't you think it's touching, Stevie?'

Stevie? Not . . . ? Shit, right now, she didn't give a damn who it was. She had to get help for Joseph. She held him closer, and saw that her hands were covered in his blood. If she didn't act quickly . . .

Nikki looked up, saw a semi-circle of jeering faces looking down at them, and her heart sank. The masks had been thrown to the ground, all except the main man, who was carefully peeling his over his head. If they didn't care about being identified, then they were certainly going to kill her. So, nothing mattered, did it? Nikki swiftly turned Joseph onto his side, checked his airway, then placed herself between him and the gang. If there was any chance for one of them, it had to be him.

She looked up at them defiantly, then saw the uncovered face of the ringleader, and her defiance turned to revulsion. The rat death mask had almost been an improvement on his distorted features. One side of his head had no hair, the ear looked as if it had been melted into something that resembled tiny cauliflower florets, and his right cheek, temple and jaw were a mass of puckered scar tissue. But the other side was just as it always had been, and she recognised Stephen Cox immediately.

'I see you haven't forgotten me, Inspector.' His twisted face smiled vindictively. 'And you'll know that I have debts to settle.' He squatted down on his haunches beside her. 'You made my life hell, DI Galena. If you hadn't driven me away from Greenborough, I wouldn't look like this!' He pointed to his ravaged face.

Nikki still had her hand on Joseph's pulse, and it was becoming erratic. She had to do something but she had no idea what.

Desperation and anger welled up inside her, and in pure frustration she vented it all on Steven Cox.

'I don't give a shit what's happened to you! You are vermin! Filthy murdering vermin, and whatever you've suffered it wasn't nearly bad enough, considering what you did to Emily Drennan. And where is Kerry Anderson? You *do* have her, don't you? You fucking little shit-bag!'

'Temper, temper.' Cox stood up, glanced at his watch, then looked across at his thugs. 'Fun as this is, we need to finish it.'

'Seems such a shame to kill her, Stevie, It'd be far more painful for her go on living, with this on her conscience.' Frankie poked the toe of her shoe viciously into Joseph's leg. 'As well as everything else in her sad little life.'

'What the hell would you know about conscience? You were born evil!' exploded Nikki.

'So they say.' Frankie's cold fish-like eyes never left hers, and she slowly removed the long wig and dropped it casually over Joseph's body. 'Poor Mr Policeman.'

Cox glared at her. 'We don't have time for this. We need to be gone. There's no time for a bloody debate.' He caught Frankie by the arm and pulled her away. 'Say your goodbyes.' He turned back to Nikki. 'Much as I'd love to stay and watch you both die, we've got a little bit of business to attend to. Benny! Get it over with, and fast!'

One of the three Flukes drew a knife, stepped slowly towards her, and Nikki's heart began hammering in her chest. She loosened her hold on Joseph, and as she did, her hand touched a rough piece of timber that lay just beneath his arm.

As the thug moved closer, Nikki saw an odd expression on the man's face, an expression of apprehension.

In that second, as she saw the man's Adam's apple move jerkily in his throat, she knew instinctively that he had never killed before, and she seized the moment.

With nothing left to lose, Nikki grabbed the piece of wood, and launched herself at him. Swinging the makeshift club with every ounce of strength she could muster, she landed a crushing blow on the side of the man's head.

Taken completely by surprise at her sudden attack, the man screamed in pain and crashed to his knees, before lurching forward and laying still.

It wasn't until Nikki saw the blood pouring from his temple, that she noticed the ugly, rusted nails sticking from the end of her impromptu weapon.

Her eyes snapped up and swiftly took in the amazed faces of her assailants, then still clutching the bloodied chunk of wood, she sprang back to Joseph, and stood over him like some fearsome shepherd protecting her lamb from the wolves.

Nikki barely knew what happened next, but she did hear a loud shout echo across from the far side of the car park. "Police! Get away from her! Now!" Then she heard the wail of sirens and saw the two remaining Flukes spin around in shock.

'Fucking blue lights, boss! What about the . . . ?'

'Shut up, you fool!' screamed Cox. 'There's too much at stake! Come on!'

Nikki saw her assailants turn and race for their cars, then she threw down her weapon and dropped to Joseph's side.

'Give my love to Hannah!' shouted Frankie, as she fled away.

'Rot in hell, bitch! You've made a big mistake by not killing me, because I'll see you dead on a slab one day!'

Nikki turned back to Joseph. His pulse was still erratic, but at least he had a pulse. She just didn't like the way his eyelids fluttered and his breath was now coming in short, ragged gasps. She ripped off her thin jacket, balled it up and pressed it firmly against the wound in his side.

'Oh, Joseph! You fool! You bloody stupid fool! Stay with me! You're going to be fine, you hear me, just fine. I'm not losing the best sergeant I've ever had, not now! Talk to me, Joseph!'

'B., best sergeant? ' Blood began to seep from the side of his mouth, but there was the slightest smile there now. 'Hon, honestly?'

'No, you're the biggest idiot I've ever met!'

'Ma'am!' Despite his weight and poor condition, Dave ran towards Nikki, then almost fell down beside her 'Are you alright?' He gasped. 'My God! Sergeant Easter!' He staggered back up again. 'Paramedics! Over here! Quickly!'

'You, and those guys in green, are the best thing I've ever seen, PC Harris!'

Joseph clung tightly to her hand. 'Ma'am! You have to know, if there was the chance to rewind, I'd do it again.' He coughed and gave a little cry of pain. 'I mean, what . . . what if she had been just an ordinary mum collecting her kid?'

'But she wasn't, Joseph.' She stroked his hand and gently pushed the hair from his face.

'But I couldn't have taken that risk with an innocent life, could I?'

'No, no, of course not.' The tears were now almost blinding her. 'But just you lie still, the medics are here now.'

He looked at her, his eyes suddenly wide with fear. 'I don't feel good.'

Nikki leant over him. 'Just you hang on there, Joseph Easter, and that's an order!'

'Tamsin. Tell Tamsin . . .'

'Tell her yourself.'

'Plea . . .'

'Joseph? Joseph!'

'It's okay.' She felt a hand on her shoulder. 'We've got him, ma'am.'

As the ambulance crew took over, Nikki felt Joseph's hand slip from hers, and she sunk back on her heels and cried like a baby.

CHAPTER TWENTY-EIGHT

Nikki sat outside the resus. room and clutched a beaker of hot chocolate. She was surprised to see that her hands were still trembling. It had been two hours since they first stabilised Joseph, but they were still not confident enough of his condition to send him to theatre.

'I put plenty of sugar in, guv, it'll help with the shock.' Dave sat across from her, stirred his own drink and looked bemused. 'Tell me, how come so many people here seem to know you?'

It was true. She was better known here by her first name, than by the staff in her own nick. And there was little point in covering anything up anymore. She was tired, sick to death of all the subterfuge. 'My daughter is in here, Dave. She's on the High Dependency Unit. Has been for a long time now.'

'Daughter? But, I didn't . . .'

'No one did. Except the superintendent, and recently Joseph, and he found out by accident.'

'But, ma'am! That's awful! I could have helped, I'm sure!'

Nikki gave a long shuddery sigh. 'You know, you really are a good bloke, Dave, but you've got enough problems of your own.'

'We all have our crosses to bear, ma'am, but it doesn't stop us lending a hand to a friend, does it?'

She looked across at him, quite liking the thought of being someone's friend. 'You're beginning to sound like Joseph.'

'That's not such a bad thing, is it?' Dave asked with a faint smile.

'No, it's not.' She stared across to the room where gowned hospital staff were still moving around her injured sergeant.

Nikki sank further down in her chair. She was so weary of sitting in hospital waiting areas, while those she loved and cared about lay on trolleys, or beds or tables, with their lives suspended between heaven and earth.

'He's going to make it, you know,' said Dave positively.

'If he does, it's down to you. I never dreamed you'd follow us, I thought you'd have gone to the docks.'

'I don't like crowds, guv. And I had a really bad feeling about you and the sarge.'

'Thank Heavens you did.'

'By the time I got there, Joseph was already on the ground, and you were yelling your head off.' Dave shook his head. 'I rang for the ambulance and told them I needed a quiet approach to the entrance as far from the river as possible. I ran back when I saw their vehicles, then I had to re-evaluate the scene, didn't I? I couldn't let those medics wade into a potentially life-threatening situation, but when that one came at you with the knife, I told them to throw on the blues and twos and decided to wade in and help. Am I glad those villains decided to leg it!'

'You came across that car park as if the hounds of hell were after you.' Nikki gave him a tired smile. 'I had no idea you possessed such speed.'

'Surprised myself, ma'am. It's funny what the old adrenaline can do.'

'Control to PC Harris, confirm your location. Over.' Dave's radio crackled into life.

'PC Harris here, still at Greenborough Hospital. Over.'

'Any news on Sergeant Easter?'

'Not yet. I'll contact immediately that we have anything.'

'Thanks. The super wants you to ring control on a landline, please?'

'Wilco.' Dave flicked off his radio and turned to Nikki. 'They want me to ring in.' His voice dropped to a whisper. 'Must be for an update on what's going down.'

Nikki straightened up. 'Then go. And ask them when it all kicks off and if they have the suspects in place.'

Dave was back in moments. 'Everything is ready. They reckon within the hour, and they have four suspects in their sights, three male and one female.'

Nikki gave up a silent thank you.

'Sorry to interrupt, Mrs Galena, but we are ready to take your officer to theatre.' The doctor, yet another who had attended Hannah, gave her an exhausted smile. 'Touch and go, but he's much more stable now, and we'd rather not wait too long. We can't afford an internal bleed, but as long as his vital signs stay as they are, he's got a really good chance of pulling through. You can wait with him until they take him up, if you like.'

'Try and stop me.' Nikki grinned at Dave, who immediately passed on the good news to their colleagues.

At the door, she faltered, her legs suddenly unable to carry her into the room. What if he didn't make it? What if there was another bleed? What if he finished up like . . . ?

'So where's the grapes?' Joseph's voice may have been weak and raspy, but it broke the binding spell.

'Still on Tesco's shelf, Sergeant. Sorry, I've been busy chasing villains.'

'Was it my imagination, or did you really call that masked thug "a little shit-bag"?'

'*Fucking* little shit-bag, actually.'

'Oh, good.'

Nikki was suddenly overcome with relief, and almost ran to his side. 'How are you feeling, you great . . .'

'I feel like I've been stabbed, and idiot is the word, isn't it?'

He reached for her hand, and she took it gladly. 'Idiot will do, until I get you back into the CID room. By then, I'll have had time to think of a few more appropriate ones.'

Joseph's expression changed. 'I'm so sorry, ma'am. I put us both in danger.' He looked thoroughly miserable. 'I can't imagine why I believed her! My instincts have never let me down before. In all my years as a soldier. . .' his words seem to dry up.

'Maybe, finally, you are not that soldier anymore. That soldier you so desperately wanted to leave behind? Perhaps you are one hundred per cent policeman now, and it's a very different job. We are fighting a different sort of enemy, Joseph, and it's not straightforward, we make mistakes, believe me!'

'Maybe.' He closed his eyes, then everything seemed to flood back to him. 'Ma'am! Was it the right ship? Did they seize the drugs? Did they get the gang?'

'Whoa! Relax! You must stay calm, Joseph! Yes, it's the right ship. But the operation can't begin until the cargo is unloaded. They have to catch the villains taking possession of the consignment. The super says everything is in place, and our rat-faced friends are waiting in the freight office, paperwork in hand.'

'Including Frankie Doyle? She was the woman who stabbed me, wasn't she?'

'Yes, Joseph, she's there, and they'll catch her. Then she'll suffer for what she's done, I promise you.'

Joseph closed his eyes again. 'Promise me something else?'

Nikki moved closer. 'It's no schmaltzy, "Tell Laura I love her" stuff, is it?'

'Far from it,' he gripped her hand tightly. 'Listen, they told me my operation is not without risk, and even if all goes well, I may be in here for some time.'

'I know that, but you are going to be fine, I have it on the best authority from your number one fan, Dave Harris.'

She looked around, and on cue, Dave lifted a hand and waved through the observation window.

Joseph smiled at the man, then turned back to her, his face deadly serious. 'Frankie Doyle. When you get her into custody, and I have no doubt that you will, do it by the book! Promise me, ma'am?'

Nikki frowned. 'What do you mean?'

'You know exactly what I mean. She's done you immeasurable damage.' He gripped her tighter. 'But don't give her one inch to play with, not one tiny discrepancy where she could have anything on you, and get herself off.' He gave her a small smile. 'I know you'd like to tear her limb from limb, slowly and without anaesthetic, but for God's sake, treat her with kid gloves! She *has* to go down! She *has* to go to prison, and she *has* to stay there, ma'am.' His breathing became laboured, but he hadn't finished. 'And don't forget, she is probably the one person who knows where Kerry Anderson is. If you antagonise her even more, she'll never tell us anything.'

Before Nikki could answer, a voice called out, 'Time to go, Joseph.'

Two porters stood in the doorway, and the doctor and a small army of nurses began organising drips and monitors for his trip to theatre.

'Don't wait around here, ma'am. Get yourself down to the docks for a piece of the action.'

'I think I've had quite enough of that for one day, thank you very much, Sergeant. Maybe I'll do as suggested, and leave this one to the professionals.'

As the bed was pushed towards the door, he called back, 'Whatever you do, don't let her win.'

She followed him along the corridor towards the lifts. 'Good luck, Joseph,' she whispered. 'I'd like to pray for you, but it doesn't seem to have worked too well recently.'

As the lift doors closed, he smiled wanly and said, 'Oh, I wouldn't say that, I'm still here, aren't I?'

Dave met her in reception. 'There'll be a few nails being bitten down at the docks right now.'

Nikki nodded. Normally she would have given her eye teeth to be a part of the raid, but not this time. This time she would prefer to keep close to the operating theatre. And anyway, a horrible lethargic tiredness was creeping into her bones. Today she and Joseph had been a hair's breadth from death, and she was feeling the aftermath.

'I think I'd like to go and spend a little while with my daughter. Would you stick around in case there is any news on the sergeant?'

'Of course. And I'll come and get you if I hear anything, either about Joseph, or from the station.'

As Nikki walked the long corridors to HDU, she saw Frankie Doyle's wicked eyes in every other person she passed. There was no doubt now that she had fully intended to kill Hannah. As it was, by committing her to a long, living death must have been even more deliciously satisfying for her twisted ego. Nikki bit back tears. Sadly, the bitch had been right. Maybe it would have been easier to die out there in the cattle market, than to keep living the sort of life she had now. If Hannah had died, she would have buried her, then grieved, and finally, as everyone has to, moved on with her life. But the night she spiked Hannah's drink, Frankie Doyle had committed them both to limbo.

At the door of Hannah's room, she stopped. Through the window she could see a nurse carefully washing her daughter's face. Hannah seemed to be awake, her eyes were open, but there was no interaction with the woman that was caring for her. There never was.

Nikki swallowed back the sob that was rising in her throat. How could she go in there and sit with her child? How could she talk inanely to her, knowing that the woman who put her there was still very much alive, and had just cold-bloodedly knifed her colleague?

She remained at the door, looking in for a moment or two more, then turned and walked slowly back down the corridor. She couldn't face her. Not today.

As she walked, she decided that Joseph was right. Everything regarding the treatment of Frankie Doyle had to be carried out by the book. There should be no legal loophole that she could squeeze through. But could she do it? The punishment meted out by the judges didn't always reflect the severity of the crime, and Nikki wasn't sure that she wanted to leave that judgment to chance.

Frankie Doyle was going to pay, one way or another.

CHAPTER TWENTY-NINE

It was just before eleven when Nikki and Dave walked slowly across the deserted hospital car park to their vehicle.

'Straight back to the station, ma'am?' asked Dave with a yawn.

'Yeah. I just hope to God they get hold of all that white stuff *and* the scum that were about to make a fortune out of it.'

'They will, ma'am,' said Dave confidently, as he unlocked the car. 'I know there wasn't much time to organise such a massive operation, but those specialist units really know their job.'

Nikki didn't feel quite so positive. She'd been part of some glorious cock-ups in the past, and knew that the slightest thing, the most inauspicious action, could ruin the whole operation. She closed the door, buckled up her seat belt and switched on her radio. 'I'll see if I can find out how it's going.'

The radio crackled into life, and her heart sank. From the shouts and barked orders that were being sent to the police vehicles in the area, things were far from peachy at the docks.

'DI Galena! Present location Greenborough Hospital, can we assist?'

'Two suspects apprehended, two on their toes, ma'am. Last seen running from the docks thirty minutes ago. No sightings since.'

'Damn! Damn!' cursed Nikki. 'Do we know who they are?' *Don't let it be Doyle! Just not Doyle!*

'No, ma'am. One is a white male, and one a young white female.'

Nikki signed off, then crashed her balled fists down on the dash board. She could barely bring herself to say the words. 'She's got away.'

'So where to, ma'am? Shall we go help look for her?'

'Where would she go? Who would help them?' Nikki was thinking out loud. 'They're going to need transport. A car.'

'Surely they'll nick one?'

'Frankie wouldn't want to damage her nail polish, but who is she with? One of the Flukes? Or Steven Cox? The henchmen could hot-wire a car in seconds, but Cox, no, probably not. We better get back to the station, Dave, and get some more details before we chase our tails all around the town.'

For a while she could hardly speak, her blood boiled at the thought of that scum on the loose again. Okay, maybe she'd lost all her merchandise, but Doyle still had her fucking freedom.

'Any cars in the vicinity of Adams Way! Lone female, possibly our suspect, heading towards the Carborough Estate.' The radio screeched at them.

'The Carborough, Dave! And fast!'

Dave hung a U-ey and drove at speed down a series of side streets that led towards the estate. 'If she gets in there, we'll never find her!'

'Don't be so sure.' Nikki flipped open her phone, punched the speed dial number for Archie Leonard, and talked earnestly for a few minutes. As she closed the phone, a cold smile spread across her face and she half whispered. 'Nowhere to hide, Frankie Doyle. The big boys are *very* unhappy with you.'

'So where should I go now?' asked Dave, looking around the deserted streets.

'Just cruise, and keep your eyes peeled. She's here some-where. It's the only place in town that she believes she may be safe.'

As the car toured the lonely streets, Nikki suddenly realised what Yvonne had meant when she said that the atmosphere was 'bad.' In a very short time, the Carborough had subtly changed. The streets that she knew so well, felt sinister and threatening. Shadows were no longer just shadows; they were pools of darkness that concealed the shapes of men. The whole place had seemed to come to life, but you saw nothing clearly.

Nikki felt her pulse quicken. They were out there. They were looking for her.

Other police cars drifted in and out of side streets. A window went down and a few negative words were spoken before the cars sighed off again.

It seemed like an eternity, but it took less than thirty minutes for her mobile to ring.

'Archie?' Her voice shook in anticipation.

The voice on the other end was slow, calm, and carried all the warmth of the Polar ice cap. 'Come to the Zig Zag café. Back door is unlocked. Tell no one.'

Nikki stared at the phone, then pressed the 'end' button.

'Where to, ma'am? Has he found her?'

Nikki inhaled, then held her breath for several seconds before she blew the air out. 'I think he may have.'

'Fan-bloody-tastic! That was a stroke of genius, guv, asking the enemy to help.'

'Archie Leonard isn't the enemy, Dave, he's a villain, but he's hung onto some sort of values. Stephen Cox and Frankie Doyle are the true enemy, and they don't have *any* friends, either in our world or Archie Leonard's.'

'So where is she, guv?'

'Close by.' She turned and looked at Dave. 'And I'm going to suggest that . . .' Before she could continue, Dave swore loudly and swiftly pulled the car into the curb.

'Shit!' Dave jumped out of the car and stared down at the front driver's side tyre. 'Jesus! Look at that!'

In the narrow side street, lay part of an improvised stinger, the sort of equipment that they used themselves to stop stolen cars and joy-riders by shredding their tyres.

'We sure aren't going any further until I change that!' muttered Dave, pushing up his sleeves.

'We don't have time!' Nikki leapt from the car. This was her golden opportunity! 'I'll go and find Archie! You stay with the car, or we'll come back and find no wheels, no radio, and possibly no engine!'

'But you can't go on your own, ma'am!' Dave looked completely torn. He knew exactly what the Carborough kids would do to his vehicle if he walked away from it. 'I'll call for back up.'

'Not yet, Dave! Think about it! I've got the biggest, baddest man on the block, plus half his extensive family, all looking out for me! Who's safest, me or you?'

'And Doyle?' he asked. 'If she's there, you know you shouldn't see her alone, ma'am. After what she did to the sergeant, and all that . . .' he looked at her, his eyes full of concern. 'You would do things by the book, ma'am, wouldn't you?'

If you knew the half of it, Dave Harris! 'Trust me, Dave. I just need to know that Archie's actually got her, or at least that he knows where she is, then I'll ring you and we'll go arrest her, okay?' Nikki looked back at him. 'Stay here, wait for my call, and hang fire on radioing in our position just yet. Not everyone thinks my trusting Archie is such a good idea, so just in case this is a blind alley, let me check it out first, okay? I can't afford any more black marks on the super's reports.'

Mixed emotions fused into one big mess on his face, but he finally nodded. 'Fair enough, ma'am. But don't take all night, will you? You may have half the Leonard clan behind you, but I've got sod all out here!'

* * *

The Zig Zag café had always been a dive, but since a gang of masked hooligans had tried to torch it, it looked more like a demolition site.

The back door led directly into the kitchen, a place that looked more suited to hosing down tractor tyres than to preparing food.

Archie stood in the shadows and waited for her. 'Did she kill my girl, Nikki? I want an honest answer.'

'Forensics prove that Lisa Jane was killed by a powerful man, Archie. Not a woman.' That was honest enough for now.

He nodded. 'But is she implicated?'

'She may well be, but I'll need to prove it.' She stared directly at him. 'And I will, of that there is no doubt.' She took a step closer to the man. 'Archie, listen to me. If it *was* Doyle that hurt my Hannah, you know that I'll never be able to pin anything on her, so I need to take her down for every other crime that she's ever committed!'

Archie Leonard placed a hand on her shoulder. 'There's more than one way to make her pay, Nikki. Walk out now, and it could all end, right here. For ever.'

'Maybe I wish I could do just that!' Nikki closed her eyes. 'After what she's done to Joseph . . .' she ran out of words for a second, then whispered, '. . . but I have to know, Archie, about Hannah. I *have* to hear it from Doyle's own lips. And I have to try to find Kerry Anderson, if she knows where that poor girl is, somehow I have to get her to tell me. And there's so little time.'

Archie stepped back from her. 'Yes, you deserve that, at least.' He glanced at his watch. 'Are you alone?'

She told him about Dave.

'I'll send one of my boys to wait with him, just in case he finds himself outnumbered by masked idiots all hankering after his police radio.'

'Don't mention that you've got Doyle, Archie. Just tell him we're alone, talking.'

'Naturally.' He smiled at her. 'I reckon you have about fifteen minutes before your colleagues ride by this part of the estate again, so,' he pointed to a door, 'she's all yours, Nikki, but if you change your mind, I'll be outside, and the offer still stands.'

* * *

The room was a grubby storeroom. Shelves packed with cheap own brand ketchup and even cheaper teabags lined one wall.

Frankie Doyle sat unmoving on the only chair. She didn't move because she was tied tightly to the back and the legs of the chair, and had a wide band of duct tape across her mouth. Her eyes were wide with fear and the parts of her complexion that were visible around the tape, were a sickly grey. Nikki found it hard to recognise her as the woman who had so recently, and so casually, stabbed Joseph.

The room was poorly lit. One greasy 15 watt bulb hung from an even greasier light fitting, and it swung backwards and forwards in the draft from an old air-conditioning unit and caused freaky shadows to move around the walls.

Perfect! Nikki closed the door.

For so long she had dreamed of this moment. Played out a thousand different scenarios of what she would do if she ever got Frankie Doyle alone in a small room. Not surprisingly they had all been violent in some way or another, and most involved considerable blood loss. Her heart should have been pumping adrenaline at an alarming pace, and her face should be contorted in righteous anger, but it wasn't.

A strange calm descended over her as she leaned back against the door and stared unblinkingly at the other woman. There was no hurry now. No one was going anywhere for a while.

Doyle tried to stare back, but blinked rapidly, and Nikki could see her throat constrict several times as she swallowed. For once in her miserable life, Frankie Doyle was not in charge and she was bricking it!

Taking her time, Nikki approached the woman, then pulled the tape from her mouth. Doyle gave a muffled scream and tears involuntarily filled her eyes, as the strong adhesive tore at her skin.

'Mm, you seem to be more comfortable dishing it out, don't you?'

'Where's Leonard?' Her voice fell to a scared whisper. 'Where's Archie Leonard?'

'Not here. It's just you and me for a while, Frankie. And frankly I'd be more scared of me right now, than of Archie.'

Nikki stood closer to her, close enough to smell stale perfume and sweat. 'Why did you hate me so much, that you wanted to kill my daughter?'

Doyle seemed completely caught off guard. Whatever she had expected Nikki to say, it hadn't been that. Her eyes opened wider and her mouth dropped a little. 'What?'

'The bad drugs. You thought they'd kill her, right?'

'Ye-ah,' Doyle looked genuinely confused, 'but what's all this shit about hating you?'

Nikki stiffened, 'So if I'm wrong about that, tell me why you hurt her?'

Doyle gave a humourless little laugh. 'Because it wasn't you, it was Hannah I hated.'

Nikki felt as if someone had kicked her legs from under her, but she kept her face stonily impassive. Why on earth should she hate Hannah?

Doyle's fear seemed to fade, and for a moment she looked quite pleased with herself. She had apparently never considered that the inimitable detective inspector may have been barking up the wrong tree for so long. 'So, you thought I did it to get at you? Well, well!'

'What did Hannah ever do to you?' Nikki asked, trying to keep the immediacy from her voice.

'What? I'll tell you what! Day in, day out! Whine, whine, whine! My mother hates me! My father hates me! He's gone to America and left me with *her!*' Frankie Doyle's eyes flared in anger as she imitated a petty, whinging voice. 'Poor hard-done-by Hannah! Can you imagine what that does to some-one whose mother and father *really* hated her?' She stared up at Nikki. 'Look at my arms! Go one, Roll up my sleeve! Either one, they're both the same!'

Although she didn't want to do it, Nikki pulled up the sleeve of the woman's silky blouse. The skin on the inside of her forearm was a grid of old welts. A criss-cross pattern of long, narrow, raised scars.

'That ain't self-harming either! That's what real hate is, and there's more! Some nice cigarette burns! Wanna see them too?'

In spite of her shock at seeing the woman's horrific scars, Nikki managed to remain silent, but Doyle was still talking.

'See, you, Inspector, never hated Hannah. You loved her. You gave her everything she wanted, and tried to keep a proper home going, even though you had your poxy stinking job. And all your ungrateful daughter could do was plot and plan to get her own back on you!' She screwed up her face in disgust. 'Oh, don't get me wrong, I couldn't give a flying fuck about *you*! I'd just had enough of your miserable, bleating offspring, who didn't know when she was bleeding well off.'

'But you don't kill someone for something like that!'

'I do. If they piss me off enough.'

'And my sergeant? How did he piss you off?'

Doyle pouted. 'He didn't do anything, except play the hero. What an arsehole!'

'There's something missing in you, isn't there?' Nikki looked at her, rather like she would a nasty smelly specimen under a microscope. 'I'm sorry for what you suffered, but it goes much deeper than that, doesn't it?' She tapped her head with one finger. 'Something's not right, up here.'

Doyle bridled. 'You can talk! You're so much better, are you? You hound people, you make their lives a misery.'

Nikki could have laughed at the comparison, if it hadn't been so pathetic. But still, Doyle's open admission that she had fully intended to get rid of Hannah had rocked her. All this time, wondering and speculating, and now she knew. She knew, but what was she going to do about it?

For a few moments, Nikki stood and just stared at Doyle. Yes, if she were honest, Nikki wanted to call out for Archie. Tell him to finish off this parasite, this damaged, compassionless creature. She *could* still do that. And the way she felt, she *may* actually do it. But one thing stopped her.

Kerry Anderson.

She glanced at her watch. How long did she have? Just long enough, she hoped. 'Were you and Stephen Cox lovers?'

'Me and that meat-head! You're joking! We were business partners.' She said importantly.

'How did he get his face burnt off?'

'When you chased him out of Greenborough, he started doing a bit of dealing on someone else's patch.' She tugged unsuccessfully at her restraints. 'They didn't take it too well, and it was just Stevie's bad luck that one of them owned a restaurant. They griddled him.'

Nikki had carefully watched her face as she told the story. But even though a good-looking man had had his face and the side of his head pressed into a searing hot iron plate, there was no compassion, no horror at what had happened, no emotion at all.

'It worked out all right in the end, though. He got rid of them and took their manor. Made a packet out of it.'

'And now, where is he exactly?'

Doyle's face darkened. 'We got split up, but he'll be back for me.'

'Oh yeah, I thought I saw a bloke outside, on a big white horse, all ready to ride in and save you!' Nikki laughed. 'Get real, Frankie! You're in deep shit and he's laughing!'

'Like I said, he'll be back. He'll find me.'

'Mm, you really weren't the brains of the outfit, were you?' She threw Frankie a piteous look. 'You fool! He'll be miles away by now. He's ditched you, Frankie. Left you to take the blame for everything. And believe me, you will.'

'Get stuffed.'

'Shall I get Archie back?'

Doyle threw her a look of pure hatred. 'What do you want?'

'Why did Stephen Cox arrange the abduction of Kerry Anderson?'

'Because I asked him to,' spat Frankie.

Nikki smothered her excitement. She *did* know about Kerry! Which meant a slender chance of finding her. 'Ah, so she was someone else who pissed you off, I suppose. Let me guess? Kerry was bright, intelligent and was making something of herself, even if she came from the Carborough?'

'Stuck up cow,' muttered Doyle. 'She had it coming. Just like the Leonard bitch. All fucking airs and graces the pair of them.'

Nikki felt nauseous, and prayed that Archie was not listening outside the door. Somehow she fought back the rising bile, and knew that she had to keep on probing. Because she desperately needed to find Kerry. 'Did Cox kill her, like he did Lisa Jane? I know you were there when he did it to Lisa Jane. You spat on her, didn't you?'

Doyle began to struggle again. 'I don't want to talk about her anymore, not with *him*, not with Archie, around.'

Nikki walked around until she was behind Doyle, then whispered. 'As I see it, this could go one of two ways. I give you to Archie, and tell him all about what you and Stephen did to Lisa Jane, or you tell me where I can find Kerry Anderson, then I arrest you for attempted murder, and a whole load of other stuff, *but* then I get you out of here.' She gave a small laugh. 'Deal, or no deal? And I know which I'd choose.'

Initially Doyle said nothing, although Nikki was pretty sure that she understood the wisdom in her words, then the woman found some sort of misguided bravado from somewhere and hissed. 'Stinking pig! Find her yourself!'

Anger coursed through Nikki's gut.

Suddenly she was tired of all this. Why was she even lowering herself to try to reason with this bag of shit!

Nikki stared at her.

Doyle was callous, lacking in all social graces, and seemed completely indifferent to other people's suffering. *And* if crossed, even if unintentionally, she was lethal. Better to walk away and leave her to the Leonard family to dispose of. The world would certainly be a safer place.

Do it by the book! Promise me! Joseph's voice rang through her mind like a clarion call.

Still staring at the woman, Nikki flopped back against the wall. But they were never going to find Kerry in time to save her, so what did it really matter? She should call for Archie.

'What are you thinking, Pig? I don't like the look on your face.'

'Shut up!' Nikki never took her eyes off her, but desperately tried to control the heated temper that was boiling away inside. In her head she saw Hannah, just as she was when they hooked her up to the ventilator. She saw Lisa Jane Leonard handing her a cup of coffee and telling her how she had been chosen to model for a sun-crème advert. She saw the stunning photographs hanging on Kerry Anderson's pod wall, then Mickey Smith's battered face swam into view, and standing next to him was young Marcus Lee. She saw the doctor's attending to Callum, the boy who got stabbed for the sake of a mask. And then she saw Joseph. And *he* filled her field of vision like an avenging angel.

By the book, Nikki! She ***has*** *to go down!*

Nikki felt a strange peacefulness enter the smelly storeroom, and swirl all around her. And in that stillness, the bitterness and the hate began to fade slowly away.

How close had she just come to crossing the line?

Maybe she would never really know, but now she didn't need to hear Joseph calling to her any more. There was only one way to deal with Frankie Doyle.

Nikki had overstepped the mark more times than she could ever remember. She'd threatened and intimidated drug dealers, she'd even given one or two a good thumping, but at heart, she was a good copper. Her whole career had been about righting wrongs. Her conscience was not going to let her move into the same category of the scum that she hated so much.

'Oi! Inspector Filth! I'm fucking talking to you!'

'And *I'm* talking to you, Frankie. So, shut up and listen.' She marched right up to Doyle. 'As Stephen Cox is now out of the picture, I am going to assume that you are the ringleader for this whole thing. The deaths, the abduction, the drug scam, everything. You will go down for life. There will be no successful appeal because no judge or jury in this land will see you for anything other than what you are; a vicious, evil and calculating killer. You won't go to a secure hospital, because everything you did was deliberate. You will die alone, in prison. One way or another.'

For the first time, Doyle seemed to realise that she really was a scapegoat. Alone and in terrible danger. Her already pale face drained to the colour of wallpaper paste, and her eyes widened.

'First, however, I'm going to caution you.' Nikki quickly untied the ropes that bound her arms, then swiftly cuffed her wrists before the circulation returned. 'Frances Doyle, I'm arresting you for the murder of Kerry Anderson. You do not have to say anything, but it may harm your defence . . .'

'For Christ's sake! She ain't dead! How can you accuse me of her fucking murder, when she ain't dead?'

'And you can prove that, can you?'

'Of course, I can! Unless that lump of shit Cox went back and finished her off, and that ain't my fault, is it?'

'Where is she?'

'Get me out of here! Just get me away from that psycho Leonard, and I'll tell you.'

The words pot and kettle came to mind, but then Nikki felt a great surge of hope. She pulled out her phone and called Dave Harris.

'Call this in, Dave, then get your arse down here pronto. I've got Doyle, and I want a car immediately, to the Zig Zag café.'

She released Doyle's feet and stood her up. 'After you.' She pushed her through the door and out through the kitchen and into the alley.

Archie waited outside, his face expressionless. 'I should have guessed which road you'd choose, Nikki Galena.' He threw her a slightly sad, half smile, then began to walk away. 'Pity.'

'You'll thank me for it one day, Archie.' She called after him. 'And thank you.'

He paused, then nodded and walked on, and in moments he had melted into the darkness.

CHAPTER THIRTY

When Nikki and Dave arrived back at Greenborough police station, and the mood was a mixture of disbelief and anger that one of their own had been deliberately injured, and elation at the fact they had secured the massive shipment of drugs, *and* taken three, now four, of five of the villains. The officers that had just returned from the raid were naturally high, the adrenaline was still pumping, and there was the usual back-slapping, high fives, but even they seemed subdued considering the high profile of the operation.

'Didn't see you down the docks, Davey-boy?' called out one young officer. 'Skiving off again? Dodging the action?'

Nikki spun round on him, but Dave put his finger to his lips, and said, 'Let them have their moment, ma'am. They don't mean no harm. I've seen plenty of action in my years on the force, done things that he'd only dream of. Forget them, you need to see the super about a search party for Kerry.'

'Sorry, but some of these gung-ho rookies make me want to puke. They need to learn to keep their big gobs closed when they don't know the full story.' She gave Dave's arm a squeeze. 'You've been a diamond today, and I'm going to make quite sure that the superintendent is aware of it.' She pulled in a deep breath. 'Go grab a coffee, Dave, and thanks for everything.'

As Nikki hurried to the superintendent's office, she vaguely wondered if Cat were still there. She doubted it, Cat's style was more subtle, she preferred the undercover, clandestine operations, not the riot gear and 'batons at the ready' kind of stuff. So, as she passed the CID office, she was surprised to see the hunched form of Cat slumped over her desk.

She pushed the door open and called out, 'Hey, not sleeping while the rest of the station parties, are you?'

'Ma'am?' Cat looked up blearily. 'Sorry, but I couldn't go home until I'd heard directly from you about Joseph. How's he doing?'

'His operation went fine, but they want to keep a close eye on him for a while. The knife penetrated his stomach and they had to resection a chunk of his intestines. They're scared of sepsis, so he'll be pumped full of antibiotics for a while to counteract any infections.'

'It doesn't seem fair, does it? A good bloke like the sarge, goes to another nick for a change of scenery, and some psycho sticks a blade in him.'

'No, you're right, it doesn't seem fair. But good news, I've caught Doyle and she may know where Kerry is, so I need to see the super right away.'

Cat brightened instantly. 'Go, ma'am! That's fantastic!'

She had expected the super's office to be jam packed with gold braid and shoulder pips, but oddly, the man sat alone at his desk, with an expression on his face that Nikki found difficult to read.

'Ah, Nikki. Come in and sit down. Thank you for keeping me posted on Joseph's condition.' He reached into his drawer, took out the familiar half bottle of whisky and two glasses. 'It's such a relief that he's pulled through.'

'You may want to put that on hold, sir.' Nikki would have wrenched his arm off for the drink, but the night was not yet over. 'Doyle needs to be interviewed, and the book states that as I have issues with the prisoner, I can't do it.'

The super looked at the whisky, then returned it reluctantly to his drawer. 'So you really have got her downstairs?

How did you manage that?' He raised an eyebrow, 'when the rest of the force failed.'

'We aren't the only ones who want her off the street, sir. Even the villains hate a loose cannon like that. It muddies the waters for their more *legitimate* crimes.'

'Ah, good old Archie.'

'Better to have that man as a friend than an enemy, sir.'

'Probably. Now about Doyle. You suspect that she knows the whereabouts of Kerry Anderson?'

'She said she does, and although she's flaky as hell, I do believe her.'

'So, let's hope the custody sergeant allows this interview as soon as possible.'

Nikki nodded. 'I know all prisoners have rights, sir, far more than they ever allow their victims, but there's reasonable grounds for believing that there is a serious risk to a girl's life, if we delay.'

'I'm banking on that, Nikki.' The super stood up. 'Come on. I know you can't interview her, but you can watch through the viewing window.' He walked to the door and held it open. 'By the way, you really should know that top brass are pretty damned pleased with you and your team.'

Nikki nodded, said, 'Makes a change from their usual vitriolic comments, sir.' And thought, *Would they be so pleased if they knew my earlier quandary?*

'Well, let's face it, you were the only one to find some sense in this whole bloody shambolic war!' He shook his head as if still astounded at what had just happened. 'And in turn, we managed to intercept cocaine with the street value of over three million pounds! You deserve more than just a pat on the back!'

'And no one got hurt on the raid, sir?'

'No. All back home safe, even though it wasn't quite text book. These hastily cobbled combined ops can be tricky.'

'How did Doyle and Cox manage to slip the net?'

'We think something aroused Cox's suspicions, but to alert the rest of them would have attracted attention, so he and Doyle went to use the loo, then they slipped out and off the radar, leaving the two remaining Flukes to carry the can.'

'Once a piece of shit, always a piece of shit.'

At the lift, the super pressed the down button. 'Remind me, this is the man you believe to have been instrumental in Emily Drennan's death, isn't it? The footballer?'

'Ex-footballer, now drug dealer.'

'I don't think he'll get far, Nikki, not with a face as distinctive as that. We've circulated a description to all forces, and to all airports and ports. I'd be surprised if he lasts more than a day on the run.'

'I wouldn't be too sure, sir,' said Nikki. 'There are more villains involved in this than the ones we have in custody. Someone will hide him.'

'We already have the names for the mask makers. Two of the Flukes have clammed up, but the one that you pole-axed has woken up singing like Aled Jones in order to help himself. Sadly he has no idea where Cox took Kerry.'

'Then it really is all down to making Frankie talk.' She stepped into the lift. 'So what was the shipment concealed in, sir?'

'Two restored classic cars. Little beauties, they were.' The super smiled as the doors closed. 'Apparently being brought in for a private collector up North. Everything was totally kosher, the buyer, the seller, the paperwork, all the real McCoy, but there was one major anomaly. The transport company that was collecting them from the dock didn't actually exist. Cox's drivers had nice smart uniforms and two sign written lorries to transport the cars, but they were as phoney as a painting by numbers Rembrandt.'

'And the drugs?'

The lift sighed to a halt, and the doors opened.

'In the hand stitched leather upholstery. All the newly restored seats were stuffed with Charley. It was wrapped in some kind of scented material to throw off the sniffer dogs, but the drugs squad found it.' Rick Bainbridge yawned and stepped out. 'We haven't had time to dig up the details yet, but it looks like a very well planned scam.'

'And one worth murdering for.'

'If you don't have one ounce of morality or conscience, it's not even an issue, is it?' said the superintendent. 'I just can't believe the lengths they went to, to keep us away from the docks. There must have been easier methods.'

Nikki followed him down the corridor to the Custody Suite. 'I think there are a lot more issues here than we know about, sir. Later perhaps, Frankie Doyle and the Fluke Brothers may collectively help us shine some light on them.'

While the superintendent spoke with the sergeant, Nikki kept well back. In any police station, the custody sergeant was King, and every officer knew it. There were so many rules and regulations that even someone of Rick Bainbridge's rank couldn't just walk in and have everything their own way, but very quickly the super turned to her and gave her the okay sign, his thumb and forefinger making a circle.

'He's gone to check her condition, but I think we are on.'

Nikki sighed with relief. 'While we wait, sir, can I just tell you that Dave Harris was a star today. If he hadn't used his initiative and acted quickly when it was necessary, I'm not sure that I'd be standing here with you right now, and I'm damned *certain* that Joseph would be in the mortuary getting reacquainted with his friend, Professor Wilkinson.'

'I'm aware of that, Nikki. *And* he gave us the reg numbers of Cox and Doyle's cars. When they drove into the docks with their import documents in their sweaty little mitts, SO19 knew exactly which vehicles to target.'

'Good old Dave! There's a lot more to him than people think, sir, and his home life is difficult, to say the least.' She looked at her boss. 'Cut him some slack, sir. Just because he doesn't rabbit on about his problems, doesn't mean he doesn't have them. Don't tell him I told you this, but his wife has early onset Alzheimer's. He has a lot to handle.'

'Why the devil didn't he say? We could help!' The superintendent looked dumbfounded.

'Ever heard of pride, sir?'

'I'll speak to him, Nikki. Privately and with no mention of what you just said. Simply to commend him on his work today, and then maybe he'll open up a bit.'

'Maybe, but don't hang by your eyelashes.' Nikki gave him a tired smile. 'What you *could* do, is make sure some of the young probationers know how professionally he acted today. It doesn't do to write off the old-timers, their experience is worth its weight in gold.'

'Point taken, I'll make sure they hear about him. Ah, look!' The sergeant was beckoning to them.

'Are you okay with this, Nikki? After what happened earlier, you don't have to be here.' The super looked suddenly concerned about her.

'I'm fine, sir, and I'm seeing this through. For Joseph's sake, and for Kerry. Let's go, shall we?'

* * *

The interview took very little time, and resulted in an irate Rick Bainbridge storming from the room growling. 'Her idea of knowing where someone is and mine are a very different thing!'

'At least we've got a clearer location to search this time, sir.'

'Did you hear that smart comment about the fucking marshes not having post-codes?'

Nikki nodded. 'I did, but the area she mentioned is well known to me. Shall I organise a team, sir?'

The super shook his head. 'Don't be daft, Nikki! You know we can't head out for at least four hours yet. It's the dead of night! Pitch black and it's now pissing with rain again! Doyle's indicated a treacherous spot in the middle of the bloody marshes! It'll be bad enough after dawn, yet alone now. We can't put more lives at risk.'

Nikki knew all that, but it had been worth a try.

'Go home! And tell your team to do the same. Grab some sleep. God knows you all need it. We'll find her, Nikki, just as soon as it's safe to get out there, we'll find her.'

'I know, sir. It's just that I'd prefer her to still be alive.'

CHAPTER THIRTY-ONE

Nikki began her short walk home, then stopped abruptly. Mickey Smith! What would he think when his hero failed to turn up to visit him? Even worse, what if he got to hear that Joseph had been badly hurt? He should be told the truth, and it would be better coming from her. She could do nothing for her own child, but maybe she could help a boy who no one cared about. With a sigh, she turned around, went back for her car, and drove to the clinic.

The night staff told her that Jonas had been fretting, unable to settle and seemed unduly frightened, even though the protection officers were with him. As Nikki pushed open his door, she was glad she had made the effort. He had helped them, and no matter how tired she was, it was only fair that they do the right thing by him.

She pulled up a chair, and gently explained about Joseph. Although she softened the story, she decided not to lie to him. After a while, the boy cried, and to her astonishment, she cried with him.

'He's special,' said Jonas, wiping his nose on the sleeve of his pyjamas.

'I know,' said Nikki, sniffing into a tissue. 'And now you two have got a lot in common, haven't you? When he's better, you'll be able to compare war wounds.'

The boy nodded. 'He will get better, won't he?'

Nikki didn't want to frighten the lad with the real prognosis, one that was far from reassuring, so she said, 'I've spoken to the doctors, and they are really happy with his progress.'

'Good. Maybe he could come here when he's a bit better. We could share a room.'

'He'd like that,' said Nikki with a grin. 'Except he'd nick all your comics.'

'Who hurt him?' The boy suddenly asked.

'Frankie Doyle,' said Nikki evenly.

'Then we've got even more in common.' He looked at her warily. 'But I really don't want to talk about that, okay?'

I knew it! she thought, then said, 'Absolutely. No questions tonight, I promise.'

'And you really have caught her?' Fear clouded his bruised face.

'Locked up in a cell.'

'And her bloke, the dealer?'

'Not yet, but we will. We got all the others, including Fluke, so you really are safe now.'

'I don't feel it. And Doyle's bloke is still free. Maybe he'll come after me in the night!'

'He won't, I won't let him.'

'But you're not going to be here, are you?' Tears filled the boy's eyes once again, and Nikki's heart went out to him. Joseph had finally made the lad feel that he had someone in this world, someone who cared about him, and then, bang, no one again.

'I've got an idea,' said Nikki softly. 'Give me a minute, and I'll be back, okay?'

She slipped out and found the night sister, and after a short conversation, returned to the boy. 'Sorted.' She smiled at him, 'You, young man, are going to get some proper sleep.' The door opened and a nurse entered carrying in a smart fold-up bed and some brightly coloured pillows and covers.

'And so am I! We're in this together. Okay, Private Jonas, old buddy?'

Mickey/Jonas gave her a relieved smile, pulled the bed-covers closer to him, then saluted. 'Understood, Inspector Nik!'

* * *

The night nurse woke her as arranged, just before dawn. After several hours spent in a camp-bed, lying next to a boy who had more bruises than a bare-knuckle fighter, Nikki had not expected to wake up feeling good. In fact she hadn't expected to even sleep. But she had. And she felt very good. She had dreaded going back to her miserable flat, a place that was only inhabited by her own dark thoughts, and Mickey's night fears had provided her with the perfect compromise.

The boy had slept soundly too, and the weak light of dawn through his window seemed to melt away his earlier terrors. Nikki felt happy to leave him. His distress had been out of proportion, but considering what had happened to him he had every reason to be scared, and there was always the outside chance, a million to one maybe, that one of the gang had sussed out their deception and decided to close his chatty little mouth forever. She didn't think that was the case for one minute, but she was still happy with the decision that she had made.

She left him with promises that she would keep him updated with news of Joseph, and that she would return at the end of the day to visit him. As she stepped out into the corridor and looked back, she saw the pathetic, bandaged child, and a feeling of intense emotion flooded through her. Some sort of a bond had developed between them when they had spoken about Joseph. Something she couldn't define, but she knew that Mickey had allowed her in, and she felt almost humbled because of it.

She waved to him, and he gave her a thumbs up.

'You really helped him, you know.' The nurse lightly touched her arm. 'He'd been agitated all evening. We were considering a sedative, but we prefer not to with paediatric head injuries.' She looked back through the doorway. 'He looks a different boy now. You and that nice sergeant would make a good team! You both seem to have the knack with a problem child.'

As the nurse walked off, Nikki smiled in amusement. Her previous reputation with young tearaways had been far from creditable, in fact most of her colleagues liked to keep her at least 100 metres from anything in trainers, jeans and a hoody! This was something of a first.

She left the clinic, called in at a small market café, and grabbed a large coffee and a bacon sandwich to go. The sleep, all be it short and sweet, had been great, now she needed sustenance to keep her grey cells ticking over. She was going to need both energy and a brain, if she were to find Kerry Anderson.

As she waited for her sandwich, she rang the hospital to check on Joseph. The nurse on the ward was cagey, but said he was comfortable, whatever that meant, and they were cautiously optimistic that he would not need more surgery. The next twenty-four hours were the testing time apparently. Nikki sent her best wishes, hung up, took her breakfast and left.

Superintendent Bainbridge had everything organised and ready when she arrived, and Nikki was pleased to see that she had Yvonne, Niall and Cat with her.

Doyle's directions had been hazy, but as she said, she had never been there, she had just listened to what Stephen had told her.

The first wave, four small search teams, were waiting for instructions, and a fleet of emergency backup vehicles were being sent to a rendezvous point on the main road above the marsh coastline.

Nikki took a look at the maps and the details of the areas to be searched, then said, 'I'll take this one, sir. It's old home ground.'

Ten minutes later, with every one of their senses switched to high alert, they moved out.

* * *

'We've already been over this part of the marsh.'

'Then we go over it again! Give me the map.' Nikki swung around in the speeding police car and grabbed the map from Niall. 'I used to live near here, and I was only a mile from here on the seabank yesterday morning.' She drew in a deep breath. 'God! I could have been metres away from her and never realised.'

'There are only three possible spots on the search record, ma'am. The old watch tower, a decrepit shack that bird watchers occasionally use, and a derelict cottage.'

'What have they said about them?'

'Watch tower and one out-building, totally clear, nowhere on site suitable to hide or conceal.' Niall turned over the sheet of paper and continued. 'Bird hide, a single room, derelict, totally clear.' He ran his finger down the page. 'And the place called Coggin's Cottage. Demolished. No longer standing.'

'Nothing else about it?' asked Nikki sharply.

Niall shook his head. 'Just a pile of bricks apparently.'

Nikki felt a rush of hope course through her. 'Then that's where we go! Yvonne! In about 500 yards, take a right at the fork in the road. Go careful, it's single-track and the reeds are high on both sides. Head towards the estuary.'

'But why?' asked Cat, looking anxiously out of the window as Yvonne capably swung the vehicle around a blind corner.

'Because although the report is right, it's little more than a chimney stack and a couple of collapsed walls, it once had a cellar.' Nikki exhaled. 'I haven't thought about that old place in years! It was strictly out of bounds, and a magnet to us local kids. It was dangerous even back then, so it's liable to be a death trap today, but that cellar was pretty well built.' For a moment she saw herself, a little kid doing what she shouldn't, slipping through the doorway and down the worn stone steps to the creepy old cellar.

'Where now, ma'am?' asked Yvonne, braking sharply. 'It looks like there's nowhere to go.'

'There's a track that leads down to the bridge. See, over there,' Nikki pointed. 'It's really overgrown, but someone has been down there recently, look! The grass is flattened!'

'If this is it, God help the ambulance crew trying to find us!' muttered Cat. 'Maybe we should go the last part on foot?'

'It'll probably be quicker. Come on.' Nikki threw open the car door and hit the ground running. 'And Niall,' she yelled back over her shoulder, 'bring a thermal blanket, just in case!' Every fibre in her body screamed out that this was the place.

Oblivious of her trouser legs snagging against tall reed grass and nettles, she ran like a hare. And in her head, she saw herself standing on the seabank, and seeing a small brown and white dog running across the marsh paths, towards the estuary! Towards this place!

A broken skeleton of a five-bar gate blocked her way, but she scrambled swiftly over it, all the time thinking about the dog. What was Kris Brown's dog? A springer spaniel. Swampy, he'd called it. But this stretch of coastline was miles away from Barnby Eaudyke, could it be the same animal? And if it was, what other reason would it have had to travel so far, but to go to find someone it loved.

'This is it, I know it!' she called to the others, hardly even knowing if they were managing to keep up with her or not.

She felt so sure because another thing had just hit her. Stevie Cox would certainly have known about Coggin's Cottage. Years ago, the Cox family had lived close to her own, but that was before Stevie found money in football, and they moved on to some posh address closer to the Wolds.

'Kerry!' Her voice echoed out over the vast reaches of the watery landscape. 'Kerry!'

The single stack of the weather-beaten chimney suddenly came into view, and although seabirds screeched and cried, Nikki heard no sound of reply. 'Kerry! It's the police! We're here to help! Can you hear me?'

All she heard was the sound of her colleagues crashing through the undergrowth, swearing and stumbling after her.

Suddenly Niall was overtaking her. 'Where's this cellar supposed to be?'

'Close to the water side, beneath what would have been the back wall. This was an eel-catcher's cottage, the stream used to run right past it.'

'Yes! There *is* a door!' cried out Niall. 'Kerry!'

'Hell-fire, not exactly a softly, softly approach, is it?' gasped Cat, as she reached Nikki's side. 'What if we find Stephen Cox sitting in there?'

'Then I stick his ugly head in the stream, and drown the fucking bastard! That's what!'

'Fine. Just checking.'

'It's jammed! Give me a hand here!' Niall was wrestling with an old, but still solid wooden door. 'Can't move it.'

'We need something to prise it back,' said Yvonne, hunting through the rubble of the derelict building. 'Maybe this'll do.' She dragged a flat metal pole from a pile of debris.

'Give it here.' Niall wedged it firmly between the door and the frame, and put all his weight behind it.

There was a screech of splitting timbers, and the door swung free.

'Good lad. Let's get in there.'

Nikki followed him down the damp and slippery steps, then almost cannoned into his back when he suddenly stopped.

'What is it? I can't damn well see through you!'

'She's here, ma'am, but . . .'

Nikki pushed him aside and jumped down the last two steps.

Kerry Anderson lay on some old fleece blankets, the kind that come two for fiver in cheap bargain shops. And beside her, cuddled in tightly, as if trying to keep her warm, was Kris Brown's springer spaniel. Even the sound of the door being trashed had not woken her, and for one moment, Nikki feared the worst.

With a little cry, Nikki threw herself down beside the girl and frantically searched for the pulse in her neck. 'Please! Please! Oh, sweetheart! You're safe now, we've got you. Come on, Kerry!' She turned and looked up. 'Radio for the ambulance crew. Tell them she has an irregular heartbeat, she's cold to the touch and unresponsive, it looks like hypothermia. Yvonne, can you remember the way back to the marsh lane?'

'No problem, ma'am.'

'Then go meet them, and escort them as far as their vehicles will go, then bring them in on foot.'

As Yvonne jumped up and ran up the steps, Nikki called out, 'And tell them to bring oxygen and all the equipment they can carry, the poor kid's in a bad way.' She swung back to the still form huddled on the cold floor. 'Niall, over here with that thermal blanket. The dog's done its best, but she needs more right now.' She ripped off her jacket, recalling recently doing the same for Joseph, and laid it over her. 'Yours too, Niall, and you, Cat. We need to get her core temperature up.' As she tucked the last jacket around Kerry's narrow shoulders, she felt the spaniel gently lick her hand.

'You're a good boy, Swampy,' she ruffled the fur under his chin, 'and if I had half your intelligence, I'd have been here a day ago, after I saw you running across the marsh.'

'Any change, ma'am?' asked Cat.

'No damn it! We just need those paramedics.'

'Should we try to get her out of this damp hole, do you think?'

Nikki chewed on the inside of her cheek. 'I'd love to, but no, I don't think we should move her. We don't know what injuries she may have. Better we leave her to the medics.'

'Pity we can't scramble the helicopter,' said Niall with a boyish glint in his eye.

'Nice one, Numpty!' said Cat, with a hopeless expression on her face. 'We're in the middle of a marsh, with nowhere to land, and the rotor blades would bring what's left of this dump down on us like a pack of cards.'

'Ah, good point.'

'Shut up, you two and do some police work while we wait.' Nikki glanced around. 'Did the scumbag who brought her here leave her food or water?'

'There are some plastic water bottles, ma'am,' said Cat. 'And a few empty sandwich boxes. Anything your side, Niall?'

'A syringe and a needle. Maybe he drugged her, the wicked sod.'

'Bag them.' Nikki checked her wrists and ankles. 'At least she wasn't tied up. Just imprisoned.'

'So how did fur-face get in?' Cat looked around.

'Here.' Niall pointed to a small channel where some sort of pipe work had once led out to the stream. 'Certainly not big enough for even a little kid to get through, and it's concrete, so she couldn't have enlarged the hole in any way.'

'How much longer?' cursed Nikki. 'If we don't get help soon, we'll only be needing a body bag to take her out in.'

'They'll be here, ma'am,' said Cat calmly, 'And soon, there's no one better behind a wheel than our Vonnie.'

And a few minutes later, they heard the sirens scream across the bleak and brooding marsh.

'Thank God.' Nikki felt the anguish begin to melt away. 'And she's still with us, so she has a chance.'

As the green uniforms came down the steps, Nikki thought that maybe for the first time ever, she had something to thank Frankie Doyle for.

CHAPTER THIRTY-TWO

'This hospital has more people in it that I know than the bloody nick! Visiting time is taking me hours!' Nikki handed Joseph a large bag of seedless grapes. 'Thought you'd start carping on if I forgot them again.' She smiled down at him. 'How goes it?'

'Fair to middling, as my mum used to say, but I'm starting to get suspicious about what they are doing with all the blood they keep taking from me.' He eased himself higher in the bed, and winced. 'And my gut is still tender as hell.'

'Ah, then you'd better give me that fruit back. Maybe they weren't such a good idea after all.' She moved a chair up to the bed, sat down next to him and pulled a small cluster from the bunch of grapes. 'Everyone sends their love, or their regards, delete which is not applicable.' Nikki bit into a grape. 'So . . . any news on when they are going to discharge you?'

Joseph pulled a face. 'Five, maybe six days. Things aren't operating quite normally yet, and some liver function test was not quite what they expected either.'

'More blood tests?'

He nodded glumly. 'I know I should be just happy to be alive, but my boredom threshold is pretty low. I need to be doing something.'

'How about concentrating on getting better?'

'Done that. I'm improving by the hour! Oh, and how's Kerry?'

'That's one resilient kid! If it hadn't been for Kris Brown's dog, I'm not sure she'd have made it.' Nikki grinned. 'I saw her earlier, and she was raving on about the light/shade juxtapositions in the Coggin's Cottage cellar! Can you believe it, she actually wants to go back there and photograph the place for her final project?'

'Incredible! But I wish her well.' Joseph moved uncomfortably. 'Have you pieced together what actually happened to her yet?'

'More or less,' said Nikki with her mouth full. 'Nice grapes. Sorry about that gut of yours. Now, just prior to Kerry's abduction, Fluke III mugged Kris Brown, nicked his wallet to make it look good, but actually took his mobile phone.'

'Ah, that answers a lot. Texting her, luring her up to the seabank, and diverting the suspicion to Kris.'

'Spot on. And lucky for them that Kris was a bit of a weirdo. I was *so* unhappy with that boy, but it turns out he was always obsessive, then his father's death made him ten times worse. He watches the heavens to be closer to his dad.' Nikki looked slightly abashed. 'I may just have to make a few apologies there.'

Joseph smiled. 'You were pretty hard on him. But going back to Kerry, why didn't Fluke kill her?'

'Flukes II and III were the worker ants, it wasn't in their remit to murder, just cause chaos.'

'So why kill Lisa Jane?'

'I'm afraid that was simply a whim on the part of Frankie Doyle. Jealousy and spite. Lisa Jane was all the things that Frankie was not. Beautiful, and loved by her family.'

'So no vendetta? No take-over? No revenge on the Leonard family for past crimes?'

'Nope, just a twisted, bitter woman without a scrap of humanity in her heart, if she has one.' Nikki thought how

241

right Rory Wilkinson, the pathologist, had been when he said she would have "a heart as cold as a gravedigger's shovel."

'And Stephen Cox? The original Fluke?'

Nikki's face darkened. 'Disappeared.'

'With a face like that! How on earth did he manage that?'

'Beats me. But I really wouldn't want to be him right now.'

'What, with the entire British police forces hunting him?'

'No, because Archie Leonard has offered a reward. A strictly unethical and totally below board offer, you understand. Right now, the Carborough looks like Dodge City, with *Wanted! Dead or Alive* posters everywhere! The faster we take them down, the quicker they spring back up again!'

'Sounds like a bit of light relief actually,' said Joseph.'

'It shouldn't be, but it is. Oh, and we are running a Mask Amnesty! Boxes of the ugly buggers have been handed in over the last few days! Mainly by furious parents, it has to be said. We are going to have a ritual burning at some point.' Nikki glanced at her watch.

'Great! You've eaten my grapes, now you want to go.' Joseph endeavoured to look miffed.

'Not without giving you these.' She reached into her bag, pulled out three copies of the Beano and threw them on the bed. 'Guess who sent you those?'

Joseph's face brightened immediately. 'How's he doing?'

'Brilliantly. He could go home soon, but . . .' Nikki shrugged.

'Social Services?'

'Not sure yet, I'm working on a few ideas.'

Joseph tilted his head to one side, 'And they are?'

'You'll be the first to know, if I come up with something more suitable for him.' She smiled. 'And now, I really do have to go.'

'To see Hannah? How is she?'

Nikki looked at him but didn't answer for a moment. Then she smiled again and said, 'Fancy a trip in a wheelchair?'

* * *

'I've never brought anyone here.' Nikki said softly, as she gently stroked her daughter's hair.

Joseph watched the girl, and Nikki noticed a tear glistening in the corner of his eye.

'It's disconcerting at first, but you get used to it,' she said. 'Don't we, Hannah?'

There was no response.

'She seems to be awake, but there are no signs of awareness, are there? Can she hear us?' asked Joseph.

'They say not. They say she is completely unaware of her surroundings, but I'm not convinced.' Nikki took Hannah's hand and gently massaged her fingers. 'She breathes for herself, she goes into a sleep cycle, and she wakes up, but it's widely accepted that any other movements or noises she makes are just involuntary.'

'This must be so hard for you.' Joseph's voice crackled with emotion.

'It was worse when she was in the coma. At least this is a slightly better neurological situation.'

'Nikki! Hello. I'm sorry, I didn't see you come in.'

'Hi, Bob.' She turned and indicated towards Joseph. 'This is a colleague of mine, skiving off active duty at present. Joseph, Bob Trainer, one of Hannah's ministering angels. Or one of her specialist nurses, as they like to be called. So, how's my girl doing today?'

'I was just going to bath her. She had a great workout with the physio earlier, didn't you, Han?'

'We'd better leave you then,' said Nikki.

'No hurry. Have you got a moment before you go, Nikki? Hannah's consultant asked me to give you a letter if I saw you. It's in the office.'

Nikki's heart lurched in her chest. *Please, not like this, not after all this time. Surely not in a letter!* Somehow she kept it together, and said, 'Would you stay with her Joseph, just for a minute or two?'

'My pleasure. Time we got acquainted. I've got *such* a lot to tell this girl about her mother.'

* * *

Nikki followed the nurse into the office. 'Do you know what the letter is about, Bob?'

She tried to keep the tremor out of her voice.

'I do actually. And I know he also wants to talk to you personally about it.'

A shiver rippled from shoulder blade to shoulder blade. She wasn't ready for this. Not on top of everything else that had happened recently. 'And?'

Bob Trainer smiled at her. 'We did a functional MRI scan yesterday.'

'I know, I consented for it, but I didn't know you'd done it already.'

'It threw up some very slight differences from the last one we did.'

Nikki stared at him. 'For the better, or . . .'

Bob rubbed his hands together. 'Let's just say that her consultant, Mr Leyton, has been in touch with the cognition and brain sciences unit at Cambridge. He wants to do further tests and he wants their expertise. That's what this letter is, an explanation and a consent form for you to sign. He would have spoken to you himself, but he's in Liege in Belgium at the university. He's taken Hannah's case to them for review.'

For a moment Nikki felt as though she would pass out.

'You know that this is not a cure, Nikki, don't you?' He looked at her seriously, as he handed her the envelope. 'But we do believe that she has some new brain activity that we *may* be able to stimulate.' He exhaled, then added, 'Just don't expect too much, she's been in this state a very long time, and that's not good, but . . .'

Nikki tried to stop herself grabbing the man and hugging him. 'But, it just may be an early sign of recovery?'

'I wouldn't go that far, but stranger things have happened in medical science.'

'If nothing else, it's a reprieve, isn't it?'

'Oh yes! It's that for sure.'

As Nikki walked back to Hannah's room, she felt as if an enormous weight had been lifted from her. It was the smallest improvement, a tiny drop in the ocean, but it *was* a step forward, not another backward slide. She felt as if someone had given her a little piece of her daughter back.

At the door, she paused and looked in.

Joseph sat, with Hannah's hand in his, and chatted comfortably with her. She saw him talk, then smile, then laugh, as if they were sharing some secret joke. And who was to say that they weren't?

Nikki stepped back from the door and watched them unnoticed.

Joseph was a natural with Hannah. She thought of Mickey Smith, and the way that Joseph had handled him. Hyperactive or not, he had got through to the boy, and very quickly.

She then saw him take a tissue from a box beside the bed, and carefully wipe the corner of Hannah's mouth. He was good man, and those around him should see past the rumours and the gossip and see the real Joseph Easter.

Nikki took a deep breath. He deserved better. Especially from his own family.

EPILOGUE

It was called the Garden of Tranquillity. Lots of hospitals have them, if you know where to look. Greenborough's was set at the back of the chapel, and could be accessed either by a door from the chapel, or by a long straight pathway that led from the car park.

In the centre, was a rectangular fish pond, its surface interlaced with oriental looking pink water-lilies, and a scattering of tiny lime-green duck-weed. All around were tall, scented shrubs and beds of brightly coloured summer plants. It was well kept, but Nikki had hardly ever seen it used. Which was a shame in one way, but when Hannah had first been brought here, it served as a private place for her to bring her broken heart, and cry unnoticed.

Today, as she entered the garden, she didn't feel sad. She felt excited, almost elated, but part of her was as nervous as a school kid waiting for A-level results.

With a rueful smile on her face, she walked across to a wooden bench with a faded brass plaque on it, sat down and wondered if she had done the right thing.

But there again, she had done rather a lot of quite radical things in the last few days, and most of them were still open to question.

The first thing she had done was to ring her landlord and give him a month's notice on her grim little 'bijou residence' in the town. She had then driven out to Cloud Fen, taking with her a builder and a decorator, and told them that they had four weeks to get her old home liveable again. She knew it would mean a very different work schedule for her, living back out on the marsh, but she also knew it was time for changes.

In the last few days, she had done a lot of hard thinking.

The dark thoughts and intentions that she had harboured when in that small room with Frankie Doyle, had scared her badly. If she had continued with her old crusade, if she had travelled much further down that ever-spiralling pathway of bitterness and revenge, without ever being forced to take a look at herself, what would she have done in that room?

Nikki shifted uncomfortably. It was the fact that she really didn't know, that had sparked off her new mission, to make some big life choices, some big life changes. Before it was too late.

The second thing she had done was to champion the cause of Mickey Smith. There had been no way on God's earth he could have gone back to his 'family,' and Nikki had been certain that a foster home was not appropriate, considering what the child had gone through. So, she had approached Archie Leonard. To an outsider it may have seemed like madness, but Nikki knew quite a lot of well-kept secrets about the Leonard family, and in particular one that involved Archie's youngest son. Peter wasn't a rogue, like most of his family. He had a home, a wife and a small business of his own. And the previous year, he had lost his only son, a boy with severe learning difficulties. The death had left a big aching chasm in the little family's life, and she had no doubt that, given the chance, Mickey could go part of the way to healing it. And let's face it, Mickey had been brought up rough, very rough. He was at home on the Carborough, and this was something that Peter understood, given his own background. Give Mickey to a nice, middle-class family, and he'd be running riot in no time! So she'd arranged a month's 'holiday' for him. It may not work, but it was worth a try, for Mickey's sake.

A warm breeze blew across Nikki's face, and brought with it the smell of orange blossom. There had been an orange blossom tree at her old home. She wondered if it were still alive after being neglected for so long. She hoped so. She inhaled its perfume, and it made her think of happier times. Nikki sighed. She was making changes alright, but it was too soon to think that happy times may come round again, although she would dearly love that to happen. One day.

She glanced at her watch. Joseph was meeting her here, in just about ten minutes, and she had some news for him. The problem was, she was not sure if it would be welcome news.

As soon as the doctors had assured him that, in time, he would make a full recovery, she had gone to Rick Bainbridge and asked if he would consider assigning Joseph to her team, as her permanent detective sergeant. The super had practically tripped over his own tongue in saying yes, but it would all hinge on Joseph. His time in Greenborough had been hardly peaceful, and whereas once she couldn't wait for him to high-tail it back to Fenchester, now she felt very different.

She touched the delicate petal of a rose that grew close to the seat. If Joseph hadn't been with her, even if only in her mind, in that stark and dangerous room, she may not be sitting here now, smelling flowers. Because no way could she have continued as a police officer knowing that she had consigned another human being, and she used the term loosely in Doyle's case, to a violent death. To protect life, that was what it was all about.

The rose felt like silk to her fingertips. She desperately hoped he would agree to stay. It was all part of her plan for a new attitude to policing her patch, and if he didn't, well, she wasn't too sure how she'd manage. She pursed her lips, and gave a little shrug. She'd know soon enough.

Nikki leaned back, closed her eyes, and breathed in slowly. It was so good to be alone like this, with the breeze and the flowers and birds singing. It was very different to the kind of 'alone' that she used to enjoy, in dark alleys, waiting for another drug dealer to walk into her trap. Oh, she'd still go after them, and she'd still catch them and lock them up, but that would just be a part of her life, not all of it.

The sound of footsteps dragged her from her reverie. She cursed under her breath, she had hoped to get time alone with Joseph. She'd never really told him that he had been the pivotal point in how she dealt with Frankie Doyle, and she felt that he deserved to know.

She opened her eyes and squinted in the sunlight. A figure was moving towards her from the lane. A young woman, tall and willowy, with a light brown hair and a curtain of a fringe hanging across one eye.

Nikki took a shaky breath, and looked again. She had not dared to believe this would really happen, but as the girl came closer, there was no doubt. *My God!* she thought, *she's actually come!*

Because that was the last, and probably the most radical thing that Nikki had done in her busy three days.

It hadn't been easy, but somehow she had traced her halfway round the world, and then, ironically, found her in London of all places. The girl had made no promises, but she *had* listened to what Nikki had to say, and Nikki had asked no more of her. Just told her where and when she could find him.

She looked up at the girl, and smiled.

Tamsin had her father's eyes. Nikki hoped that she also had his capacity to understand and to forgive.

'Thank you. You won't regret this,' Nikki whispered, then she heard the door to the chapel open. 'Time for me to go.'

She slipped quietly out into the lane and walked swiftly towards the car park. It was *so* hard not to take a look back, but this was their time, not hers.

She unlocked her car and slid into the driver's seat. Joseph had said it would take a miracle to reconcile him with his daughter. So, no one knew what this meeting would bring, but it could be that miracle. And if Joseph could have one, maybe she could too?

Nikki slipped the key into the ignition and smiled. One day at a time. Right now she'd settle for a permanent detective sergeant for her team, and if Joseph Easter didn't want the job, he'd better have a damn good reason for turning her down!

THE END

Join our mailing list to be the first to hear about
Joy Ellis's next mystery, coming soon!

www.joffebooks.com

Thank you for reading this book. If you enjoyed it please
leave feedback on Amazon or Goodreads, and if there is
anything we missed or you have a question about then
please get in touch. The author and publishing team
appreciate your feedback and time reading this book.